NOT

The

Plus

One

BELLE HENDERSON

Dedication

To all the women who have had to endure dates that don't quite go to plan. Remember, never ignore the red flags.

Thank you to my brilliant support system of loving family and friends who have helped make publishing my fifth book possible.

Other books by Belle Henderson

You Grow Girl

The Hounds of Love

What's eating Felicity Frost

Livin' La Vida Lockdown

We can Work it out

Chapter 1

I'm going to miss these sacred moments.

I sigh deeply while trying not to move too much and disturb her as I stare down at my sleepy nursing baby. After a bit of frustrating fussiness, I've been enjoying catching up on the latest episodes of *Love Island* as I feed Nancy-Ella to sleep. '*You should never feed or rock a baby to sleep, you'll make a rod for you own back.*' One of the mums told me at the baby group once, needless to say I've changed baby groups now. Anyway it works for us and that's all that matters. It's been a great comfort to her and if I admit it, an even bigger comfort to me. Except she's not much of a baby anymore, she's nineteen months and in just five months she'll be two. A full-blown toddler.

Cue defiance, standoffs and snotty tears.

People aren't exaggerating when they say time flies.

Softly, I stroke her white blonde hair then touch her soft cheek before gently removing my nipple from her mouth. She stirs and I move slowly but surely so as not to wake her. The effort of getting up off the sofa with her weight on mine is steadily getting harder and harder with the bigger she gets. This will have to stop soon but for the next few months we'll just enjoy it, savour it.

Yeah, we can carry on until she's almost two, until I'm back at work after my maternity and career break. The plan wasn't necessarily to go back to my normal job but a lot has changed since then.

I pad up the stairs and lower her into her cot as the thought crosses my mind that I'll have to take the sides off soon and change that to a toddler bed, then after that I expect I'll have to consider when's right to start toilet training. I touch her cheek again and quickly wipe my own cheek with my sleeve so that the big fat tear that's sprung out of my eye doesn't fall on her and soak her.

For God's sake, I need to get a grip. Get a life even.

I pad back down the stairs and trundle into the kitchen. Standing in front of the cupboards, I consider what to eat whilst trying to compose myself; Brie will be here soon and I don't want her to see me in this state. She'll think I've gone mad. I'll have a fruit smoothie with banana, yoghurt and honey, and a nice cup of tea. Yes, some potassium will cheer me up, give me some energy and get me feeling better but there are also chocolate muffins in the cupboard and they go off soon. Hmmmm. Wait, what's that thumping noise? I stand still in my tracks, a muffin in each hand, as the thumping continues.

I'm frozen to the spot.

Then Mum clomps towards me in her giant high heels and stands in the kitchen doorway.

'Arrrghhhh, Mum!' I scream, squeezing the muffins. I really wouldn't be good in a crisis if it were a real intruder. 'How many times have I told you not to just enter my house like that?' I say.

Mum stares at me opening and closing her big pouty lips, like a done-up rabbit caught in headlights. She always manages to make me feel dowdy by comparison and although I make a bit of effort with my appearance, mum is on a whole other level. Veneers, permanent fake lashes, the lot. She's like a Hollywood wife, except she's not married and we live in the lot less glamourous location of Swindon.

'Oh Tilly, you're so dramatic. I didn't want to wake my precious princess as I knew it was nap time. Is she sleeping now?' she asks, as she steps forward, pulling me into a hug and kissing me on both cheeks. She smells of expensive perfume and hairspray, a familiar smell, a happy smell. I wonder what smells will remind Nancy-Ella of me? Toast and tea at the moment. That's not so bad. Wholesome.

'You could just text me when you're on your way or even when you're outside and I would come down and open the door to you. It's creepy just entering my house,' I say, whilst busying myself in the kitchen.

'Yes but then I might be left loitering around outside for ages until you answered and what's creepier?' She shrugs. 'Tilly, are you alright?' She studies my face.

Why do mothers always know?

'Yes, no, yes. I've just been fretting about going back to work, that's all. It's going to be a big change for us.'

'Darling, you're not going back just yet, enjoy the rest of this time off, make the most of it and just relax. You're such a worrier.'

'I know,' I say, putting the muffins down and flicking on the kettle before stretching on my tiptoes to get the tea out of the cupboard. 'But it's not that far away.'

'You'll be fine, it will be good for you, get you back to feeling like you.' She smiles then rubs my back in a circular motion.

'I feel like me,' I croak, not convincing myself.

'You know what I mean.'

'No I don't,' I say, facing her.

'All I'm saying is you need a life outside of my gorgeous grandchild, a bit of you time and work will do that. It will be good for you.'

'Oh great, I can hardly wait.'

'Tilly!' She tuts as a manicured hand swoops a muffin off my kitchen counter.

'Mum!'

'Well you can't eat them both, sweetheart.'

'Yes but Brie will be here in a minute and I might have been saving one for her,' I say, with one hand on my hip.

'Brie, brilliant.' She claps her hands together. 'I wanted to book in with her to get a few more tweakments anyway.'

'Oh God,' I groan, whilst dunking the teabags and envisioning my mother turning into the reincarnation of a female Pete Burns.

'Don't *oh God* me. You'll understand when overnight your lips shrivel up like prunes and you begin to resemble a crinkled old paper bag. A little work does wonders for the confidence of this fragile, menopausal woman and Brie is the best,' she says, waving her arms around in excitement. Mum has literally been menopausal for the last fifteen years. Does it really go on for that long?

'Brie is the best and you are anything but fragile.' I place her mug of tea into her hands and she purses her lips, suppressing a smile.

'I won't stay long, I'm meeting a friend for lunch anyway,' she says.

'Ooooh, anyone I know? A man?' I tease. I wish it was a man, Mum's been on her own for ages. She's still not gotten over my dad leaving like he did, which was almost thirty years ago. He left the day after my third birthday.

'No no, nothing like that.' She wags her finger

playfully just as my phone beeps in my pocket.

'It's Brie, she's here,' I say, tapping a quick 'okay' back in response.

'Oh goody.' Mum rubs her hands together and I throw her a look which I hope comes across as a warning, before making my way to the front door.

'Alrighty-roo, how's my gorgeous mama bear?' Brie beams as she steps indoors and dumps her bag down before pulling me into a big hug.

'Good, good mate.' I beam back. 'Mum's here too, come on through.'

'What? Ms Loveberry? MY BEST CLIENT,' Brie says loudly, to unashamedly butter Mum up as she comes trotting into the living room swinging her hair around like a pony trying to win a prize.

'Well hello, Brie sweetheart. Am I really your best client?' Mum coos, patting down her face as if to make sure it's all still there.

'Ah yeah, without a doubt, Lil.'

'That's great because I was meaning to ask you…' Mum trails off then looks at me for permission. I smile at her and try to stop my eyes from rolling to the ceiling. 'I need a little more filler, a few tweaks,' she almost whispers. 'Just here and there.' She points to places on her already full lips and cheeks.

'No dramas, we'll go for two mil in the lips next time yeah, Lil? That will freshen you up nicely.'

'Okay Brie, whatever you say, I trust you completely. I'm in your hands, well my face is.' She chuckles, pleased with her own joke.

'Thanks and you know I'd never give you a trout pout, just subtle tweaks make all the difference, you're gorgeous Lil, you don't need much at all.'

'Thanks Brie, you're a star,' Mum simpers. 'I was also

considering a few other things but I'll email you about those,' she says, throwing a quick glance at me and then back to Brie.

'Mum!'

'What?'

'Brie, please don't turn my mother into Pete Burns.'

'As if. Isn't he dead anyway?' Brie laughs then winks at me. 'So where's my cupppa?'

'Coming right up.' I grin then leave Mum and Brie in the living room to discuss turning my mother into the next Joan Rivers lookalike whilst I make Brie a cup of tea. I scour the cupboards for a packet of biscuits and end up finding an unopened packet of chocolate chip cookies. I place everything on a tray then retreat back into the living room to find Mum and Brie sitting with their hands on their knees, pasted on smiles and radio silence. Have they been discussing me? Maybe they think *I* need work. My nose has gone a bit of a funny shape since giving birth I guess, but I haven't really thought that much about it until now. I read an old wives' tale that daughters steal their mother's beauty and I think that might be true on my part.

'Okay, let me have it then? How much filler do I need? What work do I require?' I joke, placing the tray down on the coffee table before leaning across to open the biscuits. 'But know that just because you tell me what you think I need doesn't mean I'll actually get it done. I might like my modestly small lips, fine blonde hair and characterful nose. I'm happy with my own features, because they look like my baby's.'

'You don't have tiny lips, babe and even if you did like, whatever, it's fine, you're beautiful just as you are,' Brie says softly, but her face looks a little contorted, guilty almost.

'Oh God, what is it?' I hold a cookie up to my non-tiny mouth. 'Have you booked me in to have a facial peel or something Mum? A daughter and mother joint lip filler session? MUM? MUM! How many times do I have to tell you? I want to keep my own face!'

'No darling! Absolutely not!' Mum says, mirroring Brie's expression.

'Well, what is it then?' What are they conspiring?

'Sit down darling,' Mum says, patting the space on the sofa beside her. I do as I'm told then stuff the cookie into my mouth in one go as I wait for them to break whatever it is to me. The sound of my own munching is beginning to heighten the annoyance bubbling within me as Mum begins to speak.

'We, we just…'

'Don't worry, I got this, Lil,' Brie says, putting her arm around my mum who (if I didn't know any better) looks like she's about to cry. 'Tilly love, and this is coming from the most warm and loving place...'

'Okay?' I frown and shake my head.

'We think it's about time you stop playing happy families with Billy.' There's a long pause as I use that time to sigh.

'Not this again. I'm not playing happy families with him.'

Mum and Brie give each other side eye then return their gaze to me.

'I'm not!'

'Matey, all we're saying is that it might be time to start saying no to him. I mean, how are you supposed to move on when you're always going to bloody *Peppa Pig World* and shit with him.'

'That was for Nancy-Ella's birthday and we thought it would be nice for her to have us both there.'

7

'Nice or a tad confusing?' Mum pipes up with a pained expression on her face.

'She's one year old,' I retort. 'She doesn't know any different.'

'Exactly,' Brie winces.

'Then what are you doing it all for then, darling?' Mum asks.

'What is this? Since when did you two join forces and decide to stage an intervention on me?'

'Since last week, darling,' Mum admits. 'It needs to stop if you ever want to move on and it isn't just *Peppa Pig World,* is it? He's over here whenever he fancies then drops you like a hat when he thinks something better has come along.'

'That's not true,' I mumble.

'Babe.' Brie takes a sip of her tea then carefully places it back on the coffee table. 'All we're saying is that you should set some boundaries with him and take a bit of time for you. Just because you have a baby with him doesn't mean he gets to lay down the law.'

I shake my head but don't say anything because deep down I know she's right.

'Don't you think we're right?'

'I just want her to have a good relationship with her dad, that's all.'

'I know, babe, but it's their separate relationship, not yours… anymore.'

'And you never know darling, if you begin to set these boundaries that Brie talks about you may find yourself meeting a nice man.'

'And what if I don't want to meet a man, Mum.' I lock eyes with her. She should probably think about taking her own advice. 'I'm too busy, and it's just hassle.'

'We've got Nay's wedding at the end of the summer,

that's just a couple of months. You've got a plus one on your invite,' she says with an encouraging smile. 'Wouldn't it be lovely to bring a date? A date that isn't Billy. I mean, it doesn't have to be anything serious, but you could have fun finding your plus one?'

'Hmmmm.' The plus-one was meant for Billy, one of the downfalls of planning a wedding so far in advance is that some couples will inevitably split up. And that couple to split up, was me and Billy. Nay, being too kind to take the invitation back, offered that I bring a friend or date in his place.

'A few little dates here and there,' Brie suggests, raising an eyebrow and still smiling.

'Hmmm, Maybe, it would be nice to dress up and go out, no strings. No relationship. Just fun,' I say, sounding way braver than I feel. It's been a very long time.

'Alrighty, great,' Brie says, rubbing her hands on her knees. 'We can discuss it more on the hen do.'

Uh oh no. I am not a project.

No way.

'Oh, anyway haven't I told you? I'm not coming.'

'What?'

'Okay.' Mum stands up and pastes on a big bright smile. 'I think it's my time to leave you girls to it, I'll be late for my lunch date.' And with that, Mum clomps out of my house, giving us both little waves and air kisses as she departs. So typical of my mum to stir the shit and then bugger off. I know she instigated this but it really is a case of the pot calling the kettle black.

'So why aren't you coming?' Brie asks.

'Wait, I think I can hear Nancy-Ella crying. Can you hear her?' I stand up and make my way over to the stairs to get a better listen.

'No.'

'She shouldn't be up for another hour at least, oh don't tell me she's going through another leap, she didn't nap for weeks last time.'

'Tilly. Stop trying to deflect, Nancy-Ella is sleeping just fine. Why aren't you coming to Nay's hen do? It's all booked, haven't you paid for it all?'

'Yeah, I'm going to tell her that someone can take my place, it's fine.' I don't tell Brie that I've already hinted to Gemma that I might not come. 'I just don't think I'm ready to go out yet and leave my baby. I've never left her and it's for two nights, plus I've got nothing to wear and I'm just not really feeling it.'

'Look, I get it alright, but don't you want some time with your girls? A bit of time to yourself. You've been saying yourself how drained you feel and how you're dying for more adult conversation and fun. It's gonna be amazing, Tills. Coolsbay is so stunning, it just reminds me of Oz so much. We can enjoy the beach, the bloody booze cruise and learn how to Bollywood dance, all in two days.'

'Coolsbay has a decent beach, doesn't it?' I can't believe I've never been.

'Yep, it's golden sands and it's set to be a scorcha for that weekend too. Just like the old days mate, it will be such a hoot, say you'll come please. Come on. It won't be the same without you.'

Brie and I met in Cairns, Australia ten years ago whilst doing bar work. Not your usual bar work either, we were topless barmaids. After Brie got the sack for punching a punter who tried to grope her, we decided to travel around Australia for a year together. Brie followed me back home to sunny Swindon in the south-west of England, with the intention of travelling around England but then we met Billy and Nick on one of our wild nights out and she ended up staying here for another few weeks, which turned into months, which eventually turned into years. She hasn't travelled since apart from her yearly holidays back to Oz but she's super happy. Her and Nick are the perfect match in every way. I'm a little bit envious of their relationship.

Billy turned into a big disappointment; a big disappointment that just keeps on giving.

'Yes, I do miss it, it's just… and I want to go, it's just…'

'What about Billy having the babe overnight? Or your mum perhaps?'

'Hmm, I guess I could ask him to have her here and that way she will stay more settled.' I'd have to pump a bit before and hope that she'd take a bottle for him. I guess I could start doing that over the next few weeks. She should start to stay over with her dad soon, I suppose.

'Yeah, see? It will be great. I think Emma's hired a stripper for Nay too but don't say anything as it's a surprise. Top secret,' she says, pretending to zip her lips.

'Oh God!' I throw my head back and laugh, Nay's gonna die when a stripper appears. I think of my mild-mannered, slightly timid friend and giggle to myself.

'Mate, it's gonna be mental, have I sold it to ya yet?'

'Yes, okay, okay. I'll come but you must promise to not let me snort tequila, okay? I'm a mother now not a hedonistic party girl anymore.'

I have to be sensible. Well, semi-sensible.

Chapter 2

Hey Sis,

How's it going in the land of Swine-town? Loving life here in Barcelona still, I'm literally never coming home, well not to live anyway. I'll come and visit to remind myself why I left haha, and to see you guys of course. How's my gorgeous niece? How's mum? The kids I teach here are so lush and not to blow my own trumpet but I'm just getting better and better at my job all the time. I've even picked up a bit of tour guiding on the side, now that I'm basically a local. How's Bumbrain Billy? Are you back at work yet?

Anyway got to go, going out again, on the hunt for a fit Catalonian man to sweep me off my feet. Although, I'm going out dressed as big bird from Sesame Street so not sure how successful I'll be. It's a friends' birthday and the theme is favourite TV characters from your childhood (I KNOW! PISS OFF! I'M SHOWING MY AGE!!)

Ciao for now & love you lots.
Charlie xxx

I smile to myself then exit email on my phone. I'll reply after the hen do, at least then I'll hopefully have some gossip to tell my brother. Sometimes I feel like such a bore, especially when I reply back to his Barcelona adventures about breast feeding and growth spurts. Who am I kidding? It's been pretty much three years since I've had a sip of alcohol, I'll probably be in bed by nine o'clock after two glasses of wine. Oh well, at least I'll get to enjoy a lay in and some adult company.

The doorbell rings and I pick Nancy-Ella up and balance her on my hip, bringing her to the front door with me. I open the door to Billy looking as bronzed and perfect looking as ever as Nancy-Ella begins to squirm excitedly, reaching her arms out to get to him.

'Hey, hey come in.' I hand our fidgety toddler over. She gives him one of her big toddler cuddles and my heart melts for a second until realisation sets in, and it cracks all over again. This happens every time we are together. I know I'm torturing myself.

'Don't you look pretty today,' he coos, whilst looking me up and down.

'Oh, thanks.' I blush. I must admit, I have made an effort. My hair is freshly washed and blow dried into long, soft blonde waves. I've actually put on some makeup, taking the time to highlight my hazel eyes with some gold eyeshadow, black eyeliner and false black eyelashes, just subtle ones that Brie recommended. I'm wearing a new funky shorts playsuit that shows off my best feature. The only feature that didn't change much during pregnancy, my legs. I lean my hand on the arm of the sofa and stretch my legs out, crossing them over in what I think is a seductive manner. Shame on me.

'You're such a gorgeous girl, aren't you? Daddy's eyes for sure,' he continues to coo at her, his twinkling blue eyes matching hers as he lifts her up and throws her in the air causing her to squeal and my stomach to flip over

13

for her. Of course, he isn't talking about me, he's talking to our daughter. I sit down on the sofa and fold my arms.

How silly of me.

Silly Tilly Loveberry.

'Her eyes might change to hazel like mine, it's still early days,' I say, annoyed at myself for thinking that he might have been paying me a compliment.

'Nah, she has her dada's eyes, don't you princess? The prettiest ones.'

'Dadda eyes, dadda eyes,' Nancy-Ella mimics, as Billy grins at her.

'Umm, you alright if Tim comes over later, we're gonna go over some new branding ideas for the coffee shop,' Billy says, whilst not looking at me.

'Tim that hates my guts for no reason? Yeah sure he can come and hang out in my house,' I say, attempting sarcasm. Urgh the coffee shop, the biggest bone of contention. Before Billy and I split we had discussed that I'd give working at the coffee shop a try. Despite working for a tiny company, my boss was kind enough to let me take a career break. Her words were that she'd find something for me if and when I return from my sabbatical. There was a time that Billy and I were excited to work together. Billy wanted someone to do the admin for the coffee shop and in return our mortgage would be paid, but sometimes things don't always pan out as planned.

'Dadda eyes, Dadda eyes.'

'He doesn't hate you, he's just shy,' Billy says lightly, whilst continuing to throw our baby around.

'Oh come on! But yeah, whatever when Nancy-Ella's in bed I guess that will be fine.' I can't face any arguments right now and not in front of Nancy-Ella. Timmy has never liked me which makes me dislike him because he has no reason not to like me. What's not to love?! 'Umm so, breast milk's in the fridge. I've managed to ween her onto bottles so she'll be fine taking it, one bottle before bed and one bottle before her nap. I've written a list anyway in case you forget and made up the spare room for you.'

Billy nods at me, uninterested and probably not listening.

'Bye baby girl, be good for Dadda, don't give him too much trouble.' I give Nancy-Ella a kiss before rubbing noses with her. Please do loads of massive shitty nappies for Daddy and throw in a tantrum or two for good measure. I smile a big toothy grin, trying hard not to inhale his familiar aftershave that I hate and miss so much, all at the same time.

'Dadda eyes, Dadda eyes.'

Life is good. The sun is blazing and the radio has just announced that it's the hottest day of the year so far. Brie and I are driving with the roof of her black soft top down, posing with our novelty heart sunglasses which Brie bought especially for the trip. I clutch onto my gin in a tin taking tiny sips from it every few seconds, it's strong and sour but so moreish. My face feels warm from the sun and I lean back, basking in the glory of this beautiful weather. Brie's put together a playlist of all the songs we used to listen to back in our party days which mainly consisted of RnB and a couple of Australian bands, I'd forgotten how good *Sneaky Sound System* are. I must listen to them more.

This is the life.

My skin is so warm.

This is bliss.

You would never know that just a few hours ago I'd turned up to Brie's in hysterical ugly tears. Both false eyelashes were stuck to my cheeks like two big, angry spiders had fallen out of my eyes. I felt torn between not wanting to leave my baby but also wanting to have a good time. I *am* going to have a good time.

Nancy-Ella handled my leaving better than I did. I was half expecting her to scream blue murder when I left but I guess she has no concept of time yet, she's used to seeing him in the day but tonight could prove a different story, because I've been breastfeeding she's never stayed with him. Two days is a long time, it might catch up with her tomorrow. I'll ring them tonight anyway.

'Alrighty-roo, we're here!' Brie sings as the car jerks aggressively, struggling to pull up onto the steep huge gravel driveway. Three other cars are already parked here, including a cute turquoise mini, which means we must be the last ones to arrive. A lovely, large white detached house with a navy-blue door sits at the top of the driveway surrounded by a beautiful garden full of colourful flowers. Opposite is a very similar looking house, if not a little bigger, sitting on top of a slightly higher hill. An image of *Pepper Pig* and her family driving up it in their red car flashes in my mind.

I really do need to get out more.

'Wow, what? That was quick!' Apparently Coolsbay is becoming quite the place to go for hen and stag parties and from looking at the views I can see why because just behind our house is the view of the sea, it's stunning. I take it all in, breathing in the fresh, seaside air.

'You fell asleep babe, snoring like a greedy little albino wombat.'

'Greedy little albino wombat? I laugh. 'I swear you've

become more Australian lately.'

'Mouth open like a flaming galah,' she jokes. Brie does an impression of me which reminds me of a gormless goldfish.

'I did not!' I laugh. 'This place is amazing,' I say, waving my arms in the air. 'It's so hot, I feel like I'm on holiday abroad somewhere.'

'Yep! Amazing isn't it, glad you came now?'

'Too right.'

Brie and I drag our suitcases along the bumpy gravel up to the door and ring the doorbell. I hear squeals of excitement and my body pings and fizzes with excitement. This girls' weekend may be doing me more good than I first thought and it hasn't even got started yet.

'BRIEEEEEE, TILLYYYYY.' Naomi, the bride to be, usually rather reserved, comes flying through the front door and throws herself at Brie and me along with the rest of the gang from school and college. A couple of the girls hang back, girls that I don't recognise that must be from Naomi's work. Brie said it was a fifteen-sleeper house and by the looks of it we must be filling all of the rooms. I've never been on a hen do with this many hens.

'So sorry girls, we've already started the drinking games,' Naomi confesses, followed by a hiccup. 'There's a hot tub!! In fact there's two hot tubs! We got a bit carried away.' She hiccups again.

Chief organiser Gemma throws her hands up in the air, exasperated. She makes a face as if to say she tried to stop her but failed. I can't imagine there was much effort put into stopping the drinking games from getting started, a lot of the girls look quite drunk and it's only 5pm.

'No worries lads, you'd probably need a head start

with us two in town now anyway.' Brie takes her sun glasses off, shakes her long brown glossy hair and winks at me. I nod back with all the apparent confidence of an eight-pint-a-night lager drinker but the truth is, I already feel slightly tipsy from my half a can of gin in a tin.

I wonder how Nancy-Ella and Billy are getting on?

'Come in, come in, get in your bikinis, girls, and let's party.' Nay saunters off to the living room in her black sequin bikini. The rest of the girls with their lovely figures follow and just for a second I feel self-conscious about getting out my mum tum. I'm still not back to how I was, almost but I'm not sure if my stomach will ever be the same. I still have the pouch that no one tells you about and I just want it to go. I'm not a kangaroo, I just don't have a need for it.

Gemma leads us up three flights of stairs and shows us to our room.

'I hope it's alright guys, it was first come, first served and you are unfortunately last,' Gemma says, as she opens the door to the broom cupboard that is our room.

'And where am I supposed to bloody sleep, on top of the shelf?' Brie says with a smile but I can tell she's a bit annoyed, as am I. We've paid the best part of three hundred pounds to sleep in a shoe box.

'Maybe one of us could sleep on the sofa?' I suggest, as I slide my sunglasses off and take in the space which consists of a single bed, a shelf, a small oval mirror and an inch of floor. The single bed actually looks smaller than a normal sized single bed, if that's even possible.

'Sorry girls, it all went a bit wrong, I over booked the rooms,' she says, glancing at me and I feel a pang of guilt for mentioning that I might not come. 'It's been so stressful organising a hen do for this many people.' Gemma looks as if she's about to cry and Brie pats her on the back.

'No worries, babe, we can top-n-tail, can't we, Tils? It'll be right, we'll be too pissed to care any… what the…' Brie points to my face. 'Oh dear god, Tilly mate, you might want to look in the mirror.'

'Huh?' I shuffle into the room and lean over the bed to look in the mirror. Staring back at me is not the face I left my house with.

'Oh Fuck. How did that happen?' I touch my red raw nose and cheeks and groan as I see the heart shapes around my eyes.

I've given myself my very own face peel.

'Mate, did you not wear any sunscreen?' Brie asks.

'Oh Tils, it's quite pink, does it hurt?' Gemma soothes, as she touches my boiling hot skin with one finger then quickly pulls it away like she's just burnt herself on the oven.

'Well it does feel a bit tight,' I say, putting both hands to my burning cheeks. 'But what am I going to do about my eyes? My eyes!' I say, blinking at them both like a frightened little racoon. My skin is so pale that the contrast is quite obvious already and it's only going to get worse.

'Don't worry, Tilly, Vanessa's a makeup artist, she will sort you out for tonight I'm sure, but for now you can borrow my aloe vera, stop it from getting any worse.'

'Good plan, Gem,' Brie says, biting her lip, she's definitely fighting the urge to laugh and I don't blame her.

'Yes, good plan,' I say, staring back at my face. It's not *that* bad, it'll calm down. 'I mean how can you even get burnt in a car?'

'We had the roof down; it was super-hot and the wind probably didn't help on your pasty English rose skin.

Sorry mate, it didn't notice in the bright light of day or I'd have slapped some cream on you.'

'No it's fine, I'm a grown up, a mother, I should be able to look after myself and wear proper bloody sunscreen on the hottest day of the year. I'm sure my moisturizer had sun screen in it but obviously that wasn't enough. Oh well, hand me the aloe vera then Gem, and a very strong drink.'

Gemma nods and Brie grins at me. 'That's my girl.'

The next couple of hours are spent catching up with old friends, playing silly drinking games to break the ice with the people we don't know and enjoying the hot tubs with the view of the sea as our back drop. Gemma orders in a load of pizzas which I'm thankful for as the booze is starting to go to my head. It gets to seven o'clock and Gemma begins to panic that we have taxis booked for eight o'clock and only a handful of us are ready so it's all stations go. Luckily Gemma drafted in Vanessa to camouflage my face a while ago after everyone gasped in horror at the state of me, so I'm already ready. I'm feeling like quite the yummy mummy (yuk I hate that phrase) with my little black dress, freshly blow-dried hair and fabulous immaculate, fresh-faced makeup. Thanks Vanessa! Whilst everyone else rushes around I sneak off with my new face to facetime Billy and say goodnight to Nancy-Ella.

'Hey.' Billy's face appears on the screen. Tim's already there in the background, scowling lightly.

'Hi.'

'Alright? How is she?'

'Yeah fine, she's in bed.' He yawns.

'Already? What did you guys get up to when I left?'

'Not much, just played.'

'Did she take the bottle of breast milk okay?'

'Yep.'
'Has she been missing me?'
'No, she's alright.'
'Oh okay, did you sing to her and read her stories?'
'Just stories.'
'Okay, well I'll let you get back to your coffee meeting then, bye.'
'Yeah bye.'

Urgh, Timmy, why is he such a mood muncher? I swear I caught him wincing when I said breast milk. Billy always changes into a completely different person when he's around him. It all seemed to happen so fast with Timmy. Three years ago, they met on a night out and then what felt like minutes later, Tim was his business partner. I drop my phone into my handbag then lean over to check my face in the mirror. It looks so good, now it's time to have fun, right after I pump and dump.

'What is this place?' Samantha, one of Naomi's work friends, scrunches up her nose as we enter a pub called The Mermaid's Lair. It's your typical old man pub with vintage looking décor and furniture, coupled with pictures of mermaids and other made-up sea creatures on the wall. I kind of like it. It feels like we're on holiday in Cornwall or Devon, but Samantha isn't so impressed judging by the look on her face.

'Well, I think it looks great,' says Naomi, as she squeezes Gemma's arm and the rest of us agree.

'Relax, we're just meeting here for one drink,' Brie says, as a curly-haired guy and I lock eyes. I bite my lip to stop my grin from splitting my face in two. He's insanely fit.

'Shhh, don't spoil the surprise,' Gemma hisses, having

sobered up from trying to get everyone out of the house on time. Brie pulls her into a side hug and whispers something in her ear and Gemma laughs, her shoulders instantly relaxing. Good old Brie, she's always so calm and knows just how to make light of a stressful situation.

'Yeah, well actually, maybe I've just changed my mind.' Samantha raises her eyebrows and licks her lips. I follow her gaze to find a huge group of men gathered by the bar, there's even more of them than there are of us. It looks like two stag parties, there's a man dressed up as a giant cactus, joking about with his friends and behind him leaning on the bar, is a man in a wedding dress deep in conversation with a tall friend. I'm guessing these are the stags. More than half of the men's heads swivel as we walk past them and some of them gawp over for way longer than is acceptable. They're all looking at Samantha, not that she minds from the gooey grin that she's displaying.

Out of sixteen women in their twenties and thirties she's the only other singleton on the hen do apart from me. She's stunning so I'm not surprised they're gawping, gosh even I would gawp at her. She swishes her long auburn, thick silky hair that sits just above her bum as I examine her tiny waist. She puts my blonde wispy locks and mum tum to shame but I do have a nice face and even nicer with Vanessa's handiwork to enhance my features. Just as I think this, the tall guy with big shoulders and a mop of dark curly hair, who I locked eyes with earlier, smiles the loveliest of smiles at me. I can't help but smile back and I have to look the other way to stop myself from grinning like a complete maniac.

This Mumma's still got it. This Mumma's still got it.

'You ladies here for the hen do?' a woman with a shiny bob asks. She's dressed in black trousers and a pink t-shirt with the words Cool Tours Excellence emblazoned across her chest.

'Yes,' Gemma nods.

'Excellent, I'm Suzie, come this way and I'll show you ladies to your area.' We all follow Suzie to the other side of the bar where sixteen orange cocktails await us, it looks like your typical freebie drink, very orange, very small and not very strong. Suzie explains that the booze cruise will start in thirty minutes and will last for two hours then we will be taken to Coco Lala for some dancing and I think that's where Nay's surprise stripper will turn up. Or is that tomorrow? I don't know, I can't keep track, poor Gem has had a lot to organise. The girls begin to down their drinks as I watch Vanessa delve into her handbag and retrieve the box of dares she told me about earlier whilst doing my makeup.

'This drink is rank,' Brie whispers to me, so as not to stress Gemma out any more. Curly hair man locks eyes with me again and we both smile shyly then look away.

'I know, shall we sneak off and get something else, there's no queue, look,' I say, thinking that we'll avoid the dares too if we go now. I don't want to do a dare. Just as I'm thinking I'm too old for this shit, Curly smiles at me again. I could get used to this and if we go to the bar we will be that bit closer to him. I don't know what it is but I just need to get close to him, get a better look. He's pulling me in like a magnet. It's all his fault.

'Let's do it.'

Brie and I shimmy away from the group and make our escape for a better drink, we reach the bar and order two glasses of wine. I suck my stomach in and take my time to sip my drink as Brie talks about how stressful the hen do arranging has been for Gemma while curly guy and I makes eyes at each other. We begin to walk back to the group and I do what I think is my best sashay.

'Mind out girls!' Samantha bumps into Brie as she trots past us, boobs first, clutching a piece of paper in her hand. She's making a beeline for the group of men on the stag. Cactus tries to stop her from getting too close and one of them shouts at him for acting like a prick. She laughs, eye fucks a few of the men then stops at cute curly hair man. My heart sinks as she fiddles with the piece of paper in her hand and gets down on one knee.

Ah the first dare, but I thought they were all meant for Nay.

Why is she doing them?

'You're the hottest guy in here,' she says in a raspy, sexy voice. 'Will you marry me?' Her bosom heaves and her eyelashes flutter.

Some of his mates groan and complain about him *not* being the hottest as Samantha extends her long elegant arm forward, revealing a gummy sweet friendship ring for him. He looks down at her and smiles kindly, then to my surprise, furtively steals a glance at me. It's so quick that nobody else would have noticed but I did. Is he teasing me? My heart skips a beat then drops into my stomach; he is incredibly good looking, of course he's going to say yes to the gorgeous Samantha's fake proposal. At a closer look he has the most beautiful smile and teeth and a slightly curved nose that makes him resemble a Greek god. I sigh a little too loudly, I'd love to snog his face off and so much more. I've not seen someone this fit in, well, forever.

'Urrrm I, well thank you.' He laughs a deep sexy laugh.

Butterflies form in my stomach and begin to slut drop like they've never slut dropped before. Samantha puts the ring on his finger then gets pulled into a chat with one of his friends who basically falls over himself to get to her. Curly winces then glances over at me again. *I know, I know, it's me that you want really, baby.* I've never felt so ridiculous and normally I'd be sure that it was Samantha that he wanted but the way he's looking at me is so sweet, so sincere, so clear. Wow, if there's more men like him out in the world then maybe I should consider finding a plus-one. It could be fun trying to find one at least.

Chapter 3

'Come this way ladies, it's time for the booze cruise,' Suzie sings, as she jigs about doing an excited dance for us.

It's nice to see someone so enthusiastic about their job, I bet she has a right laugh with all the hen and stag parties. I also bet she has to put up with some shit too, I think as we pass the group of men and the walking cactus who is now dancing around trying to trip up the barman. Hmmm maybe he really is a big prick.

We drag Samantha away from her ever growing fan club and Gemma rounds up the rest of group before we (a herd of women in heels, little black dresses and white sashes) follow Sadie out of the pub making the five-minute walk down to the beach and pier. We almost resemble a bunch of penguins on their way to migrate or maybe on their way to mate, just as I think this, I giggle to myself. That wine is definitely starting to kick in, I should probably stick to one drink now.

On the way down, Samantha tells us that Curly's name is George and that the group of lads also come from Swindon, which isn't that surprising as this seems the hot place to be. Swindon was also recently voted one of the worst places to go out in the UK so lots of people are fleeing in pursuit of a decent night out. Samantha tells me George is also single. Luckily she has her eyes set on someone else now, some guy called Lee who told her that she looked like a ginger *Megan Fox*. I suppose she does.

It's nearing nine in the evening by the time we've queued up and begun to board the knackered looking boat with Cool Lady painted on the side. The sun is just beginning to set and behind the boat is a beautiful display of pink and navy-blue swirls in the sky.

'Stunning, isn't it?' Brie nudges me, reading my mind. 'You don't see a sky like this often in Swindon, reminds me of Oz.' She smiles as I continue to admire the sky and push away any intrusive thoughts about the boat being able to make the two-hour cruise. What was the hottest day of the year has now turned rather windy and whilst it feels nice on my skin, especially my rather warm face, I'm not one hundred percent confident that this booze cruise is such a good idea.

My eyes dart to the large group of men joining the end of the queue, I don't recognise any of them apart from the cactus, but that means gorgeous George, just might be with them.

'Yeah, I was just going to say the same,' I reply as I slyly scan the group of men for him. God you'd think I'd never been out or seen a good-looking male before. Well I suppose I haven't, not for a very long time anyway, almost three years and I'm *not* going to do anything, I just want to admire him from afar. My bit of eye candy and secret sexy smiles for the night, that's enough for me. A little confidence kick is all I fancy really.

'Which one are you checking out?' Brie teases as she nudges me in the ribs again.

'No-one.'

'Liar.'

'Okay, the one that Samantha proposed to but I can't

see him now anyway.'

'Really? I'm surprised, he's so different to Billy.'

'Exactly.' I wink.

'Okay then ladies, come this way,' Suzie sings, as she skips along the gangway. So used to the wobbliness of it all, she practically dances down it. We begin to follow her, the first few girls thinking that they can do the same before stumbling around like Bambi on stilts. I'm next and I grip onto the ropes for dear life, pulling myself along as if I'm using a bendy Zimmer frame, my feet barely touching the ground. One of the staff holds out his hand to me which gives me the final pull to get myself onboard.

God this is embarrassing, I hope George isn't watching.

'Phew, I'm safe, I'm on the other side.' I punch the air as some of the other girls who have already made it, whoop and high five me. Brie's next and she struggles just as I did; then there's Samantha who, of course, struts down the gangway like a *Victoria Secrets* model*,* turning around and blowing a kiss to Lee as she does so. There's always one.

But where is the lovely, gorgeous George?

This is almost like a test, make it across and you get to have fun. Nay's next, followed by Vanessa, then Gemma who pretty much has a mental break down halfway across the gangway. Brie steps in and saves her by launching herself onto the gangway and practically dragging her across to the other side. The rest of the girls follow, until we're all finally on the other side. I wonder how the cactus will do, just as the thought enters my head he comes stumbling onto the gangway, throwing himself around left right and centre. The sea may be choppy but he certainly wins the title of most off his chops.

'Come this way ladies, free drinks downstairs await you,' Suzie chirps, as she bobs down below deck and we all follow her to the tiny bar which appears to be exclusively for us. Nice.

'Urgh I feel a bit sick girls,' Nay says, as we stand swaying shoulder to shoulder watching the barmen pour our champagne.

Ah Champagne, now that's more like it. Gemma takes Nay off to sit her down and put her head between her legs as I fetch her a glass of water. We drink our glasses of champagne and I'm just starting to really enjoy myself, despite the swaying boat, before we're ushered back upstairs to where a band is playing nineties club covers. Suzie tells us it's now the other hen parties turn for their drinks in the bar. We've had our fifteen minutes.

'Talk about a conveyor belt system,' Brie remarks, as I try not to snigger. Poor Gemma, she's been so stressed about this and so far it's been a tad ropey. I'm sure it will improve.

'We just need more alcohol.' I glance over at Nay who's now perched on a bench with around half of the hen do singing along to *Re-rewind* by *Craig David*. At least there's retro songs to enjoy. Vanessa shoves the dare box under Nay's nose. Brie and I exchange looks, it's time to go in search of more alcohol before that dare box makes its way over to us. We bump and sway into each other and almost everyone else we come into contact with. After swimming through the sea of people we finally get to the bar and order ourselves some much needed drinks.

'Two Sambucas please, buddy,' Brie shouts over the music to the barman as I take in my surroundings. Everyone looks smashed and it appears to be all stag and hen parties and I suddenly feel the need to get very smashed and join them. The music is so loud. I've turned into such a granny.

'Make that four,' I add, as Brie grins at me. 'It's time to get smashed.'

'Babe, now you're talking,' Brie squawks.

'Mate, I'm gonna need to get smashed to enjoy this, look over there,' I scream into her ear and point. Brie follows my finger and we cringe, laughing at the five completely naked guys proceeding to make helicopters with their penises whilst laughing hysterically. 'I mean, I'm no prude but please, is that even allowed?' I pull a disgusted face and all of a sudden feel terribly sober.

'Ah babe that's grim.' Brie leans in closer. 'Remember the wet-t-shirt competitions we used to enter all the time, you were practically naked then and you didn't care.' She laughs.

'Yeah, and I always came at least third. But I wasn't completely naked, only from the waist up. BOOBS OUT ONLY.' I point to my boobs.

'I wouldn't get your boobs out in here,' a voice booms as I look up, and then up again to see a very tall man with big arms and stubble.

'Excuse me?'

'You don't want to do that, them lot would be all over you.' He throws a thumb in the direction of the naked helicopters. 'Dickheads them lot when they go out, you can probably tell they don't get out much.'

'Yeah, same here,' I giggle. 'You with them?'

'I'm afraid so, yes.' He shakes his head then turns to speak to his other, less wild mates.

'Stag do?' I ask, when he faces me again, smiling politely. He nods, closing his eyes for a split second.

'This place is crawling with stag and hen parties,' Brie says, before clinking glasses with me. We down our first Sambucas, cheers again then down the other one straight afterwards.

'Two more?' Brie asks whilst signalling for the barman to come over again, it's not our turn but he seems to like Brie who is taking full advantage.

'Yes please, that didn't touch the sides,' I say, feeling slightly more confident in my drinking ability. I've got this, these past few years of sobriety wouldn't have taken away my ability to drink most people under the table, would it? Of course not. I'm super mum.

Super fun mum.

'Make that six,' tall man says to the barman. 'Mind if I join you ladies? Bit too mental for me over there, I'm James by the way.'

'Knock yaself out, Jameo. But we can't promise we'll be tame for too long so you might wanna scoot back to ya little lameo mates once we get going, ain't that right Tills?' Brie says, as she winks at me.

By now I'd be fast asleep in bed if I were at home. Dirty stop out me.

'Sorry, she doesn't mean it,' I say to James who grins and nods. I'm not sure if he heard me or her for that matter. 'Can I have a water too?' I ask the barman, suddenly feeling like I have to be sensible as Brie obviously has no desire to be. 'Gotta stay hydrated.' Brie looks at me in disgust. 'Also, my face still feels hot. I want to avoid heatstroke if I can.'

'You look beautiful babe,' Brie slurs, as my head begins to feel fuzzy.

'Ah, what song is this? This is a good one!' James says, whilst beginning to sway from side to side to the music, in the opposite direction to the swaying of the boat.

'You're making me dizzy, swaying the wrong way.' I giggle as we bump into each other. I steady myself as best I can then attempt to show him which way to sway whilst he sings along about a great philosopher being naughty, very naughty. Then he does the unexpected and busts out a bit of trooping. His big legs slamming down in perfect timing to the beat.

It's quite impressive.

'Alright, MC Hammer.' I laugh as he continues to sing along. 'I don't know this one?' I'm still amused by his big footed trooping.

My eyes travel to the band setting up at the end of the boat who look as if they could be a K-pop band. They're beautiful and practice their dancing in perfect unison. I only found out what a K-pop band was the other week when my brother emailed me, it's his new favourite thing apparently.

'What?' James says, out of breath as he stops trooping. 'It's a classic!' You must know it – Ebeneezer Goode?' he says, and I shake my head 'But anyone born in the nineties probably won't know this to be fair.'

'I wasn't born in the nineties, I'm an eighties baby, yeah.' I punch the air and whoop, almost punching James. Okay the alcohol's kicked in now, well and truly.

'What no way? I thought you were younger,' he exclaims, and I smile and say thank you for the compliment. This is more like it.

'Now this is a song,' I say as Brie hands me another drink and we head over to the dance floor in front of the band who are now playing.

The Vengaboys' *Up and Down* plays as people grind up and down, it's taking me way back to my school days. Meanwhile James is back to swaying in the wrong direction which is cracking Brie and I up as well as himself. He's really getting into it then the old skool dancing appears and we copy him as he pretends to shop then get things off the shelves, in-between doing the odd random massive clap. I look at his hands, they're like two big shovels.

'You're really showing your age now,' I shout over the music, as he swaps to big fish, little fish, cardboard box movements with his hands. The signature dance move from the late nineties, early noughties, so my brother tells me.

'So are you!' he teases.

'We didn't do this, I'm just copying you.' I begin to show off and slut drop to the floor. Brie joins me and we high five on the way back up.

'Just like the old days, mate.' We grin at each other.

'Shit. That was surprisingly easy,' I screech, as I drop to the floor once more, instantly regretting it as a pang *down there* reminds me not to push it, literally.

'Yeah, yeah,' James says, as he proceeds to slut drop too.

'Oh fuck, help,' he whimpers, as Brie and I look down at him bouncing on the floor on his bum as the boat throws us all around.

I laugh and bend over as my stomach begins to hurt then almost fall on the floor myself due to the swaying old boat. The sea is so rough, I wonder if it's even safe. I'm sure they know what they're doing, don't they? He reaches up to me and we each grab a huge arm before heaving him to stand up. I bet he could pick me up with his little finger and I'm not even small, just average sized.

'Yeah, maybe don't do that again mate,' Brie says, as we all giggle and James looks around theatrically to see if anyone saw him. That doesn't stop him from doing another slut drop but this time he manages to get himself up. Just.

We spend the next few songs laughing and dancing before some of James's friends join us, not the helicopter dicks, some other friends who look like some of the blokes that were in the pub, although I'm not sure as a lot of the men are dressed the same. Nay, Samantha, Gemma and some of the other girls join us. We're really going for it. Brie disappears then reappears with a tray of shots for everyone and I end up doing three shots because Gemma and one of James's friends turn them down. James also does three or four shots. I don't blame anyone for turning these down, it's tequila. Rank.

The band stop for a break as the DJ begins to play *No Diggity* by Blackstreet, the tequila warms and runs through my veins and I begin to pop my body to the beat whilst trying to stay steady on my feet.

It's the rocky boat not me, okay!

We all go mad for the music. I know we're verging on the edge of old fartness but none of us give a fuck and this is fun. Good old clean adult fun. God I've missed going out having a drink and a dance.

It's so nice to finally cut lose.

Good old clean adult fun.

Blackstreet sings about being a perfect ten and a few of the guys points to Samantha as she basks in the attention, flicking her hair and popping her heaving bosom. I look over at cactus who's looking a bit worse for wear sitting on a chair along the side of the boat; he's been over watered it seems.

Then, it all goes a bit Pete Tong. Wrong.

'AAAAH FUCK,' James shouts, looking very pale then proceeds to clomp away from the group, swaying from side to side like the BFG looking for his home. None of his mates seem fussed and are probably in no fit state to help him. What I can only describe as my maternal instincts kick in and I run after him.

'Back in a minute,' I shout to the girls. 'Don't leave

without me,' I continue, then remember we're on a boat and none of us can leave. Yes, none of us can leave this very choppy, very unstable, old boat.

Shit.

'What's wrong, are you alright?' I ask, then begin to tentatively and awkwardly rub his back as he leans over the side of the boat, sweating.

'No. No,' he says. 'Just go.' He steadies himself, holding onto the side of the boat, leaning further forward, breathing heavily.

Any moment now.

I look away. If there's one thing I can't stand, it's vomit. I know, how do I even cope with a child?

'I'll get you a water, be back in a minute.' I skip off as fast as I can to get some water and some paper towels. I can already hear the loud beginnings of retching and puking and I wince for him.

Poor bloke.

He obviously doesn't get out much either, or else he's been on it since midday. Probably the latter.

By the time I've come back to James the K-pop band are gathered by the side of the boat talking excitedly and pointing to the sea. James hangs his head in shame, coupled with what looks like sheer disbelief.

'Are you okay? What's going on?' I ask, as he looks up, wipes his forehead on his t-shirt then nods in the direction of the sea without looking at it.

I take a few steps forward then force myself to peer over the edge. The sea, covered in a little blanket of his vomit is bobbing up and down with the waves.

'Oh God,' I put my hand over my mouth and closing my eyes, desperately try not to laugh. What did he eat? 'The fish, they're feasting on your sick,' I say, pointing out the obvious.

'I know.' He nods and wipes his brow again, this time with the paper towels.

Meanwhile the K-pop band and a few other people from the ship take photos of this seemingly fascinating spectacle.

'At least they're being fed. Fed is best hey.' I grin and pat him on the back.

Chapter 4

'Urgh, my head,' I grumble, as I slowly open my eyes and stare at the ceiling. 'My breath honks. Why can I taste farts?'

I roll onto my front and lean on my elbows to talk to Brie. Except Brie isn't there and I don't appear to be in my room. My mouth opens and closes again. No, this is definitely not my room. This room is much, much bigger and there are four more beds in it with men in them, fast asleep. What is this? The next day after a gang bang? There's also someone asleep next to me. Slowly, careful not to wake the sleeping stranger, I peak under the covers then breathe a sigh of relieve. I'm fully dressed, that's a positive but then panic washes over me again.

'I've been kidnapped,' I gasp, then put my hand over my mouth, half because I don't want them to hear me and half not wanting to kill them with my breath if they're not kidnappers.

'No, you wanted to party like a fun mum from nineteen ninety-nine or something,' one of them grunts from the opposite bed, before turning over and farting, moments later he begins to snore like a steam train.

Okay, perhaps I wasn't kidnapped, but what the fuck am I doing here? This does not look like good old clean adult fun. I desperately try to piece together the night as

I try to sneak a peak at the man sleeping next to me, my eyes follow the shape of his body until I get to his feet poking out of the end of the bed. He's very tall.

James.

The fish feeder.

I close my eyes, wanting the ground to swallow me up. How did I get here? A vague recollection of us stumbling off the boat and going onto a nightclub flashes in my mind's eye, but how did I get *here*? So many questions that I don't think my brain can handle right now.

'Fuck,' I whisper to myself, as I grab my phone which is luckily on the floor beside me. I check the time, eight o'clock in the morning and there's five missed calls and a few messages from Brie asking if I'm okay and if I've pulled; a message from Billy telling me to stop ringing him as it's the middle of the night and he's trying to sleep (oh God) and a message from Samantha.

Sam: *Don't leave without me, such a good night last night, you were funny. Silly Tilly! Silly Tilly xx*

Me: *Where the hell are we/you? x* I reply as I stare down at James trying to remember how I got here. I certainly do feel like a silly Tilly. My handbag strap is underneath his head, I tug on it to move it and bring it back to me but the whole bag is wedged underneath him. I don't want to wake him. I just want to creep out of here and pretend this never happened, whatever *this* is.

'Fuck,' I cuss under my breath, as the bag doesn't budge. I lean over him and slide my arm underneath feeling around for my bag before giving it a short, sharp tug. That should do it.

'Ouch,' he yelps, stirring as I catch my nails on the back of his neck. Shit. My face, now two inches away from his. I hold my breath as his eyes shoot open.

'ARRRGHHHHHHH,' he screams into my face, with a look of pure terror on his face. Why is *he* scared? I'm the one alone in a room full of men.

'ARRRRGHHHHHHH,' I scream back, before yanking on my bag one last time then sprinting out of the room. Moments later, I sprint back again really wishing I could just teleport myself back to the other house, no in fact, back in time forty-eight hours ago, that's where I want to be, saying no to coming on this bloody hen do.

'My shoes,' I whisper, as all the other men wake up and begin to give me a round of applause.

'Hey, it's fun mum, good morning,' one of them says.

'How's your head this morning, fun mum?' another guy comments.

'Did you get through to your ex and tell him what a dick he is?' Steam train snorer asks.

Fuck, why are they calling me fun mum?

'Shit, fun mum, what's happened to your face.' All three stare at me as James scuttles around for my shoes. What the hell happened? A flashback of us dancing in the living room and someone offering me an edible occurs. Surely not. I wouldn't have done drugs. No way.

'Fancy a cuppa?' one of them asks, as he gets up and heads towards the door.

'Umm no thanks, I'm good,' I answer back awkwardly.

'I can't find them I'm afraid, house is a bit of a mess.' He winces. 'Here take mine for now.' James hands me his shoes which must be at least a size twelve, they're huge. I guess he would look strange with small feet, he must be way over six foot.

'I can't wear them, they're enormous,' I say, putting my hands on my hips.

'You can't walk back bare footed, it's fine, when we find yours I'll bring them over.'

'But I need my shoes, they're Jimmy Choos,' I whine, wondering how far I'll have to walk. Miles, hours potentially.

'Just tell him I'm looking for them. I'm sure he'll understand. They'll turn up, don't worry, you had them on last night so they're here somewhere. These will have to do until I find them.'

'Tell who?'

'Jimmy,' James says, and I don't think he's joking.

Okay, thanks,' I say, as I reluctantly step into his giant, tan shoes. 'What must I look like?'

He raises his eyebrows at me and smirks.

'You do look a little different to last night.' Charming! I bet I do look rough though. I don't even want to see a mirror until I'm back at the house.

'Yes, well, you're not perfect either, at least fish don't feast on my vomit. Where's my friend, Samantha?' I say, as his mates cheer and laugh. Ha! Take that fish feeder. He lays one of his giant hands on his heart and laughs.

'I think she's with my mate, come this way.'

I follow James through the living room then downstairs and along the corridor until we reach the last door on the left. There are men asleep everywhere. I even step over a couple of them on the corridor floor. James begins to knock on the door but not before we are treated to Samantha and her lover's pure moans of pleasure.

'Oh God,' James mutters under his breath, as we both stand there in awkward silence, looking down at the floor; until they've finished their business. I don't know Samantha that well but I know way too much about the noises she makes in bed now. Lovely.

'Comingggggggg. mate,' a male out-of-breath voice answers very loudly.

'I really hope not, mate, don't want to hear that again,' James mutters under his breath while looking at me.

I snigger and he smiles back whilst we try to ignore the giggles and loud whispers coming from the other side of the door. He has a nice smile, don't remember noticing that last night. We did have fun from what I can remember. An image of us slut dropping down to the floor pings in my memory. Gosh how many down to the floor squats did I do last night? What was I trying to prove? That this mumma's still got it or that I'm such a fun mum? No wonder my legs are sore, at least my pelvic floor didn't let me down and I didn't wet myself. But come to think of it I am a bit sore down there. I hope we didn't shag, did we? I slyly look him up and down, thinking that my memory might be jogged if we did. No, nothing is coming to me, no sex memories. But I'm so uncomfortable.

'You okay?' he asks, tilting his head at me with a silly smile.

'Yeah, fine, just tired.' I'm too ashamed to ask him if we slept together, a girl should know and I don't even remember us kissing so that's *really* bad if we did. *Good old clean adult fun*. The voice echoes in my head.

Yeah, there's no way we slept together.

'Ello, mate.' The man behind the sex moans answers the door with Samantha's arms wrapped around his waist. He looks different to the man she was with last night. She pokes her head out from behind him, still looking perfect, like a ginger *Megan Fox*.

'Hey gorg… oh Tilly…'

'Hey, Sam, good night?' I do a dramatic wink, trying to make light of the fact that we heard them bonking, loudly. 'Shall we get out of here now? Nay will be wondering where we are.' I grin and give her the wide eyes let's get out of here stare.

'It's okay, I've text her but Tils,' she says, biting her lip whilst sounding as if she's known me for years when we've only met a handful of times through Nay. I think last night is the most I've ever spoken to her in the whole twenty years I've known her. 'Tils, your face,' she says through a smirk, with that over familiarity again.

I frown as both my hands fly up to the side of my face.

'What is it?' I ask, now peering through my hands whilst hiding my face.

'Oh, I think she looks very appealing,' James quips, as Samantha and her lover giggle uncontrollably. In that moment I decide I hate them all and James the most as I watch him bend forward, guffawing loudly. Clearly he finds my poor face the funniest thing he's ever seen.

How incredibly rude and mean.

I'm sure I have a mirror in my bag. I dig around in there, pulling out my compact. If no one will tell me what's on my face, I'll just look for myself.

Shits.

'Oh nooo,' I whimper, half wanting to cry, half wanting to scream as I stare back at the sorry creature that is me. Vanessa's excellent makeup has disintegrated to reveal the true beast. My whole face is peeling and bright beacon red, especially my nose which brings out the big white hearts around my eyes. Those eyelashes have made their way down my face again. To be fair, I don't blame them, if I were my eyelashes, I'd be trying to escape my face too.

I look truly terrible.

A monster.

A mum monster.

I look like I've just had one of those chemical peels that mum wants, no, I look worse. Why didn't James tell me? He let me look like this in front of his mates and didn't say a thing. A true gent would have taken me aside and told me the truth.

What an absolute knob.

'And where's your shoes?' She laughs, staring down at my enormous boat feet. I shrug, feeling helpless.

I want to cry.

Samantha's face drops, sensing my misery before she scuttles off to put her clothes on and grab her things. She's taking ages, probably giving what's his face his final goodbye bonk. James and I stand there in an awkward silence until I can't take it anymore.

'So got much else planned for the stag?' I ask.

'Not much,' he says, looking uncomfortable. Did *we* bonk? 'Think we've got some axe throwing arranged which should be fun and then onto a casino.'

'Sounds cool.' I'd like to throw a few axes right now.

'You?' he asks, sounding genuinely interested. Stop looking at me.

'Think we've got a dance class and then a stripper for the hen, just standard hen do stuff.' I wave my hand away, feeling the sudden urge to go home. I want to see my baby, I want to be sat on my sofa giving her a cuddle, not this, being laughed at by a rude stranger.

'Sounds like my worst nightmare,' he says, attempting a joke, but I think he's forgotten that I saw those moves last night. I squint my eyes at him and he looks at the floor. Samantha finally opens the door looking even more sheepish than before.

'Bye Sammy, call me yeah.' So it is a different guy, I'm sure the one last night was called Lee, not that I'm anyone to judge. Sammy grins from ear to ear as Samantha flutters her eye lashes at him because she can, hers are still on her eyelids and not on her cheeks like mine. With this thought I quickly peel them off and stuff them into my handbag. I catch James looking at me, his eyebrows flash up and stay there. I scowl at him.

'Bye gorgeous, yeah sure, can't wait.' They go in for another snog as James and I wait painfully for it to end.

'Bye then.' James waves as we begin to walk to the stairs.

'Bye, have a nice life.' I wave and I mean it because it's highly unlikely I'll ever have to see him again.

Samantha and I leave the house and I breathe in the fresh sea air. Another scorching hot day. I don't know if my face can take it anymore.

'Have you got any battery left on your phone? Shit we should have asked them for taxi numbers,' I say to Samantha, who is already texting away with a gooey expression on her face.

'Taxi? How much did you drink last night?' She scoffs and I wonder how it must feel to be as perfect as Samantha.

'Enough,' I mutter, having no idea how much I drank. A memory of me laughing, telling James that *sleep can wait* as I order us another drink at the bar sneaks into my mind. Oh God.

'Our house is there, Silly Tilly, that's what you kept calling yourself last night.' Samantha giggles then points her arm out in front of us to the hill with the house on top of it, the house with the navy-blue door. It's our house and it's less than fifty metres away.

'But you might want to walk barefoot, in case you fall over in those.' Samantha moves her finger to my feet and I let out an enormous groan that echoes around the whole of Coolsbay.

Chapter 5

Samantha and I enter the house to a massive round of applause from the girls, all wanting the gossip from our night/morning. Nay is already on the prosecco and is having her hair braided by Vanessa. I wonder if she'll sort my face out again later? I *really need* her to sort my face out later. After giving them the low down on the morning and catching up with Nay and all the dares she had to do including doing the worm on the dance floor and convincing a stranger that she used to be a man, I sneak off for a shower and a lie down. It's only ten o'clock in the morning and Bollywood dancing doesn't start until two o'clock this afternoon. I can have a little nap before the next round of fun begins.

Hen dos are exhausting.

I find my bedroom and open the door to find Brie sound asleep in the bed. Ah yes, how could I forget, we only have one bed and were meant to top and tail last night. I creep in, take off James's shoes and grab my shower bag and towels. I've never felt more in need of a shower in my life, even after I gave birth I don't remember feeling this grotty plus I'm desperate to pump and dump, my boobs feel fit to burst.

A while later, feeling a thousand times refreshed, I arrive back at the bedroom.

'Alrighty-roo, Tills! How was last niiihgt?' Brie trills as she pulls on a pair of jeans and a jumper while I envy her flat, taut stomach. 'I tried to get you to come home but you were having none of it and anyway you seemed to be having such a hoot with that James guy, who by the way is HOT.'

'You think? I guess he was quite easy on the eye,' I say, as I picture his kind brown eyes, thick dark stubble and nice smile. He was also huge which made me feel tiny, not that it matters as I won't be seeing him again.

'Hell, yeah. When I found out Sam was going back too and they were only staying over the road I wasn't too worried about ya. Shit!' She pauses and stares at me. 'Your face,' Brie covers her mouth with her hand. I know she's laughing. I know I look ridiculous.

'Urgh, mate,' I say, waving it off. 'I don't remember that much, I was dancing on the boat, then in the club with that James guy and then I woke up in his room and there was like five other men in there.'

'Oh my God.' Brie looks horrified.

'I know.'

'Girl, are you okay?' she says taking my hand. 'Tell me everything, you're in a safe space now.'

'Yeah, I'm fine and there's nothing to tell. I woke up, couldn't find my shoes and I had to wear those big clodhopper's home.' I nod towards James's shoes. Also, my new knickers have been stuck up my bits all night and now I'm very sore. I'm quite confident there was no gang bang, it's just a case of fanny fire friction from wearing too tight knickers. Lovely. But I'm not one hundred percent something didn't happen with James, I did end up in his bed after all.

'What? I wondered who those belonged to.' She laughs, looking relieved. 'Thought that cheeky cow who stole our room last night must have brought a bloke back, I felt sick thinking about it so I'm glad that wasn't the case.'

'Someone stole our room?'

'Yeah, hasn't anyone said?' she asks and I shake my head slowly.

'I came in last night to some girl I'd never met before asleep in my bed. Nay's cousin apparently.'

'What? I didn't think she was coming?'

'She wasn't supposed to be, was she? But Nay really wanted her here so she drove down and surprised her then ended up drinking so couldn't drive back. I stayed out quite late and when I got back she was asleep in our bed.'

'Fuck, what did you do?'

'I went a bit ape shit but she was so drunk she just opened her eyes, looked at me and then slumped back down again. I had to resort to sleeping on the lumpy old couch which is why I had to have a power nap this morning. I was ragingly tired.'

'God, imagine if I'd come back too.'

'I know, I'm kinda pissed at Gemma for letting her stay. Hopefully she'll go home soon, I'm surprised you didn't notice her, she isn't exactly a wall flower.'

'But why was she in *our* room?' The tiniest room in the house.

'Me and a few of the other girls were still out and I guess she just helped herself to the empty room.'

'That's cheeky as hell.'

'Yep, I remember her saying in the group chat that she couldn't come because she couldn't afford it. Looks like you and I paid to share a single bed though.'

'Nice and cosy then,' I joke.

'I know, she's a free-loader, she shouldn't be getting

away with it.'

'True, but let's try and avoid any drama though, I've had my quota times ten already,' I say, checking out my Freddy Kruger face in the tiny mirror. I can see why that James roared at me now, I look awful but that was nasty. I don't even know him.

'I'll try, can't promise though.' She winks as I flop down on the bed, still in my towel, letting out an almighty groan that echoes around the room.

'Right, my turn for a power nap now,' I say, yawning and stretching myself out on the tiny bed. It actually feels smaller than a normal single bed. We have definitely been stitched up.

'Knock yourself out sunshine, I'm off to find the wine.'

'Good luck, wake me up for the dance class.'

'Will do.' Brie saunters out of the room, closing the door behind her.

I hope she doesn't find Nay's cousin and lump her one. My friends welcomed Brie into our friendship group straight away and they do seem to love her but sometimes I don't know if it's because they're a little scared of her. She isn't afraid of conflict that one, and she's being a lot grumpier lately, I wouldn't be surprised if she punched Nay's cousin.

I pull my phone out of my bag, eager to see how Billy and Nancy-Ella are doing. He doesn't answer so I leave a voicemail rambling on about how much I miss her and to please send me some photos of their day. I cringe as I remember James's friends telling me I called Billy at three in the morning, luckily there's no record of me speaking to him. Minutes later he sends through three photos of them at the park, along with a message saying that everything is fine and to stop fussing. I'm not exactly fussing; I'm just asking how my daughter is.

Jeez.

Maybe he thought I was ringing at three in the morning to fuss about Nancy-Ella, better that he thinks that rather than the real reason, which was to apparently call him a dick.

Drunk me is the *real* dickhead here.

I go through the photos again, one of her on a swing laughing, another of her on the slide and then again on the slide with Billy. She looks happy, really happy. I'm pleased. But hang on a minute, who took the photo of Billy and Nancy-Ella on the slide? Has the worst happened? Has he got a new girlfriend? He wouldn't have introduced them without consulting me first, would he? It's something I knew was coming but now I can't bear it.

Me: *Looks fun, give her a squish from me. Who took the photo?* I tap send, hoping I sound casual and not as stalkery as I feel. Two blue ticks and he leaves me on read, am I that obvious? I study the photos over and over before my phone eventually drops out of my hand and I pass out, dreaming of big shoes, Billy's new girlfriend who looks very much like Samantha but in a different font and big juicy kebabs.

I wake up to my stomach grumbling and the smell of pizza, it's not a kebab but I'll take it. Billy's still left me on read. I get dressed and find the living room where most of the girls have congregated and are sat stuffing their faces with pizza, garlic bread and all things greasy and breaded.

'Tilly, we saved you some of the veggie one, it's very

yummy.' Gemma smiles as I wander over to their table. She looks a lot less stressed so I'm guessing Brie's kept a lid on it so far. I scan the room for the naughty cousin but she is nowhere to be seen but neither is Brie.

Uh Oh.

'Thanks girls.' I may be a veggie but I can still dream of kebabs, okay.

'Tilly,' Samantha says, grinning like a Cheshire cat and motioning with her hands for me to come to her. I grab a few slices of pizza, plonk them on a plate with a napkin, thank Gem, then pad over to *Megan Fox*. 'Sammy just sent me this,' she giggles and crinkles her eyes up. I look at the photo on Samantha's phone, squinting my eyes until I finally figure out what Samantha finds so funny.

My shoes are being worn by a blow-up doll. My beautiful Jimmy Choo shoes that I've only worn once before, on a blow-up doll.

'Her name's Tallulah.' Samantha giggles again, enjoying this all a bit too much.

'Tallulah has good taste in shoes,' Nay quips, holding out her hand to high-five me before pouring me a glass of prosecco.

'Yes, she does.' I clink her glass with the one she handed me but really I want to tell Samantha to text Sammy and ask for my shoes back immediately. They were expensive and seeing them on that doll just reminds me how beautiful they are. I sip on my prosecco, trying to think of how I can get them back. I might just have to swallow my pride and go over there after Vanessa has sorted my face out which reminds me, I need to *ask* her to sort my face out. I slapped on a load of aloe vera when I woke up so it isn't as angry as it was but it's still a bit of a sight and will be needing a professional's work.

'You not with Billy anymore then, Tills?' Lisa, my old

friend from school, asks. We used to be close but I don't really see her anymore, different lives, different routines, different outlook and all that.

'No, not been together for a while now,' I reply. I thought I'd managed to avoid this question, I thought everyone knew. Don't they read status updates on Facebook anymore?

'Oh no, how come?'

'Oh, it just didn't work out, not meant to be.' I smile, brushing it off.

I don't want to get into it in front of everyone because I still get embarrassed saying that he left me when Nancy-Ella was just four weeks old. Not wanting to explain that it felt like everything was my fault. Not wanting to explain that we still hang out and pretend everything is okay for Nancy-Ella's sake. Not wanting to admit that since he dumped me we still slept together for a while but now even that's fizzled out since he's practically in a relationship with the coffee shop. Not wanting to say out loud that I'm slowly realising that my fun, outgoing, loveable intelligent Billy is actually a bit of a twat and only thinks of himself. That's how come.

'Aww bless you, I'm so sorry, that's *really really* shit,' Lisa says, rubbing salt into the wound as a few of the others nod along with her in agreement with concern etched on their faces. Great, now I'm the pitied single mum. Come to think of it, I must be the only single mum here.

'She's alright aren't you, babe. Brilliant mum,' Nay says.

I nod, blinking back tears. I'm fine, I'll be just fine.

We spend the next hour scoffing and drinking until all plans to go to the Bollywood dance class go out of the window when Nay is sick then decides to take a two-hour long nap. Who can argue with the bride to be? Most of us are secretly pleased not to have to go through an hour and a half of dancing around looking like a knob but there are a few who grumble because they were really looking forward to it. You know the sort, the ones that are good at dancing and have rhythm. Yes that group, including Samantha of course, and also Krissy, the cousin, who hasn't actually paid for the event. I've since found out that Krissy is also a mum and our kids are the same age, she's actually quite nice for a gate crasher. I'm not sure Brie thinks so, she keeps giving me dirty looks every time I speak to Krissy. We've been chatting about baby groups and she's even booked on to the same one as me next week, Music Bums. I'm relieved I'll have a familiar face there; those things can be so cliquey sometimes.

The lovely Vanessa has done my makeup and now we're sat around playing games as Nay gets her hair done, completely unaware that a stripper is going to turn up at any moment.

There's a knock at the door and Gemma springs out of her seat looking a little agitated. Krissy follows her which I'm sure won't help with the agitation but by the looks of it she's only trying to help.

'Think the stripper was supposed to text her, not knock on the door, he's messed her about a lot this evening. The last I heard was that he might not be able to make it as he was stuck in Wales,' Brie whispers to me, as I keep one ear on the game of *never have I ever* that's going on in the corner.

Samantha's just admitted to bonking one of her friend's boyfriends before they started dating and the atmosphere has suddenly got very tense. Uh oh, this hen do is proving to be a little stressful, I guess that's what happens when you throw fifteen women together from all different walks of life with only one person in common then add alcohol.

'Oh right,' I say, biting my lip. This should at least brighten the mood anyway, I hope. 'I'll put some music on. Something to create a sexy kind of ambience, get the stripper guy feeling his stripper game.' I scroll through my phone and select Ginuwine's *Pony*. Yeah, I've watched *Magic Mike* way too many times.

Moments later the stripper is pushed into the room. Dressed in a very nice black suit, he's wearing a mask of Mark's face (Nay's fiancé) which looks hilarious because this guy is huge and Nay's partner is smaller than her. Jaws drop, smiles appear, the atmosphere instantly changes to something more positive and Nay begins to scream with hysterical excitement.

He looks very smart for a stripper.

I thought they usually dressed as fireman, policemen etc, but what would I know? The only stripper I've seen was on someone's work do about fifteen years ago and he was around forty-five in a red thong and oiled up to the max, didn't even bother with an outfit, didn't even strip.

Brie dims the lights and I crank the music up before sitting back to relax and enjoy the show. The stripper plods into the middle of the living room, looking a little awkward and begins to side step. Ahhh this must be part of his act, the shy man at a wedding type. I like it, original.

He continues to plod.

Fifteen women cheer and clap.

Any minute now, he's going to throw out some impressive hip thrusts.

He continues to plod, his big hands slapping together

in time with the beat as his big feet step from side to side. There's now a slight hint of hip thrusting going on, any minute now he's going to throw himself on the floor and start gyrating.

'Look at those hands, I bet he has a huge…' Brie begins.

'Nice package there, love,' Krissy screeches, slapping her thigh then rubbing her hands together. Brie gives her an icy glare clearly still fuming from the room situation.

One of the girls plonks a chair down next to the stripper and forces Nay onto the seat before thrusting a can of squirty cream into his hand.

He dances around her, looking more like he's dancing round a maypole at first. Nay screams in hysteria, shaking her head.

'Nooooooo, I just want to watch, please it's too weird,' she screeches, getting up from the seat and running over to me.

'Go on, Tils. Take one for the team, you're the only single one here.' Great, rub it in, why don't you. Nay grabs my arms and propels me forward until I land with a smack, arse down on the chair.

'Ouch.'

The stripper's thrusts become a little more animated as he undoes his tie and proceeds to tie my wrists up around the back of the chair. He smells delicious, like warm cinnamon, fresh mint and musky man. It's oddly familiar. He wiggles and grinds his buttocks in my face before twirling around and slowly (a little too slowly) undoing his shirt. I'm no expert but I thought they provided them with the sort of shirts that you could just rip off. I've seen *Magic Mike*. He takes his time, still doing the shy guy act it seems before he's standing in front of me in just his trousers. His big muscley, slightly hairy torso just centimetres from my face. He gently places the can of squirty cream in my hand, unties the tie around my hands, placing his finger over mine and points it at his chest before the can explodes on him.

Screams echo around the room as he scoops some of the cream off his chest and tries to put it in my mouth.

'No way! I don't know where you've been,' I screech hysterically, before he hesitates, thinks about wiping it on his trousers, then decides to eat the cream himself instead, slipping it behind the mask.

I need to see who is behind that mask.

He whisks me off the chair, carrying me with his strong arms up into an almost dirty dancing type pose before flipping me around, making me get on top of his back whilst he does push ups.

He's so strong.

I'm so lame to be enjoying this.

Just like Ginuwine says, I'm riding my pony.

Next, he's flinging me around like a little rag doll, it's as if I weigh almost nothing to him.

It's humiliating, hilarious, hugely fun and a tad sexy, just a tad.

It would be even sexier without that bloody mask on, the last thing I want to see is Mark's face (no offence Mark). The stripper picks me up and I wrap my legs around him as he begins to bounce up and down with those strong thighs.

I swiftly grab the mask, entering a wrestling match with him until the thing finally comes away and Mark's face is left dangling around his neck like a parasite. A two headed stripper.

'It's you,' I gasp, as James smiles back at me, his eyes twinkling. He's enjoyed himself a bit too much and annoyingly so have I. But that was before I knew who it was. The man who laughed at my face.

'Hey,' he smiles that infuriating, mocking smile. 'I only came to bring your shoes back and they made me do this,' he says with raised eyebrows.

'Hmm I find it hard to believe that they made you.' I wriggle in his arms, feeling a little weirded out. He loosens his grip on me so that I can get down. My eyes rest on Gemma, who's stood there biting her lip through her smile.

'The stripper let me down, his timing was perfect and he fitted the bill.' She shrugs. I don't blame her; she just wants Nay to have a good hen do but this is so cringe. I was in this man's bed less than twelve hours ago and now he's parading around as a stripper wearing another man's face as a mask.

'We were desperate,' Krissy deadpans, then bursts out laughing. 'No, you were great! Well done.' She claps at him then at me. 'You too, Tilly.'

'You were amazing!' Samantha purrs. 'Well done James, should have bought Sammy with you. You could have performed a double act.'

'Thank you, Samantha,' James says, as he begins to pull his shirt on and button it up as we hear a series of whoops and cheers from the other girls.

'Why are you wearing a suit though?' Brie asks.

'The stag wanted us in suits for the casino,' he says as he pulls on his trainers. Funny nobody noticed he was wearing those earlier; we were all too busy looking elsewhere.

'Lucky us,' Samantha touches his arm and he gently shrugs her off whilst looking at me. I glance over at Nay, who's now wearing Mark's face. Who knew that James was hiding such a nice body under there?

Shame he isn't a very nice person.

I mumble something about getting his shoes for him before escaping off down the hallway to retrieve them.

Hen dos are exhausting.

Chapter 6

'Urgh what a day,' Brie groans, as we haul our suitcases into the boot of her car and wave our final goodbyes to the hens, minus Krissy, who left super early this morning after she had nowhere to stay and no one was willing to share their bed, not even Nay.

I took the sofa so Brie could have the bed and even though there were spare sofas Krissy ended up passing out on the corridor floor with just a tea towel for a blanket. I felt mean and ended up draping my hoody over her in the night. I know she didn't pay to stay but I can't see a person shiver like that, no matter how much of a freeloader she is, plus we're meeting up next week at Music Bums and I could do with a friend there.

'What a day? What a weekend you mean, I feel broken,' I reply, as I slide on my heart shaped sunglasses.

'Out of practice.' Brie winks as we pull off the drive way.

'Yeah, definitely out of practice.'

'Did you get that bloke's number? He had a cracking bod on him,' Brie asks, as a flashback of James's chest pops up in my mind and I shake my head to get rid of it.

'The stripper? No, no. Not my type,' I say, as we pass the house the stag do guys were staying in. I was half expecting to bump into them last night but they went to the casino and we were in the nightclub. Samantha snuck off to meet Sammy, she did hint at me coming with her but I said I felt too tired. Too embarrassed more like.

'Really? Isn't he everyone's type?' Brie laughs then honks her horn at a car that's just cut her up. I close my eyes.

'Well he didn't ask me either, so…'

'It's the twenty first century, it's okay for a woman to ask for a man's phone number.'

'I know, I just didn't want to.'

'Okay, okay, I thought you wanted to meet people.'

'I do, just not him.' I sigh. 'I'll sign up to an online thingy this week.' I'm definitely feeling more in the mood to start meeting and dating other men. This weekend has taught me that there's plenty of sexy, single men out there and some of them even paid attention to little old me.

'That's the spirit, we'll get you a plus one for the wedding in no time.

'Have you set me up on a mission?' I side eye Brie.

'I definitely have, babe, the question is, are you up for it?' She asks before changing gear then speeding down the motorway like a mad woman.

'Finding a boyfriend – definitely not. Finding a plus one – I suppose so,' I say, as a flashback of James stripping flickers in my mind.

'I'm so excited for you, babe,' she says glancing at me as I vigorously shake my head to get rid of that insufferable man stuck inside my head. Brie laughs then changes the subject. 'Have you heard much from Billy?'

'Not much at all, I've called and left messages but I've practically had to squeeze communication out of him, it's been like getting blood out of a stone trying to find out what they've been up to and how she's been without me.'

'Good though, babe. It means they've coped without you. Can't you almost taste the freedom?' Brie says, but I can't help but think she means more for herself than for me, she wants her friend back, I get that.

I smile and close my eyes, feeling the warm sun on my face. It's only ten o'clock in the morning and it's super-hot already, the radio says we're in for a scorching hot summer.

'Shit! Sun cream! Sun Cream! I squawk like a frenzied parrot, as my eyes ping open.

'Yep, slap that on girl.' Brie points to the glove compartment. 'We can't have you turning into a little racoon again.'

After plastering on a load of factor fifty I dose off for a few minutes before coming round and realising I'm being a shit, lazy friend and I need to support Brie in our dirty hangover. I offer to buy Brie a Maccy Dee's and she jumps at the chance. Two lots of fried grease and two full stomachs later and we're almost home. I just can't wait to see my baby. My boobs ache, full from milk again. It will be so lovely to bond with her later, my baby.

I collect my car from Brie's and wave her off as I look forward to cuddles and kisses from my little angel. I wonder if she's missed me as much as I've missed her. This weekend has been fun, just what I needed but I think if I had done this any earlier then I would have caved and gone home early.

I pull up onto the driveway, parking next to Billy's car. Turning the key in the lock, I wander into the hallway and dump my bags down with an instant feeling washing over me that something is off. It's too quiet. Too tranquil. Why can't I hear my baby giggling, crying? Something?

'Hello? Billy?' Nothing. I run straight up the stairs, then chastise myself, it's her nap time and I've probably woken her up now. She's not in her room though, where is she napping? Calling her name over and over, I sweep in and out of each room, my eyes going over everything like a hawk.

'Nancy-Ella, baby??' Nothing. I run downstairs; they must have gone out for a walk. It's a nice day, a nice sunny morning I say to myself to try and calm my neuroticism as my feet pad down the stairs and my heart thumps louder in my chest. I could race back upstairs and grab the cricket bat that's hidden underneath my bed. When Billy left, I felt a bit vulnerable on my own and he left his cricket set here so I thought I'd put it to good use and stash the bat away as an intruder weapon. It's not like Billy used it much anyway but now *I* might have to. No! Stop being Silly Tilly, they must have popped out to the shop or something, I think as I pace through the living room.

'Oh, hi. Where's Nancy-Ella?' I blurt out as I race into the kitchen to find Billy and Timmy looking very at home sitting at the breakfast bar wearing matching white expensive looking shirts. Timmy looks me up and down before twitching his mouth into a smile that stops before it reaches his eyes.

'Hey, we're just trying out the new coffee blend, holding a bit of a business meeting in your kitchen, hope you don't mind.' Timmy wobbles his head and grins but it looks more like a grimace. I ignore him.

'Where's my child?' I demand.

'*Our* child, thank you, and she's fine. Mum's taken her out for the day, I didn't expect you back until later. You didn't say,' Billy says with a little head wobble then takes a sip of his coffee.

It does smell good and so do the chocolate croissants that Timmy has just pulled out of the oven. What the fuck is this? Have they opened up a new coffee shop in my house? Ah I see, I won't work for them so they bring the business into my home.

Very clever.

'I text you when we were leaving actually,' I say, feeling annoyed as I observe the mess they've made in my kitchen; coffee beans and sachets everywhere. He's even bought his fancy coffee maker over.

What a wanker.

'Oh, did you? Sorry.' Billy shakes his head and shrugs but he's not sorry. Too busy loading himself up with coffee and talking shop with Timmy.

'Yeah, I did,' I say, grabbing a croissant and taking a huge bite from it. 'Hmm these taste so good, got any more?' I wolf the whole thing down in seconds. That *McDonald's* didn't touch the sides, how is it that they make you hungrier? Or am I just a hungover pig that has the appetite of a hippo for the day?

'Here try a pecan plait. I made them myself.' Timmy pushes the plate over to me, watching me with a smirk.
I hesitate for a second before greediness gets the better of me and I take one.

'Hmmm, not bad, but I'd lay off on the icing. Bit much.' I lick my fingers slowly as Timmy looks on at me in disgust. He truly does hate my guts, but he needs to get over it. I sashay over to the fridge.

As soon as Nancy-Ella is home they can both leave and stick that coffee machine up their arses. I take the milk out and begin to glug straight from the bottle. Timmy can look down on me all he wants; I can do what

I like in my own home. I've recently changed to ordering glass bottles from a local company and I'm feeling quite smug about helping the environment and a small, local business.

'Pahh, yuk, this milk is off,' I say, spitting it out into the sink.

'Oh Tilly,' Timmy smirks, 'that's *your* milk.'

'My milk?' I twirl the glass bottle around in my hand, I didn't put my breast milk in here and this is gone off, it's my old milk. 'Why's it in here?' Neither of them answer and Timmy just shrugs. They've obviously got confused and tried to feed her the wrong milk, I thought I'd labelled it clearly.

'Something amazing happened when you were away on your hen do,' Billy states, and I nod for him to continue, still gagging from drinking my own gone off breast milk. I thought it was supposed to be sweet but this tastes rank. 'Nancy-Ella has given up *your* milk, she refused it,' he announces proudly.

'I don't know why,' Timmy baulks.

'And how is that amazing?' I ask, through gritted teeth. How dare he?

'She doesn't need it any more, I gave her cow's milk instead of yours and she glugged it down.'

'From a bottle as well,' Timmy pipes up. He's loving this.

'Well she's hardly going to drink it from Billy's Moobs is she?' I snap, as they both gasp. I feel truly horrible for stooping so low but I'm fuming that he's done this and I'm also feeling extremely hungover now. How dare he just decide that she's given up.

'Hey! They're enhanced pecks, I've told you before.' Billy frowns as he looks down and prods his soft chest with his fingers.

'Well…' I say, blinking back tears.

'Yeah, she was just ready I guess,' Billy says, watching me with caution.

He knows I want to punch him – hard in the face.

'Hellloooooooo,' Billy's mum sings. 'The door was unlocked so I just let us in.'

Does no one knock in my house?

'Tillyyyy, how are you, love?' she asks, as she gently rolls the pushchair into the kitchen, leaning in for a hug.

'Good thanks, Lynne, you?'

Lynne and I used to get on so well, she's always been like a second mother to me. I miss her but it's been a bit awkward since Billy and I broke up. I know she blames me for being too stressed around her Billy.

'Yes, not bad. She's been an angel, slept all the way back from the park too. So sweet,' she coos, as Nancy-Ella sleeps soundly in the pushchair. I watch her little face and put my hand by her nose to feel her hot breath.

'How long's she been asleep?' I ask, eager for her to wake up and for everyone to go home.

'Oh only about twenty minutes, yesterday she had a two-hour nap, such a good little sleeper isn't she? Not like Billy was, little nightmare, up all night, ripping his nappy off and getting up to all sorts.' Lynne quacks on. 'I'd often come in the next morning to find a poo in the bed.' Ha! My eyes move to Billy, who's face is a livid red and so is Timmy's, probably from second hand embarrassment, either that or it's dragged up some terrible memory and he also used to poo the bed. He looks like a bed pooer.

'Yesterday?' Has Billy just fobbed Nancy-Ella off onto his mum all weekend?

'Yes, she had two hours didn't she Bill?'

'Yes, she did. I've told Tilly about the milk, Mum, told

her she's given it up.' He shakes his hair out of his eyes and stares at me. The bastard.

'Oooh yes.' Lynn bites her lip. 'I did say he should consult with you first, sweetheart but he was adamant that she didn't need it and to be honest, he was right, she wasn't at all bothered.' Lynne beams on at her son, the pooey bed golden child.

I want to scream at all of them to get out of my house, it's not their decision on what to do with my child and they shouldn't have just stopped feeding her my milk without talking to me.

'Well, she doesn't need it,' I say, trying to keep an even tone. 'But she likes it so I will continue to feed it to her until she communicates to me that she doesn't want it anymore.' I don't tell him I was planning on weaning her off soon anyway.

Timmy begins to busy himself by clearing up all the coffee crap and Billy starts to help him.

'Oh darling, you know I'm all for breast feeding but you don't want her to be old enough to start asking for it, that would be a bit uncouth now wouldn't it.' Lynne grimaces.

'Well, Lynne, perhaps she already asks for it.'

After turning the atmosphere as sour as my old breast milk everyone made their excuses and left. I spent the rest of the afternoon hanging out with Nancy-Ella who, after my daydreaming about us spending beautiful quality mother and daughter time together, is ruined by the fact that she's turned into an absolute mega beast. I mean, she couldn't be more miserable. Is this my punishment for leaving her? A grumpy baby? After a long ass day with a gross hangover and a grumpy toddler, I put her to bed at six thirty in the evening. A part of me feels guilty for being so relieved the day is over. I run myself a bath, chuck in a bath bomb and whack on a rejuvenating facemask to try and feed some moisture back into my dry, scaly face. It doesn't look so bad anymore but it feels like sandpaper. Slowly, I reach down and grab my phone from the bathmat and tap my email response to my brother.

Hey Bro, back from Nay's hen do. I'm broken to say the least. It has made me realise that I want to start dating again though. Let's just say that my mojo has been ignited and no I don't mean I'm horny. Okay maybe a tad (not that you want to know that!!) but I'd really like to meet someone, someone to just hang out with and for some company, nothing serious. I'm far too busy for that. My mission is to find a plus one for Nay's wedding, so the pressures on. Tonight, I'm going to be brave and set myself up on some dating websites. What do people even use these days?

Mum is good, although she is considering getting more shit done to her face! Please talk to her, she listens to you.

Your niece is good, teething I think as very grumpy today.

Anyway, glad you're having fun in sunny Barcelona. Please come visit soon or I may have to visit you. I've forgotten what you look like, you social media loathing nomad! Send me some pics of you, the views, hot Catalonian men, anything.

Anyway, got to go. Miss you lots, love Tils xx

P.S Billy is still. . . Billy. He looked after Nancy-Ella when I was away which is great but basically got his mum to do it all – that's cheating!

I drop my phone onto the bathmat then jump out and grab a towel. My fingers are shrivelled prunes from staying in the bath for over an hour. I pull on my PJ's, collect some snacks mainly consisting of chocolate and *Doritos* then jump into bed to catch up on the episodes of *Love Island* that I've missed. I let out a happy sigh, I love my single Sunday evenings and I'm not ready to give them up. Billy and I used to fight over what to watch on TV all the time, it's nice not to have the bother but it is starting to get a little lonely. It does suck a bit being on your own every night. A few dates would be nice.

I scroll on my phone to find some dating sites and as expected Google has listened to my every thought and conversation so has presented me with some recommended dating aps. I download one that doesn't look too sleazy and begin to navigate my way round it. After filling in the initial name, age, location, we come to the about me section, I struggle to come up with a bio. After writing and deleting it several times, I finally settle with the following cringe worthy sentences:

Just a Swine-town girl, living in a lonely world.

Love meeting new people.

Lived in Australia for a year.

I always wake up at whatever time I plan the night before without

setting an alarm.

Trash TV is the greatest form of meditation.

I love my food - come and eat with me – veggie style.

Nice and simple and not giving too much away. Not wanting to divulge the fact that I have a child, I'll tell them over chat if I like them and plan to meet them. They could be a stalker, weirdo creep and I don't want them knowing that information just from my profile. After filling out what feels like a job application, I get to the good bit. The men.

I scroll through, viewing each person then swiping left or right depending on if I like the look and sound of them or not. It's disappointing that most of the ones that look good sound like absolute knobs. It feels like I'm shopping. So now, I've swiped a few rights and all I have to do is wait to see if they swipe right for me too. It's midnight by the time I tear myself away from my phone. Must go to sleep, new toddler group tomorrow so must be on form and be bright and bouncy for my potentially grizzly daughter. Please can it not be another cliquey mum group like the last one, at least I'll have Krissy, if she turns up. Just as I'm nodding off my phone lets off an odd sounding alert.

What's this?

I grab my phone off the side and tap on the icon, thinking maybe I'll have a match but no, it's another notification. I click on the image and can hardly believe my eyes.

Oh my God.

His lovely curly hair and long eyelashes stare back at me through the screen. I gasp. It's gorgeous George – he's on the bloody dating app and he's swiped for me. He's local! In amongst all the hen do drama I'd completely forgotten about this handsome stranger and that those group of lads were from Swindon, he really does have the face of a Greek god. I quickly skim his bio to check he's of sound mind and/or doesn't come across as a complete dick and he passes the check. My mission is complete. I may as well delete the bloody app now! Swiping him back can be saved until tomorrow though, can't appear too desperate.

I close my eyes with a big smile on my face, images of his beautiful smile swirling round in my mind. Moments later my eyes ping open and I grab my phone to swipe him back.

Well, I can't let him go again.

I've found my plus one.

Chapter 7

Nancy-Ella woke up in a much better mood today and now we're on our way to the new baby group. I'm walking on air, no, I'm walking on sunshine. It's still gorgeous outside. Oh how I love summer, I've got my sunscreen on and I've got a feeling I'm never going to want this long hot summer to end.

I'm feeling giddy over someone who's merely smiled at me for just a few seconds but it's fate.

It has to be.

He swiped right for me and he lives in Swindon. I can't believe my luck. We chatted briefly this morning, his name is George (which, obviously, I already knew) and he's recently left the army but is now working for a security firm. He's thirty-three and originally from Stoke-on-Trent. I can't wait to hear him speak because I do love an accent. I'm just biding my time now until he asks me out. I know women can do all that too but I don't want to. I want to be wined and dined and I want to be the one who's asked out and that's okay, even if it is just for a few dates until the wedding comes, but who knows what could happen. *Silly Tilly, don't get carried away,* a voice echoes in my head that sounds strangely like Samantha's.

We arrive at the leisure centre and spend five minutes trying to find a space, hmm it must be popular. I'm so looking forward to this toddler group and Mum pointed out that it shouldn't be too cliquey as it's a music one, so not much time for chat. Sorry cliquey mums! Plus Krissy should be coming today too, so I'll have a friend.

'Let's go have some fun,' I say to Nancy-Ella, who's sat on my hip grinning. 'You're gonna love this, sweetie.'

'Yay mumma.' She grins, mimicking my mood as I push open the door to the leisure centre and walk down the corridor. I come to a meeting room with the words Music Bums plastered above in bright, colourful writing. Before I go in, I peer through the small, mucky windows on the doors, there's a group of around ten mums and their toddlers. The teacher, wearing pink dungarees and a blue top, looks like she's just auditioned for a place on a *CBeebies* baby club. She has her hair in blonde bunches and has a friendly, smiley face.

'Hi,' I whisper, with a smile slash grimace as we enter the room and awkwardly tiptoe over.

'Hello, and who do we have here?' *CBeebies* lady asks.

'I'm Tilly and this is Nancy-Ella.' I grin.

'Hello, Tilly. Hello, Nancy-Ella.' The room loudly chants at us making me jump and Nancy-Ella cry. Oh no, that's not a good start. *Please don't be melt down central, please don't act like the devil's spawn. An image of Billy laughing with devil horns flickers into my mind's eye.*

'Welcome, I'm Chloe.' *CBeebies* lady smiles, unphased by my child's outburst as she ticks us off her printed out list. 'Riiight, we'll wait five more minutes as we have one more to turn up and if they aren't here in five then we'll get started, I'm not a fan of lateness, is that okay everyone?'

There's a succession of nods and yeses around the room as people begin to chat amongst themselves. I look either side of me and smile to the mums, one of them looks at me blanky and the other avoids eye contact, she may have even gone as far as to edge away from me as there is now a space next to me that I'm sure wasn't there before.

Great. Maybe I just have a bitch face, even when I crack a smile.

I turn to play with Nancy-Ella but to my horror she's already ninja crawled halfway across the room. *CBeebies* lady is smiling and waving at her. Why does my child do that? How is everyone else's child still in the same spot? I call her name a few times but she ignores me. Standard. I decide to get up and calmly bring her back over, the class will be starting soon.

'Okay, I think that's enough waiting, let's start shall we?' Chloe says to the class, after looking at her watch. She smiles and waves again at Nancy-Ella as I begin to scoop her up.

Please don't kick off.

Just as I pick her up the inevitable meltdown happens. Oh no.

'Sorry, bit grizzly today, aren't you, those teeth hurting you?' I say in my cheeriest tone to Nancy-Ella, she isn't usually like this.

She proceeds to scream and lash out, flailing her arms around, really not happy. Chloe ignores us as if we aren't there and presses play on her phone as the music bums welcome song begins to blasts out of the speakers. The class starts to clap along to the sick-making tune as my child screams like she's being murdered. We dash back to our space on the floor but the door looks a lot more tempting.

Nancy-Ella continues to scream. I should have just made a run for it when I could. Just as I'm fantasising about leaving, the door flies open and in runs a familiar looking face with a screaming child that's managing to scream even louder than mine. Yes! We've been upstaged. It's Krissy, my new baby club pal, the very flustered freeloader.

She runs over to Chloe who, with a pasted-on smile, stares at her. Inside I can tell that she's silently slapping her, she doesn't tolerate lateness.

'So sorry we're late. Arthur was asleep in the car and I didn't want to wake him,' she says, as she hoists her screaming child up onto her hip. Beads of sweat form on her forehead. 'He's a beast when he wakes up but he's still a little beast anyway so I should have just woken him up and got here on time because it doesn't make a difference either way does it?' Krissy's voice has raised a whole octave since she first started speaking, her child is still throwing a fit.

An image of James's chest pops into my mind, how did I get from seeing Krissy with her screaming child to that? I shake my head to get rid of the thought. Krissy's little boy continues to wail and scream in her arms as Nancy-Ella stops her tantrum to see what all the noise is. Chloe simply nods, smiles again and continues to sing and clap as everyone joins in like this outburst isn't still happening.

Poor Krissy stands there, slightly out of breath from all the rushing around. She strokes her son's face as he continues to scream and she tries to sooth him, perspiration glistening on her upper lip. She looks as if she might burst into tears at any moment.

I feel sorry for her.

Bless her.

'Hey.' I wave to Krissy. 'There's a space here.' I pat the floor next to me and Nancy-Ella. Krissy's head swivels towards us, her face breaks into a big relieved grin before she quickly trots over to sit down.

'Hey, Tilly. God am I glad to see you,' she says, plonking herself down with her still screaming child. She looks at him then to me and gives me a look that many mothers would understand.

'Me too,' I say as the now, staring and not screaming Nancy-Ella gives her son a big toothy grin; he finally begins to calm down, much to Krissy's relief.

'I've got a secret; I hate these things. I only come for him,' she whispers, then points to little Arthur. 'So ungrateful, aren't they?' Krissy giggles as a few of the other mums give her the death stare. They clearly come because they love Music Bums. Good for them.

'Your secret's safe with me and same, totally hate them,' I whisper back.

'Right everyone it's time to get up and get those bodies moving, time to wriggle those little bums, you too mums.'

I groan inwardly as Chloe grabs her box of things and pulls out several shakers and bells and hands them out to the class before putting on another song. This time it's one that I know, *The Grand Old Duke of York*. We march around the room jangling our bells and shakers with the toddlers and they seem to enjoy it, running around and giggling. I relax a little. This isn't so bad and at least there's someone I know here. Next, we're given a colourful ribbon each to sway to the music as we sing something about walking in the jungle. It's fun, everyone's smiling and Nancy-Ella and Arthur seem to have taken a liking to each other, which is nice. This is nice.

'Hey, these props are a bit different to the ones you had your hands on a few days ago,' Krissy pipes up, as Chloe hands us the shakers and bells again.

I try to hold a snort in, I know exactly what props she's on about. An image of James squirting squirty cream all over himself pops into my mind. I still can't believe he got talked into stripping for a load of strangers and for free. What a strange man.

We wait for the teacher to prepare the next song as Krissy mimes how big she thinks one particular prop was. I snort again and we get a few dirty looks from the other mums. It's not like they have a clue what we're on about. We could be talking about the size of one of the many musical instruments here or our child's latest poo for all they know. The last song is quite vigorous and the kids really get into rattling their shakers and bells. I've noticed in this music class that Nancy-Ella is quite heavy handed compared to the other children. I wince a few times as she accidently bops Arthur on the head with the shaker.

'Sorry.' I grimace as Nancy-Ella bonks him on the eyebrow again.

'Oh don't worry about him, head like concrete that one.' Krissy laughs and I laugh along with her.

The music quickens and Nancy-Ella begins clapping her hands with excitement. She picks up the bells and jangles them in her hands, turning them this way and that, getting more excited, the more she jangles. Inside, I'm still wincing but I don't want to tell her to calm down, she isn't harming anyone. I don't want to dull her sparkle. That smile. She's having so much fun, just look at her go.

'Funny mummy,' she giggles. 'Jingle, jingle.'

'Yes,' I say, as I pick up a set of bells and jangle them gently along with her in the hope that she'll calm those hands down a bit and copy me. She doesn't, in fact her arms flail around even more until they're almost propelling.

'Gentle sweetie, gentle, like this,' I say, jangling the bell in front of her. 'See.' I take her arm and try to show her but she shrugs me off.

'No! Nanyella do it.' She flings her arms to the side then down and up, continuing the motion over and over again, getting faster and faster.

Down, up, down.

Up, down, up.

Down, up, down.

Up. . .Oh shit.

The bells have gone up but this time she's let go of them and instead of coming straight down they continue to travel up and up, flying high towards the ceiling then across, making a beeline for the poor child opposite. My mouth falls open and I let out a 'nooooooo,' as I launch myself forwards in an attempt to try and stop them from knocking the poor child out.

'Stoooppppp themmmmmm,' I yell desperately. I run forward, stretching out my arm but miss the bells as they continue to aim for this child's head. The bells are quite heavy and at the rate they are travelling they are going to knock this poor kid unconscious.

Just as I think this, Krissy launches herself in front of me and catches them.

'Oh my God, thank you so much, that could have ended very badly,' I pant out the words, as I run back to my space to grab the next weapon, another bell, out of Nancy-Ella's hand.

'She's got a good arm,' Krissy says, winking and we both crack up laughing as Chloe gives us a big blinky grin. Perhaps this toddler class won't be so bad with Krissy here.

Chapter 8

Nancy-Ella's eyes open and she yawns in her buggy as I freeze mid-unclipping her belt. She falls back to sleep and I move slowly, what I do now is crucial. Normally, if I get her upstairs and in bed before she wakes then I'm guaranteed to get a good two hours to myself.

I manage it.

Phew.

Bliss.

I love nap times, I don't know what I'm going to do without them, oh yeah, go back to work. A mix of trepidation, anxiety and a pinch of excitement wash over me as I sit on the toilet to relieve myself of a much needed wee. I feel like *Austin Powers*, will this piss ever end?

I make a strong cup of coffee and plonk myself down on the sofa to check the dating site. Gorgeous George stares back at me looking as bloody stunning as ever but he hasn't replied to my last message yet. What are the chances of him being on here and just having moved to Swindon? I still can't believe my luck.

An image of the cactus throwing himself around in the pub pops into my mind. Ahh, he must have been with the wedding dress stag group. I've also got another match! Woohoo! I click on his profile to see a very good-looking tattooed man with nice arms and good hair, he's a tattooist, cool job and has a five-year-old daughter. Okay, up front and honest about that, I like it. Perhaps I should amend my profile to say that I also have a child. Hmmm, I'll have to think about that one. He's into painting, cooking and running. Well, well, well, we have painting in common and I like to eat, I wonder what he paints? In fact, he's just inspired me.

Just five more minutes on here then I'm going to get my paint brushes out and finish off that piece I've been painting for my mum. I'm painting my late nan, a present for my mum's birthday, she's going to love it. I've always loved painting portraits and been quite good at it. I've even done a few commissions but I won't commit to too many, I want my hobby to remain as mine. It's my therapy. When Billy left I painted my own portrait every month to show the different stages of a break up and just for something to do. It's amazing how the eyes changed during that time, although they did show when I went back to him those few times, they lost their glow again afterwards. My phone pings and a message pops up from Dan, the tattooed man.

Dan: *Hey, you look lovely, long time no speak, would you like to meet up soon?*

Well, he didn't hang about but am I supposed to recognise him, because I don't.

Me: *Hey, thank you, I'm so sorry but have we met? I'm rubbish with faces.*

Dan: *Haha that's okay, I look quite different now. It's Dan Heston, I went to school with you.*

Me: *Oh wow, so sorry I didn't recognise you.*

Dan: *Yeah, I guess I've changed quite a bit. So do you fancy meeting up soon?*

Hmmm he's keen, a bit too keen? I do remember him;

think we may have even snogged a few times at the school discos. I did have a bit of a crush on him but if I remember rightly he ended up going out with an older girl for ages. He must be two years above me and was one of the cool kids, a bit of a bad boy and he always had a skinhead when I knew him.

Me: *You're a bit keen.*

I add on a laughing face. Let's see how he handles that.

Dan: *Yes, I suppose I am. Sorry, I've recently learnt that life is too short so if you want something you just have to go out and grab it.*

Me: *I guess you're right.*

Dan: *Yep, would you let me cook for you? We can reminisce about the chavy clothes and school discos.*

Me: *Yeah, okay, why not?*

Dan: *Great, next Tuesday at seven okay?*

Me: *Cool, sounds good.*

Oh God, what did I just agree to? I squirm in my seat as his address pings up on my phone. I log out of the dating app and instantly call Brie to tell her the news and fill her in on my Music Bums antics with Krissy, she doesn't pick up so she gets a garbled voice note instead.

The next hour flies by as I paint, getting lost in a haze of colours, textures and memories of my nan feeding me her yummy homemade cottage pie with spinach and shredded carrot hidden in it to make sure she was getting some vegetables into us. She admitted to that little secret years later and I remember being gobsmacked as you never would have known. I've carried on the tradition with Nancy-Ella and she loves cottage pie, although I now use Quorn instead of meat.

Nancy-Ella wakes up and I bring her down for a nappy change and a snuggle. She hasn't had the boob since being back, I haven't forced it and she hasn't asked. I wonder if she'll ask tonight. Billy's smug face flashes in my mind's eye, I hate that he's forced this, but maybe she was ready all along, that will explain the fussiness, I'm just waiting for my milk to dry up now. It appears my body doesn't want to give up as quickly as Nancy-Ella.

'Let's get you some food, hey?' I say to Nancy-Ella, as I plonk her in the highchair, switch kids TV on and give her a toy to play with whist I prepare her lunch. My phone beeps as I walk into the kitchen, it's a voice note from Brie.

'*Alrighty-roo you fucking super star.*' I press the volume down button aggressively, Nancy-Ella copies everything at the moment. '*I am so proud of you for getting a date, you go girl but are you sure about going to this dude's house? And on the first date? I mean he could be a fucking psycho for all you know. I dunno mate, I'm not sure about that. Why don't you meet at a pub or something? It'll be a bit more public and you can escape if he is a freak which I'm sure he won't be but you can never be too careful, babe. Oh. My. God. Remember that guy you dated in Oz that had a foot fetish? He was a real weirdo freak; you don't want to meet another one of those, didn't he end up taking little sneaky photos of your feet in your thongs? Uh gross.*'

I send her a text back.

Me: *It will be fine, I know him, it's not like he's a total stranger to me. Don't worry about me, I'm a big girl wombat now.*

And I also don't want to bump into Billy, he's always out and about having business meetings with Tim in pubs and restaurants, knowing my luck he would be there, so this suits me just fine.

Brie: *You're mental, just think about trying to change the location yeah? I don't wanna be looking for your body…*

Me: *I'll think about it.*

Me: *Hey Dan, do you think we could meet out in a pub or*

something instead? I'd feel bad making you cook on the first date. Equality and all that.

The message stares back at me, I re-read it a couple of times, cringe multiple times, then delete it. It'll be fine, I know him. I log out of the app with no intention of checking it until the next day, hopefully in the meantime Gorgeous George will contact me and I can arrange a date with him too. Such a hussy, but you only live once and it will be fun. This bloody app is addictive, dangerous even. I peek a look at Nancy-Ella who is contentedly watching *Pepper Pig*, before I go back to making her sandwich.

The next few days go by in a haze of nappies, toys, baby TV, housework and Billy badgering me about the coffee shop. He still hasn't taken the word no for an answer but the new package he is now offering me is very tempting. He wants me to do the HR and general book keeping as that's what I have experience in and neither him or Timmy have a clue. He's got someone else doing it at the moment but it isn't working out so well, probably because Timmy is a sour faced nubbin. I'm tempted, purely because I could do a lot of it from home and it would be flexible to work around me and Nancy-Ella. I'm very tempted now.

Urgh but that would mean being tied to him not only through Nancy-Ella but also work and he would essentially be my boss. Could I put up with that for the flexibility and freedom? I'm also supposed to go back to work in a few months. I couldn't do that to them, could I? Although I'm sure Andrea has a few people lined up just in case I don't make it back. I'm nervous about going back, Andrea is such a good boss, she told me not to worry whilst I was away but I didn't think she'd actually send me no updates at all. I've kept in touch but she doesn't give much away in the way of work, I think she thinks she's doing me a favour but I'm terrified I've forgotten everything to do with my job. The coffee shop work would be a doddle compared to my old job at Taylors Venues and Events.

'Ever think about having anymore?' Krissy asks, as she plonks little Arthur into a bouncer, his legs are getting a little too long and he attempts to jump but just kind of stamps his feet with bent knees. 'You know so they can entertain each other like this?' she continues, as she laughs at him trying to move in the bouncer. She takes him out and shows him a fire engine which he whacks out of her hand before toddling off to play with some giant foam bricks.

Krissy messaged me last night to see if I fancied taking the kids to soft play. She said we could grab a coffee and let the kids play with the toys. She called it *minimal mumming.* The term made me laugh so much I almost spat out my tea and of course, I was sold. It's a hard slog being a stay-at-home mum sometimes, but I guess I won't be one for much longer. So far Krissy and I are having a hoot, it's so nice to have a mum friend with a kid the same age.

'It is nice to see them play, they get along so well.' I say as I watch them smile at each other over by the foam bricks. 'But no, I don't think so.' I shake my head. 'I'm one and done. And besides you might get a total second child arsehole who doesn't like original kid number one so all they do is squabble and fight making it more stressful than before.'

'One and done,' Krissy laughs. 'I like it. My fella wants more but I dunno if I could go through with the birth again, mate. My vagina and bumhole were as one for a little while.' Krissy grimaces.

'Ouch,' I say, crossing my legs and wincing.

'Yeah, don't want to go through that again, bumhole and vagina have only just got over it.'

'I don't blame you.'

'Mummy bumhole, Mummy bumhole,' little Arthur says, as he hands Krissy a toy phone.

'Oh hello, is that bumhole?' Krissy talks into the pretend phone as several other mums look over. 'Yep, yep okay, I'll let him know.' Krissy puts her hand over the receiver and talks to me. 'Yeah bumholes calling, he wants his own space now, sick of sharing it with that greedy vagina.' She takes her hand off the receiver and speaks into the phone again. 'Alright, okay bye, bye, I'll let her know, bumhole.'

Krissy and I crack up laughing which sets the kids off into fits of giggles too, they don't even know what we're laughing about but they're still finding it hysterical. It's a bit late but I cover Nancy-Ella's ears, obviously I don't want her calling people bumholes.

'I've got a date tonight,' I confess, after we've stopped laughing and mouthed *sorry* at a couple of the mums giving us dirty looks. Suddenly I feel like I've known Krissy for years, she's not so bad, she's actually fun.

'Yeah? Go you!' she says, with a huge grin.

'Yeah, I'm going round his house for dinner, he wants to cook for me, apparently it's one of his passions. Brie thinks I'm bonkers for going over to his house on a first date but it's not like he's a stranger, I know him. Went to school with him.'

'Oh well, if you know him then that's alright, isn't it?' Krissy says, with a little shrug.

'Yeah, yeah it is.' And that's all the confirmation I need. Sorry Brie.

Mum's come over to babysit while I go out and hoe it up as she so nicely put it. When she let herself in I was relieved that Nancy-Ella was already in bed or Mum's face may have given her nightmares. I had to do a double take; her mouth looked like two slugs had been slapped on in place of her actual lips. She told me it would calm down and that she'd only had it done that day hence why it looked so angry. Yeah, angry or bloody over-injected. I wish she'd just stop messing with her face, I worry that soon she won't even resemble my mum anymore.

'Well, what do you think?' I ask.

Mum looks me up and down then motions for me to turn around, waving her hand like the Queen.

'Have you lost weight?' she asks, squinting her eyes at me. I smooth down my trousers and pull them up again, they have become a little loose I suppose but I thought that was the elastic going a bit.

'Maybe a bit, why? Does this look shit then?'

'No, not shit, don't put words in my mouth. I just think you have better things in your wardrobe, you want to make the most of what you've got. Show off your good bits,' she says, pointing to my legs. I throw my head back and groan.

'Come on, let's get you sorted.' Twenty minutes and three outfits later she has me in an above the knee summer dress with a floaty cardigan to match. It does look better than what I'd originally picked. What can I say, I'm out of practice with this dating malarky. 'You look lovely darling, gorgeous.'

'Thanks, Mum.'

She puts her fist into her mouth, bites down on it, shaking her head.

'Mum, not now, don't cry,' I say, as her eyes well up.

'Urgh I'm sorry, I just want you to be happy.'

'I am, Mum and I don't need a man to make me happy, a man should be a nice bonus to my life, not a necessity,' I say.

'Urgh, my own words coming back to bite me.'

'I learnt from the best.' I smile and give her a hug. 'And I'm only really looking for a plus one for Nay's wedding,' I continue. 'Now, I've got to go or I'll be late for my date.'

'Bye, bye, have fun and don't do anything I wouldn't do!' she says, as she perches on the edge of the sofa, pulling a wellbeing magazine out of her handbag.

'That's not a lot then, is it?' I laugh. 'See you later.'

Chapter 9

Butterflies dance around in my stomach as I pull up to Dan's house. I'm excited but also petrified. The last proper date I had was with Billy, many years ago. I should've had that nervous poo before I left.

His driveway is huge and can easily fit three, maybe four cars, and the house is gorgeous. A detached, mixed beige brick effect house, a garage and is that an extension? It looks like a family home for a big family. Did he say he only had one daughter? I can't remember but he's clearly done very well for himself. Extremely well for himself. The bad boy I once knew from school has finally grown up. I wonder where his tattoo parlour is? Maybe that new one in Old Town. *Tilly, calm down, you can find out about his life when you meet him.*

Cool, calm and collected, I mantra to myself as I ring the doorbell. I notice he has a ring doorbell so I make the conscious effort not to pick my teeth or fart as it could all be caught on camera and I could be cancelled before he even meets me again.

Oh the anxiety of dating. I haven't missed this bit.

The door opens.

'Hey,' Dan says, looking me up and down. 'You look gorgeous, come in.' He gives me a warm welcoming smile before stepping out of the way to let me in, he touches my arm and I shyly smile back at him.

He's still hot but he obviously didn't bring his filters with him because he looks a lot more rugged than his photos. Not in a bad way really, just older. Unless they were old photos. I wonder if he thinks the same of me? I do a quick mental scan of my photos on the dating app, yeah at least one had a filter.

'Lovely house,' I squeak, sounding anything but cool, calm and collected. My belly gurgles.

Nervous poo.

Don't even think about it.

'Thanks,' he says, with a shrug. I follow him into the living room; the smells coming from the kitchen are making my mouth water and my stomach tenses. It's just occurred to me that I now have to eat in front of this man. Suddenly, I feel way out of my comfort zone. Why did I think I was ready for this?

'Aww, is this your daughter? I ask, pointing to a photo of a little girl on a mantelpiece that surrounds a huge log fire.

'Oh no, that's my sister, although my daughter looks very much like her. Here's my daughter.' He points to another photo hanging on the wall of a cute little girl. Then either his phone vibrates or mine does but we both ignore it.

'Oh yes, she's very cute,' I say, thinking how weird it is to have a photo of your sister as a child in your house. I'd never have a photo of Charlie in my house like that but maybe that's just me and our relationship. Everyone's different.

'Drink?' he asks.

'Oh yes please, just a water will be fine.'

'No problem, did you drive?'

'Yes.' I go to follow him into the kitchen and he holds

his hand up to stop me. I wait as he continues into the kitchen, returning moments later with a water for me and a can of fruity cider for himself. My mouth waters, I could do with one of those to settle my nerves although it probably wouldn't settle my stomach.

'Dinner will be ready soon; do you want to go and sit at the table and I'll bring it through.' He motions to the dining room where it is perfectly laid with fancy cutlery, napkins and candles. So sweet.

'Sure.' I could get used to this, I think as I sit down at the table and let my eyes float around the room, admiring the décor and nice furnishings.

There are quite a few family photos, a piano, a writing bureau and some paintings, some of which must have been painted by him as I recognise a couple from the dating website. I try to rack my brains to see if I can remember his sister but nothing comes to me, she must be a fair bit younger than him.

Dan brings out the starter which consists of bread, olives and dipping oils and I nibble on those. I must be careful not to over indulge and keep room for the next two courses. Wow, he really has gone all out. I feel so special. Billy was a freezer fodder kind of guy and we would have eaten that every day if it wasn't for the fact that I cooked and liked homemade meals.

'So what have you been doing with yourself for the past few years? Dan asks. 'When I saw you were on the dating site I couldn't believe it. I thought you'd be all married up by now,' he grins. Oh God he has a gold tooth, he kept that hidden in his photos.

Buzzz.

'Was that your phone?' I ask, as I hear that low vibrating noise again and he shakes his head. Come to think of it, it doesn't sound like a phone, maybe it's his cooker alarm or something. 'I was, well not married.' I continue. 'What I mean is I was in a relationship but it didn't work out. He's the father of my child,' I say, then eye up the bread, I wonder if he baked it?

'You have kids?' Dan asks.

'Yeah, just one, she'll be two in a few months.'

'Kept that quiet.' He nods at me. 'Need to be more honest on your profile,' he says, then stuffs a mouthful of bread into his mouth.

'Right, umm…'

'Kids are amazing,' he says, with a full mouth.

'Yes, they are, and you have a little girl?' I ask to detract from me being a dishonest woman.

'Apple of my eye. Still finding our feet but she's slowly becoming a daddy's girl.'

I smile at him; I know how hard it can be on a man at the start, especially if the woman is nursing. It can feel a little excluding for them and they can feel a bit useless. I suddenly feel a pang of compassion for Billy before I swallow it back down again. He can bugger off out of my date.

'That's sweet,' I say, as the buzzer noise buzzes again but this time even louder. Dan ignores it and pads out to the kitchen to fetch our mains; he returns with spaghetti bolognaise and homemade garlic bread.

'Wow, quite the chef, aren't you?'

'Yep,' he says, looking pensive. 'I've learnt a lot over the last few years, one of those things has been learning to cook. I didn't have a clue, couldn't even boil an egg. And don't worry, I've used Quorn, I saw you were a veggie in your dating bio.' He smiles and nods at me.

Buzz, buzz, buzz. What is that bloody noise?

'Wow and thank you, what made you learn?'

'Just life, I needed to.' He shrugs and looks down at

his plate. This guy has turned mysterious all of a sudden. Do I like it or am I a bit scared? My stomach gurgles again, go away nervous poo.

'I thought about becoming a veggie for a while,' he continues. 'Couldn't give up the chicken though, but I mean chickens can't smile so they don't really count do they?' He stares at me intently and I gulp, not smiling, like one of his chickens.

'Ummm.' I'm starting to wonder if this guy is the full ticket. My eyes drift over the spider's web tattoo that's spread out over his elbow and half his forearm, he catches me looking and puts his hand over it.

Buzz, buzz, buzz.

'So, do you still see anyone from school?' he asks, with a sniff closely followed by a cough.

'Me?' Of course you, you twerp. 'Yeah, I see a few of the girls, Gemma, Naomi, you know that crowd. What about you?'

'No. I don't see anyone anymore. Cut all ties.'

'How come?' I ask, not sure if I want to know the answer. This is getting a little painful, despite the lovely food.

Buzz, buzz, buzz.

'Just not good for me,' he continues. 'Not good for my well being and where I want to be.'

A bit extreme, I wonder what happened but I feel now is not a time to ask.

We both wolf down the meal whilst chatting more about school, including old teachers we had and people that we know. He asks me loads of questions about myself, which is lovely but I'm not getting much back from him. It's a bit of a one-way street. A one-way buzzy street as that noise is still happening and it's getting quite distracting.

'So your tattoos, do any of them mean anything?' I nod towards the cobweb on his elbow.

'Why do you ask?' He frowns, almost looking pissed off. My nervous poo reappears again. What have I said?

'Oh just being nosey, amazing painting,' I say, pointing to the mountain landscape picture behind his head in an attempt to change the subject and diffuse any annoyance I've caused.

'Thanks, I painted it.' He shrugs.

'Yeah? Wow, I dabble in a bit of painting myself, but just faces, I couldn't ever paint anything like that.'

'Yeah, as I've said, I've learnt a lot these past few years, painting being another skill.' He almost grits his teeth, then looks at me, no he looks through me as that buzzing noise starts again. I look away. I think I want to go home now.

'Impressive,' I nod like a nodding dog, not entirely comfortable with the tone of his voice now. That nervous poo just won't go away. We eat the rest of the meal in silence as I try to plan my escape. Brie and Mum told me to text them with the word *baby* if I need rescuing. I might excuse myself and go to the loo in a minute but not for a poo, I'll have to keep that locked in.

'Umm where's your poo, I mean loo?' I ask, just as he's sucking up an extra-long piece of spaghetti. We both wait for what seems like hours before he finishes it and can speak. Then there's that noise again, that buzzing. I definitely want to go home soon.

'There's one in the hallway.'

'Great, thanks.' I get up and make my way to the loo all the while stressing about how close it is to the dining room table. I'm not seasoning the dessert with the smell of fresh turds. Not nice. No way am I pooing here.

I freshen up in the loo then the unfortunate happens,

I do poo. It's all that rich food and I'm only human after all. I find some bleach and bleach the loo before spraying a bit of air freshener, then washing my hands with the lovely smelling hand wash until I can't smell the offensive smell any longer. I decide not to text Mum and Brie, I don't want to worry them and I'm a big girl now, I can leave on my own terms, which I will be doing very soon. I close the toilet door then walk back into the living room to an empty table.

'For fuck's sake,' Dan grunts, making me jump.

Where is he and what is he doing? Oh no, can he smell my poo? Is he cross at me for polluting the air with my pooey aroma? I creep into the kitchen to find him sat on the floor with his back to me. In front of him, the kitchen counters are covered in supermarket packaging from the garlic bread and the vegetarian spaghetti bolognaise, ahh so not home cooked then. Dan's still on the floor, fiddling with his ankle. What is he doing? Ah ha. The buzzing, so that's where it was coming from. Dan pulls and bashes away at the thing attached to his ankle.

My stomach drops.

He's got a tag on.

Isn't that what criminals wear?

'Fucking thing.' He continues to bash away at it as I slowly back out of the room, clutching my handbag. I creep to the front door and pull the handle but on the first go I can't open it. Mum and Brie were right, and now I'm about to be murdered. I try again, this time lifting the handle up. Bingo. I'm out. I've escaped my death. Just.

'Hey, where are you going?' He appears at the door with part of the tag in his hand just as I'm getting to my car.

'Sorry, I'm not feeling good and you weren't honest

on your profile about that.' I point at his tag as I back away towards my car. 'Thanks for the meal though, it was very nice, but you didn't make it, did you?'

'Bitch,' he spits as I turn the ignition on. I reverse my car off the drive as Dan stands glaring at me and speed home as fast as I can.

I've learnt a valuable lesson from this gigantic mistake the hard way. Never again am I going to a man's house on a first date, even if I think I know them. Never, ever again.

Chapter 10

'Alrighty-roo, is he here yet?' Brie's brown eyes begin to dart around the pub as she plonks her handbag down on the floor and sits down. I can see her mind ticking over, assessing every man that looks like he might be single and ready for a date with yours truly.

'Weirdly, I've not invited you to our date.' I pout then push her glass of wine over to her. 'Our date's at two o'clock, so you have to be gone by then, alright?' I bite my lip, I'm nervous but luckily there's no sign of a nervous poo today.

'That's two hours away, damn it. Hey, is that your alluring look? It works.' Brie points at me and raises an eyebrow.

'Yes, it is. Anyway it's not like you've not seen him before, gorgeous George has a face that is hard to forget,' I say, remembering his curls and big smile.

'True, I'm so excited for you mate, this could be the one?'

'Yes, he could be the plus one for Nay's wedding, let's see.' I say, primly.

Brie raises both eyebrows and smirks.

'How's things going with Billy-Boo, have you made up your mind yet about being his bitch slave?'

'Yes, I'm going to tell him that I'm not going to be his

bitch slave.' I don't tell her that I was considering it for a bit because I was desperate to get him back for a while.

'Not if you call the shots,' Brie says.

'What do you mean?'

'Well, he wants you, so tell him what you want? Even if you think it sounds ridiculous. He can only say no.'

'Yeah, I guess I could have but it's too late now anyway, I've already told work I'm coming back.' My boss Andrea emailed me last night and before I knew it I'd replied with a *yes, when do you want me?* My brain it appears is desperate to concentrate on things not baby related.

'No way, when do you start?'

'Well, that's the thing, I'm not due back for another twelve weeks but they want me to start coming in one day a week from next week to slowly ease myself back in.'

'Sounds like a good idea and you get some adult time too.'

'Exactly, plus it's been so long, I've completely forgotten what my job is. I'm petrified.' I truly am. I can't believe nothing has changed at work in my two-year absence. How do I even formulate a spreadsheet?

'There is that too, you'll smash it though, babe.' Brie makes a fist and smiles. 'You've got this,' she nods encouragingly.

'Thanks.'

'So, I've got some gossip.' Brie leans in. 'You know Samantha.'

'Yeah?'

'You know that guy she slept with on the hen do?'

'Yeah.' How could I forget? I shake my head as the sound of them bonking plays over in my mind.

'Well he's married and she's agreed to be his bit on the side.'

'What? Is she mad? But what about the wife?'

'I don't think Samantha cares about the wife, she just wants to get laid.'

'I hate that, Samantha could literally have anyone she wants, she's the ginger *Megan Fox* but she chooses to steal another woman's husband? Not cool.'

'I know,' Brie says, taking a sip of her wine.

'Who told you this anyway?'

'Nay. Gem and I were over at hers the other night,'

'Oh right,' I say, not bothering to ask where my invite was because I know exactly what the excuse will be. *It was last minute, we didn't think you'd be able to get a babysitter at such short notice.* Sometimes I feel so excluded just because I have a kid but that's just the way it is at the moment. Charlie, my brother, reassured me that it won't always be this way. He said as soon as another mate has a kid the dynamic will change again so just be patient, be positive. So that's what I've decided to try and do.

'Yeah, Nay is so cross with her, she's even thinking about uninviting her to the wedding.'

'Really?'

'Hmm hmm. Nay thinks it's bad karma to let an adulterer to her wedding.'

'Yeah, it's not great I guess but a bit harsh maybe.' I imagine Samantha galivanting off on secret trips to Coolsbay with Sammy.

'So, how's Nick anyway?' I ask, changing the subject. 'I haven't seen him in ages.' The four of us used to hang out all the time, I miss those days, me and Billy, Brie and Nick.

'He's good, still not put a ring on it though. Honestly, what's a girl got to do to be asked.'

'You could ask him?' I say, knowing full well I'd be behaving the same as Brie.

'I might bloody have to at this rate, mate.'

'Weddings are overrated anyway, just have a baby first, join that club with me,' I say, but I appear to have said the wrong thing. All the colour drains from Brie's face.

'Well, after seeing what you've been through and the stress it places on a relationship I wonder if it's really all worth it?' She blinks back at me and I try my best not to be offended. Am I really an advert for not having a baby? I mean yeah, it comes with its stresses but overall we're happy and we have fun. I consider myself very lucky. Billy wasn't very helpful though which is where most of the stress came from.

'Completely worth it.' I smile. 'Men are just plus ones anyway, there to fill a void. Children are your children forever.'

'Mate, Billy's turned your heart black.' Brie laughs.

'Yeah, maybe.' I shrug.

'We haven't discussed your date yet?' Brie leans in and I slap my forehead with my hand. The reason I told George I'd meet him in the pub is because I am never going to another man's house ever again until I've had at least ten dates and he's verified as not being a total freak, convict or murderer.

'Well, I had a lucky escape…'

I spend the next half an hour regaling Brie with the horror story of my date with Dan and the vibrating ankle tag.

'So you reckon this guy was a convict, out on licence?' she asks, her eyes wide.

'He had to be and he was trying to hide it. I googled why that thing was buzzing and it said that it does that when it needs to be charged.'

'Ah shit.' Brie laughs. 'You would have thought he'd charge the damn thing before you came over. What if the police turned up to give him a warning halfway through your date?' Brie snorts and I giggle with her.

'I would have preferred it if they had, at least I would have been safe. The whole thing was strange, he seemed lovely on the dating app, he cooked, painted, photos were lovely, had a cool career and the house was stunning, so on paper he was perfect, but it was all a load of lies and rubbish. I wouldn't be surprised if the house was his parents.' Or his sister's, if that was even his sister. I shudder at the thought of it all.

'On paper? Girl, you watch too much *Love Island*.'

'Maybe I do.'

'I still can't believe you went over there, you're mad,' Brie squawks.

'I know, I wish I'd listened to you, that's the last time I take advice from Krissy.' I giggle.

'Krissy?'

'Oh yeah, didn't I say? I bumped into her at Music Bums.' I was going to tell her that we'd arranged it but the look on her face makes me think better of it. 'Arthur and Nancy-Ella get on really well and Krissy's actually a real laugh.'

'Nice.' Brie blinks and forces a smile.

The barman comes to clear our glasses and we sit there in an awkward silence. Well, that went down like a lead balloon.

Brie, suddenly cold, makes her excuses and leaves early whilst I wait for twenty minutes on my own for gorgeous George whilst simultaneously trying to look alluring as the time approaches two o'clock. I hope his personality is as gorgeous as his looks. I flit between checking my phone and checking the door. I feel so uncomfortable now Brie has gone, and her reaction to me hanging out with Krissy has made me feel a bit shit.

♥ ♥ ♥

Ah, here he is. Gorgeous George saunters into the pub and I watch with baited breath as he looks for me whilst I try to look cool, calm and collected as well as alluring. It's a lot to do in one go and I end up looking like a constipated rabbit so I settle for a smile and shoulders back, instead. Tits and teeth as Brie would say.

'Hey, I was worried you wouldn't turn up,' he says, with a huge smile as he gets closer to me. Shit, he's just as hot as when I first saw him. Even hotter than his photos.

Not a gold tooth in sight.

'Why wouldn't I turn up?' I simper. God, I'm so alluring.

'I don't know, just nervous I guess.' That's sweet. George asks me what I'd like to drink before sauntering off to the bar. Well, so far so good. No alarm bells ringing at this point. Whilst he's at the bar, I slyly check out his back and shoulders, watch as his muscles move under his t-shirt before my eyes fall to his pert bottom.

'Here you go, I hope that's alright,' he says, handing me a glass of elderflower pressé.

'Perfect.' I take a sip. Now what? 'So what are the chances of us seeing each other again? I never thought I'd see you again since we last saw each other in Coolsbay.'

'That was you?'

'Yeah.' Oh God this is embarrassing, he doesn't even remember me. Ground swallow me up now.

'Only joking, of course I know it was you, how could I forget you? We've got a connection.' He motions with his fingers as he looks into my eyes. *We do and I want to stay connected to you in more ways than one. What is wrong with me?* I bite my lip.

Stay alluring.

'That was a big group of stags you were out with and I thought our hen do was a lot at fifteen hens,' I blurt out then feel stupid because it was clearly two stag parties. The cactus and the bride. Never mind, it was still a lot of men.

'Hmmm, to be honest I don't know a lot of them and I'm not even that familiar with the stag. My roommate asked if I wanted to go and I said yes. I've not long got out of the army so I went along for some male bonding.'

'Yeah? And did you get that?'

'Not really, I think I like my circle small.'

'Your stag was in the wedding dress wasn't he?' I say, remembering the cactus at James's house. 'I didn't see you guys on the boat trip?' *God, could I sound any more stalkery?* His eyebrows squish together as if he's thinking for a second then he runs a hand through his curly locks. An image of James trooping appears in my mind, his big chest and hands swaying about as he grins his infuriating grin.

Don't think about him.

'Yeah, I went home,' he shrugs. 'Too many beers but if I'd known you were available then I definitely would have stayed out a little longer.'

'Ah thanks,' I simper. 'So when did you get out of the army?'

'A couple of months ago, it's been harder than I thought, getting back into civilian life but I know I've made the right decision.'

'What made you leave?' Wow am I interviewing him or what? 'Sorry you don't have to answer that if you don't want to. I'm being nosey.'

'No, no, not nosey at all, it's fine, you're curious, I like it.'

I smile but he still doesn't tell me why he left, well plenty of time left for that.

'I've got a little girl,' I blurt out, not knowing what else to say.

'Yeah? How old?' he asks.

'She's almost twenty months,' I say, carefully watching his reaction.

He smiles warmly, no hint of anger or disgust, not like Dan. 'A yummy mummy then.' He leans forward and bites his lip.

'Yeah, something like that.' I giggle.

'That's cool, I have loads of nieces and nephews, love kids, can't wait to have some of my own one day.'

'Yeah?' I'll have your babies, scrap one and done.

'Yeah.'

We spend the next hour talking about kids, the army and why he's in Swindon. He's not from here, he's from Salisbury but is lodging with a mate of a mate because it's close to his new job. I got it out of him why he left the army... because he wants to find a nice woman and settle down. Ah swoon. Well, look no further baby, here I am.

I leave the pub on cloud nine, my face actually hurts from grinning. What a twerp. We arrange to see each other again in a few days' time, this time we're going out for food. An image of James stripping pops into my mind just as I'm thinking about gorgeous George on the walk home. Oh bog off, why is he popping into my mind all of a sudden? He did have a nice chest and smile though, but he was an arse. Shit, what has happened to me.

I'm man obsessed.

I also need to remind myself that I'm just looking for the plus one to a wedding, not my life partner, but gorgeous George is already proving hard to resist.

My phone vibrates in my pocket and I quickly change it to a beep tone. I don't want to be reminded of the vibrating ankle lock ever again. Shit, does that mean I have to get rid of my vibrators? An even better excuse to find myself a plus one. I tap on the message.

Krissy: *Hey doll, hope you don't mind but one of Steven's mate's is single and I've been telling him all about you. I can vouch for him, he's a lovely guy and hot. Shall I arrange a date?*

Me: *Yeah, why not?* Can't keep all my eggs in one basket after all, I'm just looking for a wedding plus one.

As I reach the top of the hill and turn off down my street I think about how different my life was before the hen do. No dates, only play dates and days out with Nancy-Ella and Billy. My life was also way different when I bought this house with Billy, we bought in Old Town because we were party animals. Me, clinging on to my travelling days and Billy to his raving days. We could just stumble up the hill when we were done partying. How times have changed, and now I'm starting a new chapter, without Billy but not completely without him as he's still here, he will always be here.

'Hellooo.' I walk into the living room to find Billy and Nancy-Ella watching TV.

'Hey, how's Brie?' he asks, as I bend down and drop a kiss on Nancy-Ella's head. She looks tired.

'Yeah good, thanks for looking after her. Did you have fun with daddy, poppet?' Don't be daft, of course I didn't tell him I was going on a date. Nancy-Ella nods then goes back to watching *Mr Tumble's* signing. I watch her little hands try and copy him, she's so damn cute.

'No worries. I've been meaning to give Nick a bell,

haven't seen him in ages.'

'Yeah?' Maybe he's missing the double dates too, but those days are gone.

'Hey, they've opened up a new kids' farm in Cirencester, it looks really good. I've told Nancy-Ella we'll take her, haven't I, poppet?' Nancy-Ella jumps up and down in her seat with a big grin on her face. She begins to make mooing noises before mimicking all of the farmyard animals she knows, down to the sheep dog and the farmhouse mouse. I'm proud she can do them all.

'Yeah, sure.' Urgh, why do I always agree, because of Nancy-Ella that's why and he's already told her we're going.

'Hey, come into the kitchen. I've got this new coffee, it's gonna be a big seller.'

I reluctantly follow after him as Nancy-Ella slumps down on the sofa and her eyes begin to droop. Great, she's going to danger nap.

'Did she have a nap this afternoon?' I ask, already knowing the answer.

'No, she said she wasn't tired,' he says, with his back to me and I inwardly sigh.

'She always says that, you have to put her up anyway or she can't make it till bed time and falls asleep at dinner, like she's doing now,' I tell him, as he begins to potter about making the posh coffee. 'Why have you bought that thing here again?' I point to his fancy coffee machine, my irritation rising. *You don't live here anymore so stop making yourself at home.*

'Because I can't make the coffee otherwise.' He wobbles his head as if I'm stupid and hands me the coffee. I sigh again, a little too loudly.

'What it is?' he asks.

'I think that when you look after her she should come to yours now, she needs to get used to your place, don't you think?' It's time to start setting some boundaries.

'Yeah, but it's not really set up for kids, and plus she likes me coming here, she feels comfortable with daddy here.'

'She does, but she would feel comfortable eventually at yours too, if you let her.'

'What do you think then?' he says, ignoring my suggestion as he sips his coffee, he's even bought his own fancy, stupidly large, rainbow stripy mugs, my average size mugs obviously not good enough. 'It's a caffe cream with an extra shot of expresso, half a shot of cinnamon syrup, steamed milk and chocolate sprinkles.'

'Hmmm nice.' I try not to roll my eyes to the ceiling. Are people's tastebuds so finely calibrated that they would actually order this? I take a sip and grudgingly gulp down my bitter thoughts, it's actually really good.

'Here.' He hands me a cake. 'Tim made them, *Mars Bar* tray bake, they're selling like hot cakes.'

'Lovely.' I take a bite then devour the thing in minutes. I forgot to have lunch and now I want another one. They are bloody delicious.

'Wow, I'll tell Tim you loved it, he'll be pleased.' He chuckles and pats his ever-growing belly. He's going to turn into a traybake at this rate.

'Will he?' I say, a little too sarcastically.

'Yes. Of course he will. Have you thought any more about my offer?' He takes a bite from his tray bake. The caramel gets stuck in his teeth and he picks it out before sucking every single one of his fingers. He's not that attractive anymore, not since I've opened my eyes to how badly he treated me and how he always put me last against everything, including his mates and beloved coffee shop. There's much more to life than Billy, it just took me a little while to realise it.

'Yeah, I have. I don't think I'm going to take it.' I can't look him in the eye.

'You don't think or you've made your mind up?'

'I've made my mind up,' I say, regaining eye contact. Well done Tilly, not so silly anymore.

'Is it because of us because that's not the reason why we split up and I know you think it is but it isn't, don't just waste a good opportunity because we split up.'

'No? Then what was the reason?' I say, as I poke my head round into the living room remembering all the arguments we had about the coffee shop before Nancy-Ella was born. It's stunning at the coffee shop; I love it there but the first time I said no is because I didn't want to ruin our relationship any further by us seeing far too much of each other.

Nancy-Ella is fast asleep, just ten more minutes and she might still go to bed on time.

'The spark went, didn't it?' he says, so matter of fact. The superficial knob nubbin. Yes, the spark went when I was four weeks postpartum when I needed him the most.

'Yes, yes I guess it did,' I agree as my eyes focus on the caramel he's managed to get all over his chin this time. 'Anyway, thanks for looking after her, I'm going to have to ask you to leave now?'

'Why?' he laughs.

'Because I have stuff to do and I have to start putting up some boundaries with you.' I put my hands on my hips, it feels good to tell him what's what for once.

'Boundaries?' he says, in a high-pitched voice with a hint of a smile.

'Yes. If you're here all the time and bringing your

coffee machine round then how am I supposed to move on and meet someone?' I wait for a response but he just continues to chew on his traybake. 'Yes, it was going to happen sooner or later so it may as well be now. I'll come to the farm with you and Nancy-Ella this time but after that we should just do separate outings with her, we can't continue to play happy families, because well, we're not,' I say, with a betraying croak in my throat.

'Oh.' Billy jerks his head as his nostrils flare then I see his eyes fill with tears of frustration. 'Okay, if that's what you want,' he finally manages.

'I do want,' I say, softly as Billy blinks back his tears. 'No. I think we *need* to, if either of us are going to move on, it's what we have to do.' I put my hand on his arm, as Billy nods and picks up another square from the tray bake. He offers me a slice and I oblige.

I'll miss those sweet treats.

Chapter 11

Today's the day. After the best part of two years off, I'm back at work and sitting in the grey and yellow reception. Andrea, my boss, owns a small office inside the huge angular building where ten other businesses also work. I scan the list next to reception and at least three of the businesses have changed, along with the receptionist who at least seems nicer than the last one who was easily getting on for one hundred years old and incredibly grouchy.

I almost feel like I'm starting a new job and in a way I am. At least I can ease myself into it before I go back part-time in a few months. I turn my phone off, cautious that I don't want the dating app to go off in my handbag as I'm filling out my returning to work forms.

George and I have text a couple of times since our date but we've made no firm plans to meet again yet. He's VERY slow to reply and a little flaky so in the meantime I've let Krissy arrange a date with her husband's mate. Well, I haven't got very long before the wedding and what if I ask George to be my plus one and he cancels the night before or worse, he doesn't turn up? Maybe Krissy's husband's mate would be a safer bet.

Since Billy and I had our chat we've arranged that Billy will have Nancy-Ella every other weekend as well as

Monday and Tuesday nights. I now have a lot of spare time to myself, almost too much spare time. I may as well spend it by finding my plus one for Nay's wedding and the rest of the time I can busy myself with doing what I love, painting. Mum's present is almost finished and I'm so pleased with it, I hope she likes it.

The receptionist looks up and smiles before checking the time on her smart watch. Yes, Andrea is late but being early was never her thing, funny because we work in events and being on time is pretty essential.

I let my mind wander to my next date as pre-work nerves begin to set in. Krissy suggested that we go over to hers so it's a bit less pressure, I quite like the sound of that so this weekend I'll be on a double date with my new pal. A pang of guilt hits me in the stomach, I haven't spoken to Brie since we met at the pub, she's off with me and I think I know why, Krissy. But what am I supposed to do? Not make new friends because Brie doesn't approve? I know she was a little cheeky on the hen do, gate crashing our tiny bed, but I'm sure it was just a misunderstanding. Gemma probably just assumed I wasn't coming.

'Tilly, welcome back, it's so nice to see you again,' Andrea's loud voice booms, as she appears in front of me.

She shakes my hand before laughing at the ridiculousness of it then pulls me into a big bear hug. Her smile gleams, and she looks genuinely pleased to see me, which is both nice and a relief as we had a slight disagreement before I left but really I think she was stressed about the amount of time I was taking off and having to find a replacement.

'It's nice to be back,' I say, as we fall into step and make our way to the office. I struggle to keep up with

Andrea's huge strides, taking two steps to her one. I feel like a little rabbit running next to a greyhound.

'I'm so chuffed to be coming in one day a week to start with. Motherhood is fab but exhausting, not that I'm coming here for a break or anything,' I say, gently elbowing Andrea in the ribs. She laughs a deep throaty laugh.

'How is the babe?' Andrea asks, as we slow down outside the office.

'Yes, she's fab thank you, a real little character.'

Andrea takes the key out of her bag and unlocks the office door.

'Oh wow.' I gasp as we walk inside.

Everything is white, shiny and minimalist. She's had it all done out, it looks very fancy and chic. Her grand desk sits at the back of the office whilst two smaller desks are tucked away in the corners. One of those desks must be mine, they look nice, I'm looking forward to laying all my stationery out and switching on my laptop. I actually feel quite excited to talk to my clients and suppliers again.

'It was in need of a makeover. Ah it's lovely that you've got yourself a little family now, I know you wanted that for a long time,' she says pointedly, as she sits down behind her desk and motions for me to take a seat opposite her.

'Yes, well it is lovely but it hasn't really worked out between Billy and I.' I sit down. 'We unfortunately split when she was a newborn.' Best to get it over and done with now, I've learnt from my mistakes.

'What? Oh gosh, I'm so sorry,' Andrea says, watching my face for signs of emotion. She's probably wondering why I didn't tell her sooner, even though we didn't message about work we kept in touch. I guess I thought Billy and I would patch things up. Or rather, I hoped we would.

'Yeah, it's complicated but I'm okay, we're okay, it just wasn't meant to be and at least Nancy-Ella won't remember us ever being together so she won't know any different, will she?'

'That's true. I'm so sorry though, what a shame.' Andrea takes a sip from her water bottle then sets it on the side, watching me the whole time.

'Yeah, well… it is what it is.' Did I actually say that? I hate that saying. 'The office looks nice, very chic,' I say, deflecting the attention away from me and my failed relationship. I don't want or need any more sympathy.

'Oh yes, thank you, I'm glad you like it, although I'm hardly here anymore. I spend most of the time on the road, tapping up new business, and buttering up our old clients, it's so nice to be able to see them though.'

'Oh, wow, what happed to Fabien?' The one I warned you about.

'Fabien was…' She taps the desk with her fingernails and I can tell she's trying to think how she can be diplomatic because he was a total tool which is why we almost fell out. I caught him gossiping with the hotels about the clients and Andrea dismissed it. '…I'm afraid to say, not the right fit, he took a lot of sick days too in the end and I ended up having to step in and do a lot of the business myself. I was apprehensive about employing anyone else for a while because I didn't want to make the same mistake again but anyway, enough about that. I have some exciting news.' She purses her lips together and claps her hands.

'Oh yes?' I say, my eyes flitting to the two desks. She's employed someone else, I knew it. I chew on the inside of my cheek. Andrea is a lovely boss but she doesn't always have the best interviewing skills which means that the blaggers are often able to pull the wool over her eyes, fooling her into thinking they are qualified and capable when really they're just all mouth and no trousers.

'Yes, actually he'll be here any minute so I can introduce you. He's certainly got the gift of the gab, great with the clients but he's also fab with the events too, extremely organised and perfect attention to detail.'

'Oh fab, sounds just well, perfect,' I say, wondering who this amazing man is. He sounds almost too good to be true and no one has perfect attention to detail, not even me.

'He's been here for about six months now and is already doing a superb job. As you know Rose, who was originally covering your maternity, has just left to have a baby of her own.' Andrea half rolls her eyes, forgetting the company that she's in, then smiles at me.

I actually had no idea that Rose had left. I didn't receive any updates whilst I was off so I really am walking back into my job, blind. I smile back at her. It will be fine. Andrea though flawed, is a fair and caring boss.

'That's lovely for Rose and I can't wait to meet the new guy. What's his name?' I ask, wondering if she's employed another Fabienesque person.

'And here he is.' Andrea's face lights up and she bounces about in her seat like she's suddenly developed an itch. 'Talk of the devil himself,' she continues. 'Tilly.' Andrea stretches out her arm to draw attention to her shiny new employee. 'I'd like to introduce you to your work colleague.' Andrea beams behind me as I paste a huge smile on and swivel around in my chair to greet the new guy.

'James.'

My jaw drops and for all the wrong reasons.

'Well, hi, Tilly.' James raises his eyebrows and beams

from ear to ear. My eyes fall to his dark grey suit and patterned tie with specs of yellow and grey, he matches the reception decor. Looking entirely different now with no beard, he also looks annoyingly fit. Fit, very cocky and in my personal space. Again.

'Well, well, hi James,' I say, matching his enthusiasm whilst trying not to grit my teeth. I feel my cheeks burn red and we both giggle nervously.

'You two know each other?' Andrea wobbles her head, not missing a trick.

'We met on a b-b-boat,' James stutters and shakes his head, his confidence faltering for a moment. Hah!

'We were in Coolsbay at the same time, both on hen and stag parties, small world isn't it?' I cut in with a winning smile, sounding way cooler than I feel. Perhaps I should have gone to work at Billy's bloody coffee shop. Is it too late to change my mind?

Fuck.

He's from bloody Swindon, another stag do from Swindon. For a moment horror washes over me, does he know gorgeous George? No, it was definitely two stags and James was with the cactus. George with the bride. I compose myself.

'That's wonderful,' says Andrea, after she's invited James to sit down so we can have our first cosy little team meeting. 'So you've already done the team bonding then?' She smiles then raises an eyebrow. Oh no, this is so cringe. I hope she isn't assuming the worst, which could have happened, except I can't remember. *Good old clean adult fun.* 'James is going to be helping you organise the events but he'll also be out on the road checking out new locations and visiting prospective clients.'

Good, at least he won't be here all the time then and I can have some time to myself. An image of him dancing in his suit as the fake stripper flickers into my mind. I shake my head to get rid of the thought.

'You okay, Tilly?' Andrea asks.

'Yes, very much looking forward to working with James and showing him the ropes if he needs me to.' I smile my best professional smile at him.

'Likewise.' James grins.

I don't need him to show me the ropes. I've been doing this job for years, what can he possibly show me? I smile and nod at Andrea as she begins to list all the amazing things that James has been doing in the past six months that he's been here. Seems he's quite the schmoozer with the clients, I wonder if he throws out his dance moves to charm them. *Big fish, little fish, cardboard box.*

'So, what did you do before you came here then?' I ask James.

'I was regional sales manager for the Lilly boutique hotel chain. I know a lot of the local hotel managers really well from networking events so I know how they work, which is an advantage for our business,' he says, tapping his nose as Andrea nods and smiles along. But has he planned an event? Does he know what he's doing? Sales are different to planning. I press my lips together.

'Yes, I agree, it's so important to build good working relationships with them.' And they know me as their supplier not another competitor so I'm guessing I probably have a better relationship with them. Don't be stepping on my toes wise guy, I've been doing this job for years.

'There have probably been quite a few changes since you've been away, Tilly.' Andrea looks at me pointedly. 'In terms of management with the venues and clients I mean, but I'll let James fill you in on all of that when I'm gone as I need to be with a client in the next hour.' She checks her watch.

Great, now I really do feel out of it.

I wish I'd insisted on being kept in the loop when I was away on my maternity leave and sabbatical but Andrea told me not to worry about work. She said that there was no point in filling me in on anything until I was back as it may change again and she didn't want to stress me out I was pleased that she had given me that privilege as I would have thought that a small company would have wanted to have kept in touch and asked for my advice from time to time. I thought my knowledge was valuable but it turns out, I'm very replaceable at work. Having said that, can I really blame her? I guess she was just protecting the business in case I didn't return. My eyes sneak a look at James and I quietly inhale his aftershave which is wafting in the air like a sedative to my boss.

'Great, look forward to catching up on all the news,' I say to James, in my best business voice.

He fiddles with his reception matching tie then smiles back at me. His clean-shaven face makes him look much younger than I thought he was. He could even be younger than me.

'Perfect, I'll leave you guys to it then. Have a great first day back and I'll see you next week as you'll be gone by the time I get back.'

'Okay great, thanks Andrea, see you soon,' I say, looking much more pleased than I'm feeling.

'Bye, guys.' Andrea waves before picking up her handbag and striding out of the door.

'Bye,' James and I sing in unison.

Andrea seems to love him but apart from me she does seem to favour the men. Not being bitchy, just an observation. If Fabien had been a woman he would have been out of the door much sooner, she let him get away with stuff for far too long because he was charming and loved to dish out the compliments to her.

'Umm where do you want to do the catch up then? Your desk or mine. Probably best if we do it at yours as you may want to show me some stuff you've been working on,' I say in what I believe to be an authoritarian voice, as I get up and hover between the two desks. I'd quite like the window spot, I love being by the window and this one has a nice view of the fields. I edge towards the one I want and tap my fingers on the desk.

'Yeah, good idea, got lots to tell you I'm sure,' James agrees, then gets up and moves to the other side of the big desk where Andrea was sat. He begins to move her mouse around and tap on her keyboard. What is he doing? Who does he think he is?

'Umm we should go to our *own* desks, I don't think Andrea will like you playing about on her laptop.' The cheek of him, I'm going to have to watch this one, just like Fabien.

'Oh no.' He shakes his head and widens his eyes. 'This is my desk.' He taps his fingers on the table then stretches his arms up behind his head before leaning back on his chair.

I will him to fall off it but he doesn't, instead he balances on the back wheels like a school boy, going backwards and forwards as he grins. Is he teasing me?

'What?' I say, slamming my hands down on his desk. I take in the huge desk and fancy chair that I thought was Andrea's. It's almost twice the size of the other two.

'Yeah, she gave it to me.' James laughs. 'I can't fit my legs under them tiny little things, they're not built for men like me.' He leans back even further, this time he does wobble a bit. A small gasp escapes him as he steadies himself, that'll teach him.

'Well, a man like you should be very good at your job then,' I say, squinting at him. Is he for real? Taken my job so it seems and the good desk.

'Look it's not my fault I've got the good desk,' he says, reading my mind.

My face must be so transparent so I rearrange my features into something that I hope resembles indifference.

'I'll let you borrow it when I'm out of the office, if you want?' He grins, I think he's being kind but he could be being facetious. I can't work him out. Work James is very different to drunken stag do James.

'No thanks, you're fine. I like to be by the window anyway.' I smirk as the image of the K-pop band taking photos of the fish feasting on his vomit pops into my mind. Before I can stop myself, a little giggle escapes me. Woops.

'Cool.' He laughs a little nervous laugh along with me, if he knew what I was laughing at, I doubt he'd be laughing. 'I'm looking forward to working with you, what are the chances, hey?'

Yes, what are the bloody chances?

Chapter 12

'Hey you, looking hot,' Krissy squeals, as she opens the door and I step into her house.

I'm wearing a red skirt and top combo; the skirt is long and I feel very hippy in it especially with the flat sandals. After a week of running about after a toddler, heels are the last thing I want to wear. Although it may have something to do with the fact that I wore heels on my first day back at work and even though I hardly walked in them, my feet suffered for the rest of the week.

James. I still can't believe he's my new colleague, I must tell Brie when I see her next.

'Aww thank you, you look lovely too,' I say, returning the compliment. And she does look lovely, she's wearing a long, colourful maxi dress and huge heels. Her hair, bundled up on top of her head together with her large hoop earrings remind me of a wacky fortune teller.

'Steve has gone out to collect Nathan so they'll be here any minute. I'm so excited for you and for me.' She snorts, puts her hand over her mouth and nose. 'Sorry, I haven't had a night off since the hen do, so I'm a little hyper.'

The hen do; I surprise myself by feeling a little stab in my guts. It appears I'm still a bit uncomfortable about her not paying and gate crashing our bedroom but she seems so nice, I'm sure she has a reasonable explanation for what happened. Surely it must have been because of me and my unwillingness to commit to coming. Yes, that must be it.

'No need to apologise, I know how you feel.' Apart from my disastrous date with Dan, I haven't had a night out either. An image of him swearing at his ankle tag infiltrates my thoughts and I shudder at the thought of it. I wonder what the next girl will think of that, I wish I could warn them in some way, it's not like the police would be interested because he actually didn't do anything wrong. Dating apps could do with a ratings and review system because he would be a one star with the review: Steer clear if you want to avoid package meals, criminals and curfews.

'Drink?' Krissy asks, as I follow her through to the living room. Krissy lives in a much larger house than I was expecting, I mean she has an island in her kitchen so she must be doing alright.

'Yes, please,' I say, eyeing up her impressive drink's cabinet. Krissy points to a bottle of Palma Violet Gin. 'Perfect.'

She gets busy making the drinks as I casually nose around at her house. It's a very nice house, apart from the kitchen island and expensive drinks cabinet, she has a very large leather sofa and glamourous chandelier light fittings. She doesn't look like she's struggling money wise which is the only excuse I can think as to why she gate crashed the hen do but still, looks can be deceiving, I guess.

'Ta daaaaa.' Krissy hands me my gin in a big fancy glass loaded with frozen berries, an umbrella and a metal straw.

'Wow, thank you.' I take a sip and almost spit it out,

it's potent.

'Would you mind if I have a bit more tonic please, Krissy or I'll be off my face by the time they get here.' I giggle nervously.

'Yes sure,' she laughs. 'I forget not everyone drinks like me.'

Krissy and I sip or rather gulp down our drinks whilst we compare notes on our kids and I fill her in on my first day back at work. Krissy screams when I tell her about James. She also reckons I should demand the big desk but he literally only has it because he is so tall. I need to stop being petty and learn to get along with him. An image of him stripping pops into my mind again. What is wrong with me? I'm going to have to stop these thoughts before they get the better of me or worse, before James sees me getting embarrassed when he speaks to me. Cool, calm and collected, that's what I need to be. Not good old clean adult fun that probably wasn't even clean. The front door opens and I jump in my seat. What if I've developed PTSD concerning James popping up in every area of my life?

'They're here.' Krissy hops up and scuttles to greet them like Bambi dancing on ice. 'Hey guys,' she says, hurrying over to the two men and kissing them both on the cheek. I only know which one Steve is from the photos in her hallway, otherwise it would be hard to tell as both look equally in awe of her.

'Hi.' I get up and give them an awkward little wave.

'Tilly, this is my Steve and this is Nathan.'

I wave at them again as they both smile. Steve leans forward to shake my hand and Nathan follows suit, it all feels very formal. Krissy motions for Steve to come into the kitchen with her to prepare more drinks while ushering me and Nathan into the lounge. I know what they're doing, they're leaving us alone to get acquainted. This is cringe.

'So how long have you known these guys?' I ask, when Krissy and Steve have left us but are no doubt still in earshot.

'I work with Steve but known them both for years, they're a great couple, Krissy's a real laugh.' He nods to himself.

'Yeah, she is. Though I haven't known her long, we met on her cousin's hen do, but we have a lot in common. Our kids are the same age and yeah, like you say, Krissy's a real hoot.' I wring my hands together, I want to sit down on the sofa but what if he continues to stand up and talk to me, that would be weird.

'Yeah, she said you had a little boy.' Nathan sniffs and shakes his head, moving his hair out of his eyes before his eyeballs swivel to the left and over my head. I resist the urge to turn around to see what he's looking at and instead ask him another question. This dating/finding a plus one lark suddenly feels quite lonely. This is meant to be fun isn't it?

'Little girl,' I correct, but he isn't listening. 'Do you have kids?' I ask, smiling. I stretch my neck a little, moving my head up to his eyeline. There, you have to look at me now, Nathan.

'Sorry?'

'Do you have kids?' I ask my lame question again.

'No, no, not yet,' he answers.

My phone pings in my pocket, I doubt he'd mind or even notice if I checked it but I don't because I'd feel rude. I'll save that for my toilet trip shortly. Moments later Nathan's phone goes off and he swoops into his pocket to check it without a second thought. I take that as an opportunity to check my phone too.

George: *Hey, how are you? Fancy meeting up again soon?*
Me: *Would love to.*

George: *Great, when are you free?* I toy with the idea of texting him back RIGHT NOW! I already feel like I want to escape this evening. It's quite clear who Nathan has his eyes on and it's not me. I quickly think when I have an evening to myself again.

Me: *Monday evening?*

'Here you go, kids,' Krissy says, as her and Steve sashay back into the room, her face falls when she sees us both on our phones.

Shit, this isn't going well. Krissy places down four very potent looking cocktails. I'll have to make this last or I'll be off my chops before I know it. I didn't eat much for dinner either.

The rest of the evening goes a little better, Nathan warms up and gives me a bit more eye contact, I think he may even be flirting with me at one point. He's easy on the eye but I'm not sure if he's my type, mind you, does he really have to be? I'm only looking for my plus one after all, not my life partner; the four of us could actually have quite a giggle at the wedding.

We have a good laugh taking the piss out of each others' music taste as Krissy starts taking song requests and searching for them on *YouTube*. More cocktails are consumed and watching the music videos turns into dancing which then transitions into full blown karaoke. Krissy gets up first and sings *Born This Way* by Lady Gaga, she's actually a very good singer, I wasn't expecting that. Then it's Steve, followed by me, then eventually Nathan who belts out Robbie Williams's *Angels*. We score our performances out of ten, it's a real hoot. I'm enjoying myself; it reminds me of my double date days with Billy, Brie and Nick, they always liked karaoke too.

Krissy and Nathan get up and do a duet of *Shallow* by Lady Gaga and Bradley Cooper. Their voices complement each other and they play the parts very well, looking longingly into each other's eyes and even leaning in for a swift kiss on the lips at the end. Steve claps and whoops at their performance, either he's being a little too enthusiastic because it is extremely awkward or he's very drunk. Hmm probably the latter.

Next we play Mr and Mrs which was a good way to get to know more about Nathan. We do all combinations, Steve and Krissy, Nathan and me, Steve and Nathan, Krissy and me and so on. Weirdly Nathan appears to know more about Krissy than Steve does, on paper anyway. I refuse the last few cocktails and have a glass of water as the room is beginning to spin. Nathan offers to make me a cup of tea which I gladly accept, it also means that we get a little alone time in the kitchen as Steve and Krissy fight over which game we should play next.

'How do you take your tea?'

'Just milk please.'

Nathan grabs a couple of mugs out of Krissy's cupboard, he's very at home here.

'Sweet enough?' he says, not turning around. 'Same as Krissy takes hers.'

'Right.' A bit of a strange thing to say, maybe he's still feeling nervous. Krissy said he was shy, although he didn't look shy whilst he was belting out Robbie Williams or when he was being Bradley Cooper.

'So, you having a good night?' he asks, as he flicks the switch on the kettle.

'Yes fab, it's been great meeting you and hanging out with all of you guys.' Even if you do only have eyes for

Krissy.

'Yeah, we should do it again,' he says, pouring the water into the mugs.

'Yeah,' I reply, a little a taken back by his sudden keenness but flattered none the less. I guess we could meet again, as a foursome. We could just be friends, yeah I think I'd like that.

Nathan grabs the milk out of the fridge and I wince as he pours it over the teabags, but that's okay, even though it's wrong you can't cancel someone for doing that. What he does next though, will haunt me forever.

Nathan picks up the sopping wet teabag with his forefinger and thumb and I watch in horror as he begins to squeeze it and the juices run over his grubby fingernails. The teabag pulsates between his digits and saliva gathers in my mouth before he goes in for a second dunk and squeezes it again.

The fingernails!

He's infused his cup of tea with his own fingernail dirt. Yuck. He won't do that to mine, surely he's going to use a spoon.

Please use a spoon. Please use a spoon.

Nathan doesn't use a spoon, instead he goes through the whole process again whilst I watch in gagging revulsion.

He's talking but I can't hear what he's saying, something about Krissy and Steve and how they're his go to couple.

I can't drink that.

He can never make me a cup of tea ever again. Thank God, I came out here to witness this or I would have been none the wiser. I could have been drinking his dirty nail infused tea for months without knowing. At this thought, I feel the bile rise up through my gut.

'Here you go.' He smiles, handing me the tea, oblivious to just how unhygienic his tea making skills are. I really do feel sick.

'Thanks.' I cup the mug and force a smile but it probably resembles more of a grimace. He watches me. Oh fuck, he's waiting for me to take a sip, to tell him it's a nice brew. He's waiting for tea validation.

'Excuse me,' I manage, setting the mug down before bolting off to the toilet in the hallway.

Krissy and Steve exchange concerned looks as I stumble past them, all of my concentration going into not being sick in front of them. I get inside the toilet and vomit all of the cocktails up as well as dinner and by the looks of it, the last five meals I've eaten. It's truly horrific and all because of a bloody teabag.

Chapter 13

'Babe, that is absolutely rank, I'd totally be sick too,' Brie says, as I finish filing her in on my latest dating episode, teabag gate. I tap the screen to put her on loudspeaker whilst I make myself a coffee and simultaneously Nancy-Ella's porridge. Today is going to be a very long day. My head is banging and despite puking them all up, I keep tasting last night's cocktails.

'Really? You don't think I'm being a drama queen?' I ask, as the smell of porridge makes me heave.

'What, you? No way! No honestly, mate. I would be chundering like there's no tomorrow but I guess that's what you get when you let Krissy organise a date for you.'

Ooooh. I won't tell her that I think he actually had eyes for Krissy then, that will make her even less popular with Brie.

'Ahh she isn't that bad,' I say.

'She isn't that good either,' Brie quips back. 'So when's the next date?' She quickly changes the subject but I haven't missed that she's being quite nasty about Krissy, it's in her tone, and Krissy doesn't deserve that. Apart from falling into the wrong bed, she's done nothing wrong to Brie. I suddenly feel quite protective over my new friend.

'Monday, but not with Nathan, I probably won't be

seeing him again any time soon, but with the gorgeous George. He's taking me out for a meal.' And he actually replied fairly quickly for him, just forty eight hours this time, not that I'm counting.

'Nice, you're really getting into finding your plus one.'

'Yeah, I guess I am. I'm really looking forward to it, he certainly has potential.'

'Amazing, let me know how it goes. Look I've got to go. I've actually got your mum coming in, any minute now,' Brie says, and I stop stirring the porridge.

'Again? What's she having done?'

'Umm, she hasn't told you?'

'No.' Looks like she'll be on her way to looking like Jackie Stallone sooner than I thought.

'Then I better not say,' Brie says quietly. 'Client confidentiality and all that.'

'But Brie, it's me, your best mate, your client's concerned daughter.' I say, sounding more whiney than I intend to.

'I know but I can't, it wouldn't be right, babe.' Brie is sticking to her guns. That's it, I've had enough.

'I can't let her continue to do stuff to her face, she's starting to look not like my mum.' An image of my mum with her new plump lips and super smooth skin flashes into my mind. Wrinkles give character and I liked hers, why does she feel the need to change herself so much?

'What are you saying? That my work is shoddy?' Brie says, in a staccato tone. Brie and I never argue, we've always had quite a jokey relationship, we take the piss out of each other and in the past, if we've disagreed about stuff, which was very rare, we always just talked it through and agreed to disagree or one of us compromised. We always said we were low maintenance friends, no drama's but now it feels very different.

Something in the air has changed lately.

'No, no, not at all but, this is *my* Mum. I worry about her and I don't want her ending up looking like Pete Burns,' I say, in an attempt to make a joke of it but it falls on deaf ears.

'There you go again, insulting my work. God, you speak about your mum like she isn't of sound mind or something but your mum is a smart woman who can make her own decisions. Just stop trying to control her like she's your baby,' Brie says, raising her voice.

'I don't talk about her like that at all, I just think she's got carried away and she needs me to talk some sense into her.'

'She doesn't. Look, why don't you concentrate on your own life instead of interfering in other people's all the time.'

'What?' Part of me thinks she's joking. Any minute, she'll laugh. There's a huge pause before she speaks.

'I've got to go, bye.' And with that, Brie hangs up the phone.

Blinking back tears, I frown and shake my head before testing the temperature of the porridge on my lips. It burns just like Brie's words. I interfere in people's lives? Is that really what she thinks of me now?

'Nancy-Ella, breakfast is ready, time to get into your highchair,' I sing, in an overly cheerful voice as I bring her porridge into the living room.

'Nancy-Ellaaaa?' I sing again, half expecting her to jump out from behind the sofa. She loves to hide, this one.

'Is she in herrreee?' I put the porridge down on the highchair and walk over to her toy box. Tentatively I knock on the lid, she's never normally this quiet for so long. Shows she's growing up, better concentration span and all that.

Oh but, she's not in there.

'Nancy-Ella?' My eyes swivel around the living room as I try to think where she can be. 'I've got some yummy porridge for you, with honey,' I say, as I check behind the curtains.

'Mumma, Mumma,' I hear her shout. 'Mumma.'

'Nancy-Ella, where have you been hiding from me, you cheeky little monkey. I'm coming to get youuuuuu.' I jog towards the bathroom, half expecting the whole bathroom to be turned upside down with shower gel, toilet roll and toothpaste everywhere. It wouldn't be the first time either. 'Fuck's sake,' I mutter under my breath, as I get to the ominously closed bathroom door. I take in a deep breath and open it.

'Mumma, dook.' Her little face lights up in a big grin as she stares up at me from the potty, she gets up and points to it clapping her hands.

'Oh my, you clever girl.' My hand flies up to my mouth as I fight the urge to cry happy tears. She's so sweet and I feel so bad for expecting the worst. She has in fact gone for a wee on the potty, albeit the tiniest of wees but she's managed to pull down her nappy and park her bum on there and I haven't even shown her how yet. Is my child actually a genius? This has got to be a fluke. She picked the potty herself because it had a picture of *Peppa Pig* on it but I was actually saving the potty training for next year. The first people I want to tell is my mum and Brie but they're both busy, probably complaining about me interfering in their lives. My boobs begin to ache again so I reach for my breast pump on top of the bathroom cabinet, then put it back again remembering that I shouldn't be expressing if I want my body to stop producing milk. I found out from lurking in one of the new mum Facebook groups that my milk should now dry up in seven to ten days. As tempting as it is to express, I must leave the tits alone.

After a long day mumming it with achy, slightly leaky boobs, I finally slump down on the sofa. Nancy-Ella's in bed, it's only six thirty in the evening but we've had a really busy day and I don't think it will be long before I go to bed myself. After breakfast we painted for a bit, I even managed to finish my mum's painting before chilling and watching *CBeebies* whilst I had a lay down for all of ten minutes. We wolfed down lunch with half of it landing on Nancy-Ella and the walls behind her, then we went out for a walk where we met with Krissy and Arthur at the park. When I filled Krissy in on my argument with Brie, she said she was being sensitive and I have every right to look out for my mum. I also gently told Krissy that Nathan was lovely but not my type, Krissy was relieved because apparently, he had said the same about me. I didn't tell her that there was no way he was ever going to fancy me when he was clearly in love with her. We went home and Nancy-Ella had just over an hour's nap whilst I did some housework and enjoyed another ten-minute lie down. The afternoon was spent playing hide and seek and making animals out of playdough. Then it was meal time again, bath and bed and now I'm completely exhausted, emotionally and physically.

I stick on *Love Island* and poke at my belly fat whilst they all skimp about in their thong bikinis and gossip about who they are going to pull for a chat. Those bikinis must be so uncomfortable, I think. Wow I really am sounding like a mum, a couple of years ago I wouldn't have thought twice about their thong bikinis. Once upon a time, I may have even been brave enough to wear one. Now I just want to wear my comfy granny pants, that is unless I have a date of course. I'll have to wear something a bit sexier on my next date with George, just in case he invites me back.

I think about the contents of my knicker drawer, I still have several pairs of my old maternity knickers, maybe it's time to invest in something less capacious. But at this rate, I'll be sixty-seven by the time he invites me over. I mean, there's taking it slow and there's taking it SLOW. I'm pretty sure he doesn't use his hands to dunk teabags or is a criminal with a curfew so I think I'll be alright. I pick up my phone and begin scrolling for outfit inspiration for my next date. I click on a video of two girls in the same outfit who claim to be different sizes, although they look the same size to me. They snap their fingers and change outfits from a summer dress, to shorts and a vest top to a jump suit. I'm just thinking that I might purchase some new shorts when an email pops up from my brother, Charlie.

Hey Sis,

First of all . . yuck . . I do not need to hear that you're hungry for dick. Vom! I literally had to stop myself from vomiting up my paella when I read that. TMI – too much information, sister.

Secondly sorry for the slow reply, I've been a little busy with ahem someone. . . okay I've met someone, yes me! Who was sworn off relationships after that absolute loser Carlos that I called my boyfriend shat on all of my expectations of love when I caught him with his pants down with that hussy Lewis behind the Sagrada Familia. But enough about him, I want to tell you about Gethin who was visiting Barcelona with his friends. They booked me for a walking tour of the gothic quarter, it was my last one of the day and I ended up having a few drinks with them. It's been a super fucking whirlwind, sweep me off my feet ridiculous soppy, lovey dovey holiday romance. I feel a little silly to admit this but I am ABSOLUTELY BESOTTED, it's only been a matter of weeks but Gethin feels the same way and I am completely lost without him. He's gone back now hence why you're hearing from me (sorry but love comes first darling haha) I am absolutely devasted, I'm even considering coming home, he only lives in Swansea so not far from Swindon at all. What is wrong with me?? I am scaring myself here, sounding like a complete psycho but…

I LOVE HIM. I LOVE HIM. I LOVE HIM. If I had social media I would be so dangerous, I'd be stalking him day and night and all of his ex-boyfriends too. Lucky for him that I don't. Anyway, enough about me and my life as a lovestruck maiden. I'm not feeling as dramatic as I sound, I just know there's something wonderful for me waiting round the corner, you have to think like that don't you? Have you been on any dates? Have you found your plus one? I've attached some photos of me and Gethin – what do you think?

P.S. I spoke to mum and she said you were overreacting and that her face is in Brie's safe and capable hands, so that told me (and you). I video timed her and she looked completely fine so maybe it's calmed down now? Anyway I'll keep video calling to keep an eye on her ever-evolving face. Also, give my little munchkin a kiss and a squeeze from me. Gunkle misses her badly.

Love you lots Charlie xxx

I click on the attachments to see three photos of my brother posing with Gethin at various tourist attractions in Barcelona. Gethin is tall, dark and handsome and they look very happy together.

I'm beyond envious.

I begin my reply, typing my approval of Gethin and telling Charlie about all my dating disasters and the potential plus-one, George. I even tell him about James and the fact I've soothed him whilst he vomited, shared a bed with him, had a strip show from him and now I have to face him every week at work which in a few months, will be three days a week. I send the email then zone out watching TV. Hours later I wake to the TV blaring and dribble on my sofa cushions. It's three o'clock in the morning and I have to be up for work in four hours.

Bugger.

Today, I've dressed in my power suit, Andrea doesn't mind us being casual if we're not seeing clients but after seeing James wearing a suit, I'm not going to turn up in my comfies and give him any reason to think I'm an unprofessional slob. Plus it makes me feel good and makes a nice change to dress up even if the heels are a little painful. I look good and I'm ready to face the day. Strutting into the office with a bright smile on my face, I expect to see Andrea and James deep in conversation masterminding some fantastic event that I will have no involvement in other than making the teas and coffees.

'Morning, nice weekend?' I say breezily, as I put my bag down by my desk. I can see his big legs poking out from underneath the desk as he sits down slouched behind his screen.

'Hey, yeah, just a quiet one with the boys, you?' he asks, poking his head out from behind his screen. He looks tired and his clean-shaven face has now developed stubble.

'Yeah, same really, quiet one with my little one,' I lie, suppressing a cocktail-tinged burp, that stuff is still repeating on me and I'm still not feeling quite right, never again. I pull out a photo of Nancy-Ella and pop it on my desk, it's time to start making my desk feel homely and looking at her little face every time I'm here, will keep me going.

'Who's that?' James pokes his head out from behind his screen, nodding towards my photo.

'Who's what, nosey?' I tease. Why is he watching me?

'The photo on your desk.' He gets up and sashays over to me, I avert my eyes as his pelvis directly meets my eyeline. He picks up the photo and surveys my daughter as I try not to breath in his fresh, minty shower gel smell and hint of a musky aftershave.

He smells delicious, like his bed on the hen do. An image of him laughing in my face plays on my mind. He may smell nice but he's not a very nice man. 'Aww, how old? She looks just like you,' he says, pretending to be nice.

'Really? People always say she looks like… she'll be two in a few months,' I say, stopping myself from talking about Billy. We don't need to get too personal, after all we're just work colleagues.

'Yeah, she's your double,' he reiterates, and I give him a genuine smile. No one ever says that, they all say she looks like Billy. I glance over at his desk and notice he has a photo of his boys. He sees me looking and goes to fetch it. 'Here are my two, they're five and six.'

'Aww cute, they look so different,' I say, as I look at the boys in the photo staring back at me. One is very fair with blonde hair and blue eyes and the other is dark with brown eyes, like James. They both have his big smile.

'Yeah, like chalk and cheese! Same mum though, I don't work that fast.' He laughs a deep, throaty laugh. 'He's like me and he's like their mother, chalk and cheese personalities too,' he says, as he points to each of his sons, clearly proud of his offspring. I let out a strangled sounding laugh which instantly makes me blush. Where did that come from?

'What's the plan today then?' I ask, feeling very uncomfortable.

I hate not knowing what's going on. Whilst James has been stood here an email's popped up from Andrea asking me to liaise with James about today's work. I watch him as a slightly smug looking smile spreads across his face. I hope he doesn't start to think he's my boss with all this knowledge, power and giant shiny new desk.

'Well, it's a fun one.' He rubs his hands together. He has huge hands and I tell myself off for wondering if the rest of him is in proportion. If I hadn't been so drunk that night then I may just remember. 'We have a new client who wants a team building event but he doesn't want it in Swindon, he wants us to present him with a couple of options but I was thinking one of them could be Coolsbay.' He clears his throat.

'Really?' I outwardly cringe.

'Yeah, I know it's very hen and stag do orientated...' He blinks as if he's distracted by something. 'But it also has stunning hotels with amazing views and they could do some cool stuff down on the beach. I was thinking a Baywatch themed sports event.' He grins and nods. He's so smug and seemingly a bit stupid.

'Are you joking? Baywatch?' I fold my arms and shake my head.

'Yeah, it's a young company and I think they'll find it a laugh. There's a company that runs beach themed team building in Coolsbay. Trust me, it's going to be fantastic.'

'Okay,' I say, not convinced.

'So yeah, we also have to find three more smallish sized venues in or around Swindon, so pubs or restaurants that have meeting rooms that we could sell to our clients.'

'Surely they would just book directly with those types of places?'

'Yeah, but we package it up and do all the hard work for them and the venue so we sell it to both. It's a little bit more but worth it.'

'Alright, was that Andrea's idea?'

'No, mine. I thought I could go out and visit a few venues and you could have the fun bit with the team building event.'

'Sounds good to me,' I say, glad I won't be playing any part in finding pub and restaurant meeting rooms which sounds like a complete waste of time. We are a venue finding company that specialises in special events. Booking meeting rooms in pubs and restaurants doesn't fit in with our brand, I'm surprised Andrea has even agreed to it. But something tells me she agrees to everything that James says.

'Oh, by the way Andrea gave me your number, said it was a good idea we swap in case we need to liaise on an event or something,' he says, as he studies my face. 'I've messaged you so you have mine too.' he nods towards my phone on my desk, expecting me to check it. I don't.

'Okay.'

'Right, I best get to it then.' He sashays off to his desk as I scowl behind his back as well as trying to avert my eyes away from his tight trousers which are doing a very good job of accentuating his perfect backside.

What an infuriating self-assured man.

Chapter 14

Mum's getting an unexpected visit from me on the way home from work, I'm excited to be able to surprise her with the finished painting of Nan. It's Monday so Nancy-Ella is with Billy which means I can make the most of my freedom and not worry about what time I'm home, it feels good to be spontaneous.

My stomach rumbles loudly and I swig my water bottle to try and quieten it down. I'm absolutely bloody starving but I resist the urge to eat any snacks that might be rattling around in my handbag as I'm going out for dinner tonight, with George.

Work was okay, I'm enjoying being back and getting into the swing of things even though I am finding it exhausting. Today I'm feeling pretty proud of myself, I've already put together a proposal for James's *Baywatch* thing but I also put together two more proposals of my own which I think the client might prefer. We'll see.

I get to Mum's and have to park on the road because there's already a car parked in the space next to hers. It's probably one of her gal pals, she's a social butterfly my mum, although I don't recognise the car. There's no answer so I bang again and put my ear to the door where I hear muffled voices. I grab my phone out of my bag and send her a message.

Me: *Mum, surprise it's me and I'm outside, let me in xx*

I have a key but I'm not about to do what everyone else seems to like to do to me and walk right into her house. I do peer in through the window though, then wish I hadn't.

Mum is doing up her dressing gown whilst laughing and kissing a man. His head as shiny as a conker, glistens in the sun coming through the window. What the hell. Yuk. I'm just about to head for my car and drive off when she answers the door with a very sheepish looking man in tow.

'Hello darling, Jeff just came by to say hello, didn't you Jeff?' She gives him the death stare; he has no option but to comply.

'Oh yes, yes, I did. Well hello, and I guess goodbye now, Lillian,' he says to my mum, before glancing at me. 'Nice to meet you.' Jeff looks down at his feet rather than at me, then trots out of the door and into his car. This is beyond embarrassing. I've interrupted my mum having an afternoon quickie.

'Mum?' I smirk as she steps back and lets me in, huffing and puffing. I set the painting down in the hallway, I'll show it to her once I've found out who Jeff is.

'I wasn't expecting you. You should have called.'

'I did call, you didn't answer.' I chuckle.

'Oh, did you? Bloody thing must have been on silent.' We both know that it wasn't on silent. It was probably in the other room whilst they got busy.

'Mum, who was that?' I ask, pointing a thumb at the door. I'm secretly pleased for her, it's about bloody time.

'Just a friend.'

I raise my eyebrow and tilt my head. She lets out a big sigh though her slightly inflated lips. Charlie was right, they don't look that bad now they've calmed down.

'Okay, it's Jeff. We met at my local yoga and meditation group, he's a very nice and interesting man, he's been all over the world,' Mum says, her head wobbling a little.

'Wow, I'm pleased for you, Mum. But you don't have to squirrel him away like a dirty little secret.'

Mum gasps and I cackle. I WISH Charlie was here to see this.

'I'm not,' she says, then turns away from me, hunching her shoulders.

'Mum?' I put my hand on her shoulder but she moves away from me.

'I just didn't want you to meet him like this, I didn't want to introduce you yet,' she says, as I move closer and put my arm around her.

'Why not?'

'Because I didn't want to let you down, I wanted to give it more time.' She sniffs not looking at me and my heart breaks for her.

'You'd never let me down, Mum. It's your life, it isn't my business what you do.' My own words echo in my head. Her face too isn't really my business. Maybe I have been a bit of an interferer like Brie said. I feel like a complete hypocrite.

'I know, but I didn't want to introduce you to someone only for them to decide I'm not for them and then leave us in the lurch.'

Like Dad did. She means like Dad did.

'Come here, Mum.' I give her a big hug. 'Sit down and I'll get you some tissues.'

'There's some there on the table.' She points at the coffee table. 'Don't use the toilet tissue, darling, it's got a strong coconut balm, too strong on my delicate nose.'

'No worries.' I reach over and grab her a load of tissues and she honks her nose, which sounds as delicate as a ship announcing its arrival at a new port.

'Thank you.' She sniffs and I smile.

'Mum, don't be so hard on yourself.'

'Really?'

'Yeah, you're only human, you're allowed to have fun.'

'Thanks sweetie. I just don't want to cause any upset to you and Charlie, you know. I don't want you to get attached and if it doesn't work out then it's horrid for you.'

I study my mum's face. I think she feels extra protective because Dad left us so young. She made a promise to herself not to date anyone until we were grown up but she hasn't really bothered until now or at least as far as Charlie and I are aware. She always used to joke saying she'd prefer a roast dinner when we mentioned her getting a boyfriend. It was our family joke.

'It's up to you who you see, me and Charlie aren't little kids anymore, we can handle you having a boyfriend, even if you want to see a few different men, it's okay.' Not too many men, though. A terrifying vision of my mum becoming the local dominatrix haunts my mind. What the hell? I really do let my thoughts get carried away with themselves sometimes. I close my eyes, desperately trying to get an image of my mum cracking a whip out of my mind.

'Thank you, sweetheart. He really is lovely. I'm just horrified that you've caught us like this. It's ghastly.'

'Me too.' I laugh and Mum manages a little giggle. 'But we won't mention it again, yeah? Hey, good job I didn't just walk in on you like you do in my house, hey? It could have been a lot worse.'

'Yes, I won't do that to you again, I realise it's wrong now, darling. Sorry.'

'You've got yourself a deal. I'll make us a cup of tea and we can toast to new men and new boundaries.'

'New men?' Now it's Mum's turn to raise an eyebrow at me.

After I've made us a cup of tea, I tell Mum all about my quest to find a plus one and all the dates I've been on so far. She laughs at the teabag incident, and is horrified when I tell her about the guy with the tag and that I went to his house for dinner on the first date. In hindsight it was a bit of a silly thing to do. I'm a little surprised that she doesn't already know as I thought that Brie may have already told her, it's not like she has client confidentiality with me as I'm not her client, but she is my best friend and is loyal. Have I been that loyal to her? I think of Brie's face when I told her I was hanging out with Krissy, could she be feeling left out? Jealous even? Mum nods with encouragement when I tell her about the gorgeous, yet aloof, George.

'I'd better go soon,' I say, as Mum finishes giving me a mini lecture about dating safety. 'Got to pop home and get ready for my next date with George.' I'm looking forward to it but this dating lark is exhausting, half of me would rather climb into bed and catch up on *Love Island*.

It's proving tiring getting back into the swing of things at work too. I've had to familiarize myself with all the new booking forms and just typing an email seems to take me twice as long as it did before, my brain has turned to mush since having a baby. Baby brain definitely is a real thing and I think I'm allowed to claim that until she's two, so I'll milk it for all it's worth until then. Plus there's James, I kept sneaking looks at him to see what he was up to and every time I looked up he was looking straight back at me, that may have slowed me down somewhat.

'So let's have that quick toast then, before you go, to new men and new boundaries.' Mum raises her teacup and clinks it against mine.

'To new boundaries and new men,' I say back to her, changing the order on purpose because I think boundaries should definitely be put before men. I've learnt a lot so far on my dating journey and setting boundaries is definitely my biggest learning curve so far.

I say goodbye to Mum but not before giving her the painting, it's not her birthday yet but it's finished and I couldn't hold onto it any longer. She cries again and says how much I look like Nan and how much she misses her. I tell her that *we* look like Nan, three peas in a pod and she nods in agreement, quietly studying the painting.

After a quick shower and a change of clothes, I'm feeling a little more rejuvenated. My boobs also look enormous today, they even look a bit perkier. Gorgeous George is not going to know where to look. I've opted for a dress and a cardigan to tame down the boobs a bit, however from the side I'm resembling a blow-up doll. An image of the blow-up doll wearing my Jimmy Choo shoes pops into my mind. I burst out laughing, that was a good hen do, and now it's less than two months until the wedding. Time flies when you're dating all the men/freaks of Swindon.

The restaurant looks quiet as I give George's name for the table. He's picked well I think, as the smiley waitress shows me to where he's already sitting. I do my best sexy walk over to the table as he casually looks up from the menu and watches me. Billy was always too much of a cheapskate to come here, he always wanted to go to the same *two for one* place that served undercooked chips and slimy burgers. Once he got the coffee shop all eating out got cancelled as we were always saving money to pump into that, so this is a real treat that I'm going to fully enjoy.

'Hey gorgeous,' George says, as he lifts his hand to stroke his hair back, he really is so very attractive.

I thank the waitress and sit down opposite him.

'Hey gor… George.' Shit.

'Were you about to call me gorgeous George?' George teases, and winks at the waitress who's hovering around to take our drinks order. She smiles back at him, batting her eyelashes and simpering.

'No.' I smirk and sit down, busying myself with looking at the menu.

'It's okay, it wouldn't be the first time.' He winks at the waitress again and both her and I giggle.

Is he flirting with her or me or both? Stop being so insecure, Tilly, if she wasn't pretty, you wouldn't give two hoots. Get a grip. We give our drinks order and she trots off to get them.

Good.

George is all eyes on me again.

'So, how are you? Looking lovely,' he says, with a sexy grin as I shrug off my cardigan and give him my best sexy smile back. Although I'm a tad nervous so it probably resembles the same look I pull when I break wind.

'Thanks, you don't look so bad yourself,' I reply, coyly.

'Gorgeous?' he asks, biting his lip.

God, why is he so damn sexy?

'Don't push it,' I say lightly, trying to be cool. 'It's lovely here, I've not been before, have you?'

'No, my housemate suggested it, said I should make an effort and choose this place if I want to impress you.

'Did he now? This housemate sounds alright. What have you been up to then?'

'Not much, just working really and going to the gym, what about you?' Not much and yet he takes days to reply.

'Yeah, same, not much. I've started back at work, so that's been cool.'

'Oh, yeah, what is it you do?' he asks, looking up from his menu.

Should I slip in that I need a plus one for a wedding or is it too soon? Definitely too soon Tilly, you've met him a handful of times.

Cool, calm and collected.

'I work for a small venue finding company for special events, we work with a lot of big corporate companies. It's fun, sometimes we even get to organise some huge parties, which I obviously love.'

'I'm sure you do.' He smiles at me and my knees quiver slightly underneath the table. 'What do you fancy then?'

You, you sexy thing. 'I'll have the mushroom and asparagus risotto please.'

'Oh, sure you don't want a steak? It's kind of their thing here?' George looks over at the waitress and she comes trotting over instantly with a big, bright smile pasted on her face.

'Umm, no thanks. I'm a vegetarian so no steak for me.'

'Oh.' George makes a face at the waitress and she mirrors him, both disappointed in my non-meat-eating skills. She flutters her eyelashes at George as we give our orders. I guess I better get used to this, women throwing themselves at him, he is very attractive. After we've ordered she bounces off and George turns his attention back to me but not for long. A big party of eight enter the restaurant including a new-born baby and a baby under one.

'Aww,' I say, as the waiter brings them over to sit on the large table next to us. The newborn is being cuddled by his mum and is slumped over her shoulder with a muslin underneath him to catch the dribble. So sweet, I miss that stage and have the sudden urge to tell the mum how fleeting it is and to make the most of it, but I don't. Instead, I watch the family sit down and they're so close to us that we might as well be sat with them. There's no hint of social distancing in this restaurant anymore.

'Feeling broody?' George grins as he spies me cooing over the baby.

'Naah,' I say, despite my ovaries kicking me. 'One and done, mate.'

'Mate?'

'Sorry,' I giggle. 'It's what my friend and I say. One and done.'

'Okay,' he says, not smiling. Shit, he wants kids. Of course he does but I only want a bloody plus one. Well. At least I've been honest and open, he may not want to see me ever again if he's looking for *the one*, what a shame. The newborn wakes up and begins to cry that high pitched newborn cry and my boobs begin to ache.

God, they really do ache.

'Here's some appetisers for you guys.' The waitress places some pitta bread, crudités and dips on the table. 'On us,' she continues, gazing at George, making it very clear that they're free because of him. I thank her then reach over and grab a cucumber stick. The waitress hovers for a second, her eyes lingering on my dress.

'It's from Next,' I say, catching her eyeing my cleavage, Christ, I'm even attracting the women now with these bad boys, either that or she's judging but I won't assume the worst.

'Oh right, great,' she says, before glancing at George and then swanning off. The newborn continues to cry, it's not very loud but the baby sounds in pain. The mum shushes him and rocks him back and forth. Poor mum, those days are so hard when they can't tell you what's wrong. It wasn't that long ago that Nancy-Ella was that tiny.

My boobs continue to ache, I must be starting my period soon.

'Christ, that's a loud cry,' George says, a little too loudly as the woman continues to rock her baby. She looks at me and I smile my best sympathy smile. She smiles back and mouths the word *sorry*. I shake my head and mouth back *don't be*.

'Really? That's nothing trust me, come again when they're a few months old and find their voice.' I laugh as the older baby begins to cry as if I've somehow summoned them to a crying competition. Shit, I must have jinxed it. I giggle nervously again but as I laugh I feel a huge release in my chest.

Fuck, have my tits burst through my bra?

Two babies are now crying, and the whole restaurant is looking at the table. Poor mums, and I don't suppose they could have left them with anyone else, probably breastfeeding.

'Woah.' George points to my chest. 'Your boobs,' he gulps.

'Okay, yes, they're big, calm down, don't get too

excited in public,' I quip, trying to laugh it off.

'No.' He shakes his head, pursing his lips, looking serious. 'There's something coming out of them.' I look down at my boobs and low and behold they are indeed leaking milk for the crying babies. My good old trusty concerned boobs want to feed these strangers' babies. I mean, what on earth? It's quite amazing really but I can't think about that right now. This is beyond embarrassing.

'Oh shit, my milk.' I instinctively grab a couple of napkins and stuff them down my dress whilst George looks on with his mouth gawping open. He must think I'm insane or my boobs are insane or maybe even both. I don't know who's cringing more, me or him.

We spend the rest of the meal eating as fast as we can so we can get out of there. I go to the toilet to check my boobs out, they've calmed down now but why did they have to have a moment of madness in front of the gorgeous George. I'll be surprised if he wants to see me again. The babies screamed throughout pretty much the entire meal so it was quite hard to make conversation.

We leave the restaurant and I wonder if this will be the last time that I see him.

'So do you want to come back for dessert?' he asks, as we leave, giving me a cheeky grin. It's very tempting.

'I'd love to but I have an early start tomorrow so I best head home.' It is a complete lie but I just want to get home, have a bath, get in my comfies and sort my tits out.

Today has been a very eventful day.

Chapter 15

Today is meant to be my day with Nancy-Ella but instead, I'm playing happy families with Billy at the farm he promised we'd take her to. We've seen all the animals, gone through all the different animal noises and now we're having a bite to eat outside. Nancy-Ella is sitting on my knee wolfing down some *cardboardesque* crisps and Billy is opposite us picking at a cheese sandwich. The smell of manure dances around in my nostrils, it smells so good and has really given my slightly fuzzy head a good clear out. I take a sip of my coffee.

It's really been quite a pleasant day, perhaps we can do this. There's not a law to say we can't hang out as a family for Nancy-Ella if we're not actually together, in a relationship. And if either of us get a new spouse anytime soon then they'll just have to deal with it, these are modern day relationships so pretty much anything goes, doesn't it? I smile at Billy and wonder what he's thinking. Is he missing me? Us? Does he regret doing what he did? I hope so, but is he seeing someone else and that's why he's not come back to me, just keeping me at arm's length? No. Don't backtrack, Tilly. Boundaries. That chapter is over. I smile again, trying to work him out, instead of smiling back at me though, he frowns, his little snub nose pointing upwards.

'I don't know why you buy that stuff?' Billy says, throwing a finger at my coffee, reminding me why we split up.

I let out a big sigh.

'It doesn't need to be fancy for me to enjoy it,' I say evenly, and Billy looks the other way at some couple holding hands. All he thinks about is his bloody coffee shop, no wonder we broke up. He didn't have time for me. He's probably not seeing anyone else; he doesn't have time.

'So the coffee shop has just won a couple of contracts, it's super exciting news.'

I rest my case, the bloody coffee shop.

Billy flicks his hair out of his eyes and purses his lips together. He's looking a little less attractive these days, a bit baggy around the eyes, a few pounds heavier around the belly, must be all that fancy creamy coffee. I like it. I'm not so much under his spell anymore, there was a time when I was so attracted to him and in love with him I would have done anything to keep him. A memory of me crying and begging burns my retinas and makes me shudder; I'm never going to stoop that low again for a man. *But why are you here then?* a little voice in my head says. *For Nancy-Ella.* One last time.

'Oh yeah, for what?' I ask, as I carry on contemplating whether I still fancy him or not. I study his face again, his slightly snub nose and thin top lip, maybe he's always looked like this but I had my rose-tinted glasses on the entire time, the entire ten years. I've definitely met way more attractive men recently and some seemingly nicer, but just some.

'Can't say right now but you'll soon see,' he nods smugly.

'Why bother saying anything if you can't say?' I snort.

Is he for real?

'Oooh, someone got out of the wrong side of bed.'

'I didn't, I'm just pointing out the obvious. Anyway, we best get going, it's time for this one's nap,' I say, not falling into his trap of an argument.

Those days are gone.

My feelings for him, also gone.

I get back home and carry Nancy-Ella up to bed.

My phone was beeping the whole time around the farm, so much so that I eventually had to turn it to silent. There's only one group that will go off like that, one group with way too many women in it and that's the hen do group aka Nay's wedding. Shit's really been kicking off with the backlash of Nay giving Samantha an ultimatum about coming to the wedding. Nay sent a huge long private message to Samantha expressing her concerns about her behaviour with regards to sleeping with a married man. She said that she couldn't have her at the wedding if she was still engaging in adultery with him as it will taint her big day, so yeah, it was a roundabout threat.

Sam sent a grovelling text back to Nay and has now called off her fling with Sammy but I can't help but think that it's all a bit mean. Since when did becoming a bride give you the right to dictate other people's private lives? And I'm surprised that Nay is acting like this, she's normally so chilled and laid back, it's just not like her but then weddings do tend to bring out the worst in a person sometimes. There, I said it, the term bridezilla is there for a reason.

Brie was going through her pink hair stage a few years

ago when one of her friends from Sydney got married. The bride asked her to dye her hair back to a natural colour for her wedding but Brie wasn't even a bridesmaid. Of course Brie did nothing of the sort, in fact she dyed it an even brighter shade of pink much to the bride's dismay and rightly so. Who do these brides think they are? I'm pretty sure they haven't spoken since.

I miss Brie. I hope she's still not mad with me. I wouldn't like to choose between a new friend and an old one. My mind wanders to James, it would be interesting to know what James thinks of all this, after all the man in question, Sammy, is his friend, he was on a stag do with him. James must have known that this guy was married, he was mates with him which almost makes him guilty by association. My phone pings again and I tap to view it, expecting to see more drama from the hens, but instead, it's my boss.

Andrea: *Hi Tilly, hope you're good? I have been chatting with James and we think it would be very beneficial to arrange a familiarisation trip to Coolsbay. I'd like you both to go together on this trip. Call it a team bonding exercise as well but there's also a lot you can learn from each other, he really has the gift of the gab with people. Have fun and please arrive a little earlier on Monday if you can so we can make the most of the day, would seven AM be okay? James is staying over Monday night as it's a bit of a trek and you're welcome to do the same if childcare permits and come back Tuesday. Let me know if you can do and we can sort hotel arrangements.*

I tap my reply before I think about the logistics, there's no way he's getting all the credit for this one. Those were my proposals, even if one of them was his idea. Gift of the gab? I can gift the gab just as well as him.

Me: *Hi Andrea, what a fantastic idea, I'd love to go to Coolsbay on a familiarisation trip. I'll sort something out childcare wise and come back to you asap to confirm.*

Billy has Nancy-Ella Mondays and Tuesday so that isn't a big deal, I'd just need to sort out Tuesday day as Billy works, so she's normally back with me and then at his for the night. A quick phone call to Mum and it's all sorted. I'm desperate to phone Brie, she'll die when she hears I'm going to Coolsbay with the guy whose bed I ended up in on Nay's hen do. Come to think of it, I'm dying thinking about how I'll survive the insufferable James for a whole twenty-four hours.

Coolsbay, here I come, again.

Me: *Hi Andrea, all sorted. I'll see you Monday.*

Andrea: *Fabulous, that was quick! Don't be daft I won't be in that early but have a successful familiarisation trip. James has arranged all of the appointments so you just need to turn up and go along with him.*

Me: *Great, looking forward to it.*

He really is prize pet, I'm not sure why I'm required to go as it seems he could easily do all of this on his own, however I'm glad I got asked. It will refresh my memory on familiarisation trips and risk assessments and I bet the forms have changed for that too.

I click on the hen do chat and read all the messages about the wedding and people's opinions on Samantha. Isn't Samantha in this chat? Perhaps she's left. I send my two-pence worth and say that whilst I get where Nay is coming from, Samantha's relationship status shouldn't be of anyone else's concern and it's all a little unfair. Brie pipes up and agrees with me then calls everyone out for being jealous bitches because Samantha looks like (in her words) a fucking goddess and most of us would happily die if we could be reborn to look like her. I snort to myself, Brie does have a way with words, I'll give her that.

♥ ♥ ♥

The next few days are spent enjoying time with Nancy-Ella, it seems the potty training was a one off. I see Krissy at Music Bums and tell her about it and she almost scoffs saying what do I expect and that she isn't even two yet. Krissy is quite off with me the entire time. I thought she looked tired but thinking back, I did try to make a joke about us minimal mumming but she didn't laugh, instead she looked agitated and didn't say very much for the rest for the session. I was going to invite her over for a cup of tea afterwards but thought she'd probably say no given today's mood so in the end I didn't bother.

Instead, I messaged Brie to see how she is, but she leaves me on *read*. It seems I've pissed off both new and old friends now and here's me thinking I would have to choose between them.

A trip away to Coolsbay could be just what the doctor ordered, just a shame it's with James and not gorgeous George. It hasn't been long but he hasn't messaged since our date, probably put him off with my milky udders. Miss Unpopular. At this rate, I'll have no plus one by the time Nay's wedding rolls around as well as no bloody mates. Woe is me. This dating and having a social life lark is truly exhausting.

Chapter 16

Monday Morning – Coolsbay familiarisation trip

The office building car park is packed full as I circle round and round searching for a space. I squeeze my car into a space that might not be a space around the back of the building right underneath our office window. James is already in there, beavering away at his laptop. He's keen, I'll give him that.

'Good morning,' I sing, as I swish my hair and strut into the office feeling like a shiny mannequin, all flustered and sweaty from the stressful parking. I'm also wearing a rather tight skirt that I've just realised is actually quite hard to walk in. I try my best not to walk like a robot and fail.

'Morning,' he says, without looking up and without a smile. I drop my bag down by my desk and switch on my laptop. I thought we were leaving straight away but I'll give him a few minutes to finish whatever he's doing. He furrows his brow and taps away aggressively on the keyboard.

Twenty minutes go by with copious amounts of huffing and puffing from James. I try to catch his eye to see if he's alright but every time I look he's either not looking or he's just looked away.

'For fuck's sake,' he mutters under his breath again, as his dark eyes frown into the screen. Something about the way he says that is alarmingly attractive but I suppose it has been a while.

Enough!

I've had enough of this.

'James, are you alright? It's just that you've been looking a bit stressed all morning,' I say carefully, peering over my screen as his eyes finally meet mine.

'Sorry, I just have to get this thing finished for Andrea, she wants these proposals sent to the client before we go this morning.'

'Need any help?' Because I've been sat here filing my nails for the last twenty minutes and you could have asked.

'Umm, would you mind?'

'Not at all.' I get up from my desk and sashay over to him careful not to fall over in my super tight skirt before pulling up a chair. James delves into the detail of what he's struggling with and I feel happy that my expertise and experience can help with his issues. Just thirty minutes later and the proposals are ready and good to go.

'Right, you ready?' I say, with a winning smile as he shuts down his laptop and runs his fingers through his hair. Why does he look so attractive today? Probably because the last male I saw was Billy at six thirty this morning and he looked rough. Timmy was also over at that ungodly hour dropping off some invoices or something, doesn't he have email? He looked a bit sheepish, like he was up to something, I don't trust him.

'Ready for Coolsbay, round two baby,' James blurts out, then looks shocked at himself. 'Whoops, sorry.' He looks at his feet and I smirk.

'Who says there was a round one,' I retort, before

waltzing out of the door to wait for him outside. I'm not sure why but I wriggle my hips a little more than I normally would, something about him makes me want to tease him and I'm quite enjoying it.

Round two, the cheeky git. There most definitely wasn't a round one, was there? I stand by my car, sunglasses on and arms folded. I'm excited to go on a fam trip and meet with clients, I'm starting to feel like me again and I like it.

'Do you want to take your car or mine?' he asks.

'Oh, I was going to take my own car.'

'Really? I thought we could share, there's no point in us both driving, that's just silly and we'll save on fuel expenses for Andrea too.' There we go again teacher's pet, so annoying.

'Okay, yeah, sure, I don't mind.'

'I'll drive then if that's alright, I love driving.' He puts his sunglasses on and clicks his keys to unlock his car. The car beeps. 'Nice shades by the way.' He grins and I offer him a small smile before pushing them a little further up my nose. In my hurry getting ready this morning, I grabbed the wrong sunglasses, the heart shaped ones.

'Sounds good,' I say. Because I bloody hate driving long distance anyway.

'Cool, let's go.' I get into the passenger seat and breath in the fresh car smell.

'New car?' I say, running my hands along the leather seats.

'No, I've just had it cleaned, figured we might be going together so I wanted it to be pleasant.' He adjusts the rear-view mirror with his huge hands and my eyes fall to his thighs encased in tight, grey trousers, they're almost twice the size of mine but it's all muscle.

'That's nice, thanks.' That really is quite sweet. Billy's car is full of old coffee cups and rubbish, it's a right mess. I basically had to wade through it to get to the passenger seat when we went to the farm, luckily the back seats weren't as bad so Nancy-Ella wasn't sat in dirt, or I would have offered to drive my car.

'Let's rock and roll,' he says in an over-the-top American accent, he nods his head and his sunglasses fall onto his nose. Smooth.

'You're such a cheese ball.' I laugh as he reverses the car out of the car park. This might not be so bad.

My phone pings. It's gorgeous George. The day is getting even better.

'Is that your partner? Tell him you're in safe hands with me,' James says, keeping his eyes on the road. He bites his lip.

'Just someone I'm dating.' I smile coyly as I open the message.

George: *Hey sexy, when are you free next?*

Deciding to reply later I close my phone, and drop it back into my handbag. Mentally I'm calculating how many dates I'll have to have with George before I can ask him to be my plus one to Nay's wedding. It would be weird to ask him now, we haven't even kissed.

'Ah, right, thought you might be married or something,' James says, more to himself than to me.

'Hmmm.' I don't ask why he would think that even though I want to, but I'm guessing he's referring to when we met. Did he make a move and I refused? I doubt it but this is so cringingly awkward. I wish he wasn't so blasé about it all. 'So what brought you to taking the job at Taylors?' I say, in an attempt to change the subject.

'I fancied something different, I'd been in sales for years, predominantly regional sales for hotels. I'd been with the same chain for nearly fifteen years and I needed something a bit less demanding if I'm honest, the pressure does take its toll especially with everything else that was going on.' He doesn't say it but I assume he means splitting up with his wife or girlfriend. 'I met Andrea about a year ago at an event and I guess I was in the right place at the right time, she'd just let that guy go, hmmm Fabien?' he says, stroking his stubble. 'And seemed a bit desperate.' He laughs a deep throaty laugh and my knees tingle at the vibration of his vocal cords.

'Ah yes, Fabien, he was a bit of a blagger from what I've heard. So you don't think events can be demanding then?' He has no idea.

'Yeah, of course, but it's less hours than the hotels. I was doing over seventy hours a week and it wasn't fun, it probably helped in my relationship breaking down if I'm honest,' he says, focusing on the road.

'The mother of your kids?'

'Yes.'

'How do you get along with her now?' Oh shut up Tilly, you're so nosey.

'Yeah, fine. It was rough for a long time but we get along just fine now, it's for the boys' sake, isn't it?'

'Yeah, I'm not with Billy either. I mean Billy is the father of *my* child.'

'How's that going?'

'Complicated, he wants us to hang out as a family still and go on days out and stuff.'

'Really?'

'Yeah.'

'Do *you* want to?' he asks.

'Not really, but I went for the sake of my little girl. Anyway I've put a stop to it now. Boundaries.'

James nods at my reply and I look out of the

passenger window at the rolling countryside views. TLC begins to play on the radio and I reach over, turning it up. 'Love this one, classic,' I say, resisting the urge to sing about wanting no scrubs. TLC had boundaries too.

'Yeah, love a bit of old skool RnB,' he says.

I glance at the screen which displays 'Radio nineties' and a smile plays across my lips as I remember our dance off, I should have guessed.

We drive in silence for the first few songs, the only noise coming from the radio blaring and the aircon until *No Diggity* by Blackstreet begins to play. I groan inwardly. I remember this song from the boat trip and James's slut dropping. I wonder if he does too? Perhaps not, because he sings along quite happily until the song ends and something comes on that neither of us have heard of. It's a female soul singer, she has a beautiful voice and we both enjoy it whilst we drive along the beautiful country roads.

'Tilly, Tilly.'

I open my eyes and frown at him, what's he doing here? Oh yeah, road trip. I mean, fam trip. He grins, and I'm sure I hear a giggle escape him.

'I thought I'd stop and grab us a coffee, what do you fancy?' he asks.

'Oh yes, sounds good, but could I have a tea please?' I'm so sick of bloody coffee I think, as I mentally pour a cup onto Billy's lap.

'Yes, sure, I'll get this.' He pads off to the coffee shop and I pull down the mirror to assess the dribble situation. Honestly, every single time, I can't help but fall asleep in the car. I'm worse than my own toddler. The first thing that strikes me is I still have my sunglasses on and the sun is blaring. How long have I been asleep?

'Oh no, God please no, not again,' I whimper as I

slowly peel the sunglasses away from my face, holding my breath and bracing myself for the worst.

Phew.

It's okay.

I'm sunburn free, it's too early to get burnt anyway. I check the rest of my face for makeup smears and spots, it's all clear. Thank God, imagine having to meet a client with heart shaped sunglasses marks around my eyes. Not professional. I have another look just to double check. Nope, all good.

'Here you go.' James's face pops up by my window as my sunglasses fall onto the floor.

'Argh, you made me jump.'

He hands me a cup of tea and a croissant.

'Thanks.' I enjoy the aroma of the croissant and my stomach rumbles back loudly.

'No worries.' He smirks. He sneaked up on me on purpose, the git.

Another hour on the road consists of us chatting about our clients and suppliers. James brings me up to speed on a few things and also tries to restrain himself from singing along to every single song that comes on the radio. Well, he doesn't restrain himself that much.

We arrive at the hotel, well bed and breakfast really but it looks very nice. I'm quite enjoying this trip now and the sun is shining. This is turning out to be an amazing summer and not just the weather.

This time last year I was a mess, still mentally getting over the trauma of a horrible birth and Billy being an absolute unsympathetic arse. I'm sure this wasn't the case with the weather but it felt like rain clouds just followed me around everywhere. I don't remember being out and about enjoying sunshine. This year the weather is just glorious, I've never known a summer like it.

James jumps out of the car and retrieves our suitcases from the boot. I resist the urge to tell him that I'm perfectly capable of carrying my own suitcase. For a big guy, he's quite nimble and I marvel at him as he picks the suitcases up as though they weigh nothing. I follow him to the door of the B & B which looks like an old cottage. From the outside, I'd be surprised if it has any more than six rooms. I wonder why he picked here and not one of the big swanky hotels.

'Hello lovelies, James, is it?' A lady with a big wholesome, slightly weathered face greets us as we enter the hallway. 'Just in time for a spot of lunch. We've just baked some cheese scones, fresh out of the oven and you're in luck, your room's already available,' she says, as we follow her down the hallway into the kitchen where she goes behind the kitchen table and begins to tap on her laptop. A little tabby cat perches next to her and looks us up and down, judging the tourists.

'Right, so while this old thing loads up, check out is at eleven AM and breakfast is between seven and nine thirty AM. We do serve dinner but you'll have to book that, would you like to book?' She looks at us both expectantly.

'Umm?' James looks to me.

'It's okay, we'll eat out, we've got clients to meet so it might be a late one.'

'Righty ho, well if you change your mind then just give me a call or turn up, we're very relaxed here, okay? Your room is number four and here's the key, there's also a key on there to the front door. I don't have a curfew like some do round here but if you could just keep quiet and respectful if it's late then we won't fall out.' She smiles and her cat miaows at her in agreement.

'Great,' James says. 'Thank you.'

'Fab,' I say. 'And is my room ready too or should I just leave my bags in James's room for now?' I smile expectantly.

'Sorry, what?'

'My room. We have our own rooms,' I say. The manager slowly shakes her head and looks at James. I turn my gaze to him and all of the colour drains out of his face.

'I definitely booked two rooms, with your colleague,' he says, not flinching. 'I'll just get the confirmation, I'm sure I have it in an email.' James reaches into his pocket and frantically taps on his phone.

'I wish I could give you two rooms, but we're fully booked,' she says to me, with a fraught expression on her face. 'I can try a few hotels for you but there's a music festival going on, it's always packed.' She picks up the phone and begins to dial out. James and I wait and I can feel the heat radiating off him as he scrolls on his phone. After several phone calls, the quest to get another hotel room is not looking good.

'I'm sorry, there's no availability but I've asked them to call me if they get any cancellations,' she says, with a hopeful smile.

'Thank you for trying and it's okay, we'll sort something out,' I reassure her with a kind smile, but inside I'm freaking out. I can't share a room with him. Not again!

'Ah see, two separate rooms,' James says, showing her his phone. The owner takes his phone, takes a few seconds to check the email then nods and gives him his phone back.

'The confirmation is for two occupants and two breakfasts and one standard room, see.' She points to the confirmation that James is still looking at and low and behold she's right.

Shit. My mouth falls open. This does not bode well if you work in events.

'Oh f….'

I rest my hand on James's arm to silence him whilst he stands there slowly dying of embarrassment.

'It's fine, these things happen,' I say to the manager. 'Do you have a spare pull out bed or something we could bring into the room?' It's not ideal but it'll be fine and it's only for one night. One of us can get changed in the bathroom and we can sleep in separate beds. There, sorted. I hope I don't fart in my sleep I think, as I let a silent one slip. Better out now than out in the night, loud and proud.

'Sorry no, we don't. We're maxed out this week, my lovelies. Music Festival. The only thing I can offer is a reclining chair type thing, at the moment there's a rocking chair in there but I can see if I can swap it for the recliner,' she says, giving James a quick once over. She's probably trying to size him up to see if he'll fit in it.

'Okay,' he says, then looks at me with concern flashing in his eyes. 'I'm so sorry, I could have sworn it said two rooms.' Beads of sweat are forming on his forehead.

'No worries, it's not the end of the world,' I say, trying not to sound annoyed. It's an easy mistake to make I guess and better that he made it with our booking rather than a client's but oh my good God this is so awkward. I mentally go through my suitcase trying to figure out what I'll wear in bed tonight. I'm pretty sure my tiny nighty won't be appropriate now.

'Let me show you to your rooms, I mean room.' The owner winces, clearly as embarrassed as James is.

We follow her up the narrow staircase, across squeaky floor boards then up a small step to the room. James trips on the step then bonks his head on the roof of the door frame and I stifle a laugh. Bless him, I almost feel sorry for him. The room is lovely, tiny but beautiful, decorated in white and pale blue stencils of boats, with crisp cotton sheets and a stunning sea view. It really is lovely… for a couple.

'So there are extra pillows in the wardrobe, towels on the bed and I'll sort that reclining chair out for you,' the owner says, backing towards the door to make a quick exit. I notice her eyes dart behind me before she leaves and I swiftly follow her gaze.

Great.

The bathroom has a bloody transparent door. How am I supposed to poo?

'Thank you, that's great,' James and I say in unison to the owner as she shuts the door. We stare at each other.

'I'm so sorry, you must think I'm a right half-wit,' he says, biting his lip.

'Why would I think that?' I tease, and he looks at his feet. 'It's alright.'

'Obviously I'll take the chair.'

'Are you sure?' I ask, relieved that he's offered.

'Yeah, I owe it to you.' James plonks himself down in the rocking chair, his knees almost reaching his chin and I try not to laugh again.

'Well it wouldn't be the first time we shared a bed but thank you.' I smirk and his eyes almost bulge out of his head.

Chapter 17

After the initial awkwardness of us both needing the loo and the other one having to wait outside the hotel room whilst we did our business, James and I set off on our appointments. First stop is the big fancy hotel to meet the manager and check out their function rooms. I wish we were staying here. James's personable chatter woos the manager and he manages to get a good deal for our client as long as they book within the next three weeks. The pressure is on then.

Next, we meet with the surfing company who offer to give us a free lesson, I decide to sit that one out but revel in watching James as he plays at being David Hasselhoff, running into the sea with an enormous surfboard almost as big as him. James frolics and splashes about in the sea until he eventually masters the waves, he looks so powerful out there and I feel like a bit of a spoilsport for not joining him. Afterwards he chats to them about the possibility of hosting a beach team sports event and what the alternative would be if the weather is rubbish. The surf company advise that surfing would physically be enough for an afternoon as it is very demanding but one of the instructors suggests that prior to surfing the delegates go on a small treasure hunt in teams to find *Landmarks of Coolsbay* and the elusive

Coolsbay Stone, which is a beautiful blue, green and purple stone, unique to Coolsbay.

We visit my venues for my team building ideas and I'm so glad we did as they aren't at all what they look like on the websites. Sometimes you have to see these things in real life to really grasp how they are and it's a saving grace that we are able to visit as the *Baywatch* theme is looking like a real winner. I shouldn't, but I feel a bit silly, James obviously has an eye for this stuff and I might be a little rusty, although I wouldn't admit that to him. So now that's two of us that feel silly, James for booking one hotel room and me for picking crappy venues for team building.

We conduct the relevant risk assessments on the new extra detailed forms, take photographs and butter up the surf company and hotel to get good terms and conditions. All in all, it's been a very successful day but now all I want is food, a glass of wine and my (or should I say our) bed.

'So where do you fancy heading for dinner?' James asks, as we drive back to our B & B. We've just finished discussing how the day has gone and sent our thoughts to the client. If I was away on business on my own I'd be happy with a Co-op sandwich and a packet of crisps in the hotel room but I suppose it would be nice to go out for a meal. It's not often I get to enjoy that luxury, apart from this week making it two meals out, with two different men.

'I don't mind, I'm happy to just have dinner at the place we're staying at if you are?' I say, watching the sea view from my passenger window.

'Yep, sounds good, I'll go and speak to the manager when we get back so I can reserve a table,' James says.

'Sounds good.'

We drive in silence for the next few minutes as I enjoy more sea views. Coolsbay is so stunning and the sky is so clear today, I never want this summer to end. I definitely suffer from SAD – seasonal affective disorder – in the winter, cold weather just doesn't suit me and yet I live in bloody England. My thoughts turn to Brie who moved to England from Australia, not knowing anyone other than me. I send her a quick text, life's too short to hold a grudge against my best friend. My comments must have really offended her and she's right, I have been too concerned with Mum's face. I pull my phone out of my handbag and begin to type.

Me: *Hey Brie, hope you're okay? I'm so sorry I upset you the other day, I didn't mean to insult your work, your work's great and so are you. Hope to hear from you soon, miss you. xxx*

I get an instant reply.

Brie: *Alrighty-roo, I'm so sorry too, I shouldn't have gone off on one down the phone. I've been having a stressful time and I think it just got the better of me. I didn't want to burden you with what's been going on as you've been busy with all your stuff. Free to meet up soon? Xx*

Me: *Of course, would love to meet up soon. Hope everything's okay. I'll message you when I'm back from Coolsbay, here on a work trip . . . with James. Xxx*

Brie: *What? Where it all began haha. Yes! Message me when you're back and we'll sort something out. P.S. You don't interfere in people's lives; I was just feeling extra sensitive.*

Brie: *Is he stripping for you yet? I want all the details.*

I smirk then drop my phone back into my bag whilst making a mental note to reply to George later. I would feel ridiculous replying back to him straight away given how long he takes. I'll reply later. Give him a taste of his own medicine.

'Pardon?' James says out of the blue.

'Huh?'

'Sorry, I didn't hear you, did you say something?' he asks.

'No, nothing,' I reply, paranoid that I read one of my messages from Brie out loud.

'Oh, I thought you did,' he smirks and I give him the side eye. What is he up to?

We arrive back at the B & B and I tell James I'm going up to the room to freshen up so to take his time booking a table for dinner. I take the key so that he'll need to knock for me to let him in. By the time he's back, it's been way over an hour which I'm not going to lie, has been lovely. In that time, I've had a poo (of course) showered and washed my hair, got dressed and done my hair and makeup. It's been really enjoyable and relaxing. Definitely more time than I get to myself at home with Nancy-Ella trotting about. Most days I try and have a shower in the morning with her playing on the bathmat with her toys or we have a bath together. I'm usually too tired to have a bath or shower when she's gone to bed so the morning is when it's done and it's always a mad rush.

'You look nice,' James says, as I let him in.

'Umm thanks, what have you been up to?' I ask, a little taken aback by his forward compliment. This may be a couple's room but we aren't a couple.

'I just took a walk along the harbour, took some photos, see.' James gets his phone out and scrolls through the photos on his phone.

'Wow, beautiful,' I say, as I study the boats lined up along the harbour.

'Yeah, but look at the name of this boat.' He scrolls back a few pictures then zooms in on one beautiful boat and I gasp.

'Oh wow, that's so cool, I never see my name on

anything.'

James nods as he zooms in further on the yacht with the words Tilly's Dream emblazoned across it.

'Yeah, I thought so too. I had a chat with the owner, really nice bloke. He's going to take us out on it after dinner.'

'Really?' I laugh.

'Yeah, we need to fully immerse ourselves here in the Coolsbay culture, make the most of it. Who knows, a client might want a yacht trip one day and he does private hire too.'

'Okay, if you say so.' I smile nervously, so much for going to bed after dinner.

'So dinner is in half-an-hour, would you mind if I…' He nods towards the bathroom, indicating his need to get ready.

'Oh yes of course, get ready. I'll go for a little walk, maybe check out Tilly's Dream.'

'You do that.' He smiles and my knees wobble a little.

Oh for God's sake, Tilly, it's just a boat and he's just a nice-looking man and this is work. Strictly work. It's not a thoughtful romantic gesture, it's not as if he's driving the boat and serving me champagne and strawberries whilst he does it. It's for research purposes only. This is strictly business.

We arrive for dinner and the manager and owner of the B & B whose name we've now learned is Fern, shows us to our table in the dining room. For a small B & B the dining room is large and the front section is almost all glass windows. I feel as though we're in a goldfish bowl and even though it sounds strange, it's quite cool, like we're the ones looking out onto the world doing the watching, not the other way round. An old man walks by and nods to James and me, he smiles as if he knows something and continues on by. In the distance I can see families heading home after a day out at the beach or in town and little colourful seaside houses are dotted all around the landscape.

'Thank you,' I say to Fern, who hands us both a paper menu then scuttles off to see to another table. 'I could live here,' I say out loud but not meaning to, as we sit down at our table.

'It's gorgeous isn't it, must be so different to living in Swindon,' James replies, as he wedges his knees under the table.

'Definitely different to living in Swindon, I haven't seen a 99p shop or roundabout for over twenty-four hours and that's got to be a good thing.'

'Yeah, but the magic roundabout is something else, sometimes I go that way just so I can spot the people that aren't local.'

'The people closing their eyes and hoping for the best?' I laugh and wonder if we know any of the same people, he's a few years older than me but it's possible. George is from Swindon.

Oh God.

'The specials today are lobster linguine and spicy seaweed crab salad with new potatoes and oh before I forget, did you still need that recliner?' Her eyes dart between James and I.

'Yes please, the rocking chair's lovely but I don't know if my back could take it to sleep in.' James winces and rubs his back as if it already hurts at the thought of sleeping in it.

'Bless you, big strapping man like you should sleep in

a bed.' Fern puts her hands on her hips, incredulous.

'Well it's my fault, so I should definitely sleep in the chair.' He laughs and Fern and I chuckle with him.

'Oh dear, what have you done?' she asks, as her eyes widen and I cringe in my seat.

'We're work colleagues,' I inform her before she starts to think that I'm a complete bitch who normally makes my big strapping husband sleep in a rocking chair on our honeymoon or whatever she thinks this arrangement is.

'Oh, shame.' She raises both eyebrows and smiles. 'You make a nice couple.' Fern drops that bomb then plods off to the kitchen leaving me and James suitably red-faced.

She plods back a few minutes later, seemingly revelling in the uncomfortable energy as we order our drinks and food. James has the lobster and I order vegan scallops in garlic butter sauce. Whilst we wait for our food James and I talk shop for a bit and send some updates to Andrea. When our food arrives it looks amazing and I salivate at the aroma.

'So what are your plans for the rest of the week?' James asks, as he finishes a mouthful of lobster.

I take a sip of wine and savour the taste. I've never tasted wine like it, apparently it's the Coolsbay house wine, brewed at their very own vineyard.

'Not much, spending time with my little one, catch up with Mum and my best mate, oh yeah and Music Bums.' I let out with a groan.

James laughs and screws up his face in puzzlement.

'Yeah, it's a baby group but with musical instruments, Nancy-Ella is a bit heavy handed so it can be a bit lethal at times.'

'Oh yeah? I'm intrigued.' James says, as I watch his deep brown eyes sparkle. His eyes are the most symmetrical shape, with quite a lot of lid on show, reminding me of half-moons. Mr half-moon eyes.

I tell him all about mine and Nancy-Ella's escapades at Music Bums and how she almost took another child's eye out with a shaker. He roars with laughter and I find myself giggling too, it might be the wine, the setting or both but I'm actually quite enjoying myself, no I'm really enjoying myself.

'What about you?' I ask. 'Any plans?'

'No, just work and I might go to the gym a couple of times if I can be arsed. Just hope my housemate hasn't left the house in a complete mess and there aren't too many randoms hanging about when I get back.'

'Oh no.'

'Yeah, I've already had a word with him about it, I think I'll be asking him to leave soon anyway.'

'Really?'

'Yeah, it's not working out, he's a mate of a mate and we just don't really get along. He's also a bit of a womaniser and brings a different woman back on the regular. It's a bit uncomfortable.' James makes an uncomfortable face and rubs the back of his neck. I watch him, finding it hard to imagine him having a one-night stand.

'Sounds it, speaking of womanisers, that bloke that pulled my mate on the hen-stag do, Sammy? I've since heard he's married?' Uh oh, this wine has made me a bit brave. Should I ask if he knows George? I feel my eyebrow raise and swiftly bring it down again, I shouldn't judge James for someone else's actions but a man is known by the company he keeps.

'The girl that came back with you to the house?'

'Yeah.' I grimace.

'He's married?' James asks, his knife and fork mid-air.

'Do you not know him?' I ask, ignoring the question.

'Not that well no. I didn't know he was married anyway, perhaps he's separated though?' James shrugs and gets back to tucking into his dinner.

'Yeah, perhaps he is,' I muse. 'It's none of my business anyway, I'm just being nosey.'

I carry on eating my dinner which is probably one of the best meals that I've ever tasted. I order another glass of wine and James orders a beer. This is oddly nice but also quite strange, it feels like we're on a date but we're not and now we're going on a yacht trip to watch the sunset together, but it's definitely not a date, it's a business trip, a very nice business trip.

Oh Tilly, the situations you get yourself into. I should have stayed at home and let James do the fam trip alone, now I'm being a romantic and catching feelings for the person who I thought was trying to steal my job.

James and I stroll down to the beautiful harbour and we spot the yacht with Tilly's Dream emblazoned across it. The yacht is stunning, sleek and from what I can make out, is decked out with an oak interior. It's also much bigger than I'd imagined.

'Good evening, Gerald,' James says to the man on the yacht.

'Good evening young man and is this the lovely Tilly?' A man in his seventies with a long, grey beard and loads of smooth white hair combed over to the side, jumps out of the way to let us on board. He holds his hand out for me as I step onto the yacht. I gasp at the sheer shininess of it all. I've never been on a boat as fancy as this in my life.

'Yes, I'm the lovely Tilly.' I grin as James and I lock eyes. James goes crimson and I quietly giggle. 'Thank you so much for letting us on your yacht, that's so kind of you.'

'That's alright my lovely. I love showing it off, one of the perks of being old, retired and having money and time to spare. Plus if your name's Tilly then you automatically get a free ride. She's named after my old gal,' he says, tapping his hand on the side of the yacht. 'Her name was Tilly too; God rest her soul.' Gerald smiles wistfully then shakes his head. 'Right we best get going if we want to catch the sun setting. I know just the spot to get the perfect view.'

Gerald gets behind the wheel and motions for James and I to sit just behind him. He brings in the anchor then switches on the engine as we sail off into the sunset, quite literally. Gerald points out all of the famous celebrity holiday homes as well as a couple of celebrities who live here full-time.

'Now *he's* been a right pain in the neck,' Gerald says, as he points to a large, white mansion surrounded by tall, iron gates. 'Wants to buy land and build more homes on it, them ugly ones too for holiday use only, the locals have signed a petition to stop him but money talks, doesn't it? We'll see,' Gerald says, more to himself than to us.

James and I exchange sympathetic looks for Gerald. Coolsbay is so unspoilt, it would be a shame to spoil it with more housing, especially if it isn't in keeping with what's already here. My eyes drift down to the sea and I see something pop up in the water.

'Oh my God,' I squeal. 'Dolphins, I saw a dolphin.' I flap my arms as if I have my very own fins and James roars.

'Oh yes, the Coolsbay dolphins. They've been here for centuries, ever so friendly, different breed to the common dolphin you'll find in the rest of England. These ones are unique to Coolsbay, if you look closely they have a purple hue about them and they absolutely love my homemade feed.' Gerald chucks James a bag of feed and we scatter it into the ocean for our new found friends. They jump and flip all around the boat, squeaking and whistling as they follow us. This is like a fairy tale, am I dreaming on Tilly's Dream?

'This is amazing, so magical.' I throw another handful of feed into the water and watch a baby dolphin poke his head out just slightly. 'Wow.' I feel so happy, so free, Coolsbay is my happy place. I've just decided.

'It's amazing,' James says quietly, with a slightly croaky voice.

I glance at him, expecting to see him smiling back at me, but he isn't. I bite my lip. Oh no, he's actually looking extremely pale.

'Are you feeling alright?' I ask as, James bends forward to put his head between his legs.

'For fuck's sake,' he mutters, as I move my hand onto his back and rub it up and down soothingly. Please don't be sick, we don't need your homemade fish food.

Please don't be sick.

'Pulling up now my lovelies.' Gerald steers to the left and a minute or so later he drops the anchor. 'Now, this is the spot to get the perfect view of a Coolsbay sunset,' he continues, before clocking James and chuckling. 'Haven't got your sea legs yet? Here you go.' Gerald tosses James a small tablet and James hesitates. 'It's just ginger, but a big dose of it. You'll be sickness free in minutes, I promise.'

James swallows down the pill and stays with his head

between his legs for a few more minutes. Gerald and I chat about Coolsbay for a little bit before he presses a button by the wheel.

'I don't do this often,' he says, as a secret door underneath the wheel begins to open. 'But you're very special guests and I have thoroughly enjoyed myself in your company.'

The door opens to reveal a fridge and he's only got bloody champagne in it, bottles of the stuff. What the hell? He presses another button on the opposite side of the steering wheel which releases a draw with champagne glasses, real glasses too, not the plastic ones that we had on the hen do boat trip. Now *this* is a boat trip. Nothing will ever be able to compare to this. And is that music I hear? As we pull in closer to the shore I begin to hear crowds screaming and cheering. In-between the cheers, the wind carries over the sounds of a familiar song, it sounds like the new one from *Harry Styles*. No wonder all the hotels were fully booked with him in town.

'Are you feeling up to doing the honours, big man?' Gerald asks, as James slowly lifts his head up. I begin to hum along to Harry and give James a little thumbs up to check that's he's okay. He turns his head to the side and smiles back at me. This is really quite lovely.

'It's okay, I'm an expert,' I say proudly, reaching over to pull out a bottle of champagne. They're all exactly the same so I'm confident this is what he meant.

'Go for it, Tilly,' Gerald chuckles. 'A real girl with gumption, just like my old gal, God rest her soul.'

What a nice man.

I untwist the wire then begin to twist the cork which doesn't move a millimetre. 'Umm do I need a corkscrew?' I ask, I'm not actually an expert at opening champagne, prosecco maybe.

'No, just twist it my lovely, that French stuff can be a bit stiff.'

James and I giggle like children as I continue to pull and twist on the cork. My boobs jiggle all over the place as I sway this way and that to get a good grip on it. I'm glad Gerald has his back turned or he'd be getting a right eyeful by now. James on the other hand is looking out onto the water, averting his eyes and being polite, although his shoulders are bobbing up and down, so he could be laughing. I continue to hum along to Harry, trying to make out that this isn't hard at all.

Twist.

Pull.

Twist.

Pull.

My humming along to Harry is replaced by grunting as I really begin to struggle. James offers to take over, clearly feeling better from his ginger pill but I've signed up for this now, I won't be defeated by a bloody champagne bottle. My boobs swing from side to side and my hand chafes but I finally begin to feel a bit of friction and movement. Yes!

Twist

Pull, a bit more.

Twist

Pull, that should do it.

Twist

Pull – COME ON!

POP.

The champagne is open.

'Ouch.' And the cork has hit poor old Gerald on the back of the head.

Oh yes, it's open all right and half of it has gone up my nose and all over my chest. I cough and splutter making the most hideous of snorty pig and foghorn noises. I've never had that much fizz go up my nose before and it's bloody well taken my breath away and washed out my eyeballs in the process.

James finds me a tea towel out of the glasses' drawer and begins to dab me down. Without thinking, I grab it off him and blow my nose on it. Oh dear, this gorgeous dreamy elegant boat trip has just gone massively tits up.

Chapter 18

My head reverberates on the springy mattress as I flop onto the hotel bed and cover my eyes with my hands. I've had a shower, whilst James paced the corridors waiting to be let back in.

He said I looked like a million dollars tonight but only because I was covered in the very expensive champagne, Christ it's probably not far off that. I groan, it could only happen to me. It's boiling hot and now I have to sleep wearing the B & B dressing gown because the only nightwear I've bought is highly inappropriate for a work colleague to see me in.

'Oh God, I could have killed the poor bloke, it hit him on the head,' I moan, as James sniggers from the reclining chair. He's been doing a lot of that this past hour and a half, sniggering at me and my drowned rat, champagne-soaked self as well as humming Harry Styles back at me.

Bloody git.

'He found it funny, don't worry about it, these things happen.' He grins and I shake my head.

'I'm glad Gerald did find it funny; it could have been a lot worse, couldn't it?' I close my eyes again, my mind betraying me with images of Gerald being catapulted off the boat by the champagne cork.

'A lot worse,' James agrees, and laughs as he perches next to me on the bed to take his shoes off. Afterwards, he rests his hands on his thighs but one of them, accidently or not, is half touching my thigh. My leg tingles with his touch. He looks quite sexy in his suit. Apart from my underwear, I'm naked underneath this dressing gown. Betrayingly, my mind begins to imagine his hand creeping further up my leg.

No!

This can't happen. It won't happen. Strictly business. Ten minutes ago I was finding him bloody annoying but he isn't that annoying. I'm starting to realise I just didn't give him a chance.

'It was fun though apart from the incident that we won't speak of ever again,' I say, motioning at zipping my lips.

James bursts a big raucous laugh, which sets me off with a huge snort. Attractive. We both silently giggle for a few minutes like children who've been fed too many sweets. He holds his stomach and I let out a happy sigh.

'We've had a successful work trip and the company hasn't been so bad.' I'm trying my hardest to be serious as I lean forward through fits of giggles. My stomach hurts now. I hope I don't wet myself. Will I ever stop laughing?

'It was truly ridiculous. The whole thing, ridiculous,' he says, when he finally catches his breath.

'I am ridiculous.' I shake my head.

'In a good way.' James's half-moon eyes twinkle with warm humour.

He leans closer and I let out a little gasp. My lips part as his lips move closer, just centimetres away from mine. I close my eyes, surrendering to his kiss. This. Whatever this is. Let's do this. My hand moves onto his thigh and he smiles, but his lips don't ever meet mine.

'What's this in your hair?' He gently pokes at my head and my eyes ping open to see him frowning in my face, inspecting me like I'm some kind of rare sea beast.

I suddenly become very self-conscious and begin to pat my head all over.

'What? What is it?' I jump up and run to the mirror in the bathroom, frantically patting my head to find whatever it is that James has found. My hair, I knew I should have washed my hair, but I was lazy, just giving it a quick rinse. A scorpion, a spider, something gross, a jellyfish?

Oh no, a bird shit.

I pull and tug at the hard mound until eventually something falls into my hands. It's not a bird shit, thank God. It's a stone. A beautiful, shiny stone, a purple, blue and green looking stone. The Coolsbay stone. How did that end up in my hair?

'I've found the treasure. I've hit the jackpot,' I squeal, feeling way more excited than I should feel about a bloody stone. 'Look,' I say as I pad back into the bedroom. I hold up the stone and James gets up to inspect it.

'Wow, the elusive stone, you must be special,' he murmurs.

My knees do that jelly thing again.

'I must be.' I flick my hair slightly and a hint of a smile plays across his lips, amused. Then as quickly as it happens, it disappears, replaced with a frown.

'Yeah, I'm just going to grab a shower if you don't mind, but it's late so don't worry about leaving the room, just turn away or something,' he says, grimacing, perhaps regretting his offer. Another shower? He wasn't the one drenched in champagne.

'Of course, I'm very tired, I'm sure I'll fall asleep anyway,' I lie.

I most definitely will not fall asleep, knowing that he's less than a foot away, naked in the shower, but I will close my eyes and imagine him in there. There's nothing wrong with that, is there? I suppress a smirk, feeling like a sneaky pervert but a happy one.

James pads into the bathroom and closes the bathroom door but it's pointless really, I can still see, not that I'm going to peak. I roll onto my side and close my eyes, imagining him getting undressed, minutes later I hear the shower start up and moments later the movement of the water running off his body. I imagine the soapy lather foaming all over him, the manly scent of his shower gel, and I long to get in there with him and help him get clean.

I sigh to myself. If only I was that brave but it would be completely inappropriate and very dangerous. Boundaries. I have to respect other people's boundaries as I expect them to respect my new set of boundaries and that does not involve jumping in a work colleague's shower with them whilst on a business trip. Although it would be very nice, it's probably best not to.

I roll onto my front and reach for my phone. I wish I could take this bloody robe off, I'm boiling even with all of the windows open, but I must remain professional. I mindlessly scroll through social media before remembering that I haven't responded to George yet. I'm surprised he wants to see me again after the leaky boob incident but I'm glad he's not bothered by it, shows that he's a real man, not fazed by a real milk maiden. Ironically, I think my milk has completely dried up now because it hasn't happened again. It's the end of an era. I tap my reply.

Me: *Yes, would be nice to meet again, what do you fancy doing?'*

George replies instantly, now that's more like it. It appears me giving him a taste of his own medicine has sped up the replying process. He may be in with a chance to be my plus one, although it's not as if I have anyone else in the running.

James comes out of the shower, padding over to his chair to faff around in his bag. In my peripheral vision I can see he just has his boxers on and I focus with everything I have not to crane my neck to get a better look. I *can* make out that they're black and very tight.

George: *Tomorrow night? Would you like to come over?*

Tomorrow night, I am of course child free as it's a Tuesday. Wow, come to his house – I don't know about that, it's only been a few dates. Well, I suppose I could go over for an hour or two, at least I know he definitely doesn't have a tag and he probably isn't a psycho murderer. It would be nice to see how he lives although why do I care? I just need a plus one, not a boyfriend. Oh fuck it. Stop overthinking everything Tilly. But it's getting increasingly harder to think straight with a giant, solid James stood very close to me in just his boxers. He's back to being infuriating again.

Me: *Sounds cool, what time?*

George: *Great, any time after seven x*

'I'm shattered, do you mind if I turn the lights out?' James asks, as he reaches down to get his bed sheet and pillow. Bless him, that doesn't look too comfortable and I feel mean for hogging the whole bed. For a moment I consider asking him to share with me but then think better of it.

'NO,' I shout without meaning too. 'Sorry, I mean, no, I'm shattered too,' I continue, busying myself on my phone. He tilts his head towards me, smiles and then reaches up and switches the lights off. The last image I see before I close my eyes is James in those glorious boxers.

I awake to my mouth feeling as dry as the Sahara Desert. I slowly open one eye, scared of what I might see. James is up and dressed, clattering about packing his bag, he strides into the bathroom to clean his teeth. I sit up and quickly pull my dressing gown around me, shit, it must have come undone in the night, hope it wasn't open all night. My boobs out on display.

'How did you sleep?' I ask nonchalantly, rubbing my eyes as he walks back into the bedroom. Just act normal.

'Not bad, you?' He stops and looks at me and I squint at him, slightly. Asking him with my eyes, have you seen my boobs?

'Like a baby, must be all that fresh sea air,' I say evenly, watching him.

'Yeah, same,' he says, breaking eye contact to zip up his bag. 'I'm gonna go and get some breakfast so you can get ready.' He nods towards me, keeping his eyes on my face then walks towards the door.

'Okay, thanks.' He definitely didn't see anything. Phew, got away with that one.

Half an hour later, I meet James downstairs for some breakfast, he's checked us out and instead of eating has spent his time chatting with Fern, about where sell's the Coolsbay stone from what I can gather. He's waited for me. That's sweet. We wolf down our perfectly cooked fry-ups then hit the road to drive back home. I message Billy and Mum to see how Nancy-Ella has been and they both send me back some photos and reassure me that she's been fine. I miss her so much and can't believe I have another evening without her. It's been fun and gone quickly but at the same times feels like I've been away forever. Oh well, at least I'll be busy this evening.

I steal a glance at James as I ponder on whether I'd still be going to George's tonight if we'd kissed. I guess we'll never know. Even though I slept like a baby last night I still can't help but fall asleep on the way home. I definitely have car narcolepsy. Is that a thing? It's embarrassing anyway, I always dribble way more during car sleeps.

I wake up to James yawning and stretching. He looks tired and I feel guilty. I thought he said he slept well although I'm not convinced now, that chair didn't look very comfortable. A pang of guilt hits me, I should have offered to sleep in the chair, it would have been okay for me, comfortable even, but the bitch in me wanted to teach him a lesson for fucking up the room bookings. The bitch in me that thought he wanted my job but really there's plenty of work to go round, there's no need for him to steal anything. We say our goodbyes in the car park and James promises to fill me in with our client's feedback next week. Fingers crossed they book.

Later I shower and get changed, then drive over to George in North Swindon. It's a smart three-story house, newish and nicely decorated. He says that he has the run of the third floor and hardly ever sees his housemate other than when they bump into each other in the kitchen. He has his own living room, bathroom and bedroom, so he has his own space, which is good.

We have a pleasant time chatting about this and that and we even share a kiss. It's okay but no sparks fly which wasn't what I was expecting, given how I felt the first time I saw him. Nevertheless, I ask him to be my plus one and he says yes. With a surprisingly heavy heart, I've completed my mission.

I thought I'd be more excited.

It's only on my way out that I notice it and if I had my eyes closed when I was kissing George for the second time then I never would have seen the photo of two little boys staring back at me, one blonde, one brunette, one blue eyed, one brown. My heart drops into my stomach.

'They your kids?' I squeak, already knowing the answer.

'No, they're my housemate's, hilarious little chaps they are too.'

'Cool, what's your housemate called?' I ask, trying to keep an even tone but I sound strained as my heart races and sweat beads form on my forehead.

'Jumbo, Jimbo,' he replies and I stare blankly at him. 'Yeah, James, he's in his bedroom, I'd offer to introduce you, but he's a bit of a grumpy bastard.'

Chapter 19

My hands grip the steering wheel before I repeatedly bang my head on it.

'Shit!' The car horn makes a loud HONK, making me jump. I stop banging my head but James's words continue to play over and over in my mind. His housemate, who we now know is George, the man that I'm dating and have just asked to be my plus one, is a womaniser. He has a different woman over almost every night, sometimes two. Yuck.

They were on the same bloody stag do; how did I not realise they were on the same bloody stag? But there were two stags dressed up at the pub, the cactus and the man in a wedding dress? Perhaps the cactus wasn't a stag after all and he really was just a prick, as his mates said.

Come to think of it, George was a little hasty in getting me out of the door just then. I feel sick. Should I wait and see if he actually has someone else lined up to come over after me? At least I could use that as an excuse to bin him off. I wait for a good twenty minutes, my legs shaking with adrenaline.

No.

What's the point in torturing myself? I fasten my seatbelt and check my blind spots but as I begin to check both wing mirrors something catches my eye. At first it's the car, a turquoise mini. Frowning, I try to remember where I've seen it before. Then it's the long ginger glossy hair swishing from side to side as she searches for a parking spot.

Oh my good God. It's Samantha, the ginger *Megan Fox*. Perhaps Sammy lives round here too? Or maybe she does. I sit and wait. I even hold my hand up to wave at her but she doesn't see me, too focused on finding a space. I stay very still as she finds a spot directly outside James and George's house. She steps out of the car looking as stunning as ever in a short dress and the highest of heels. My heart sinks as she heads towards the door. George and James's door. I don't know what I'm more upset by, the fact that James has answered the door and was there the whole time I was or the fact that she may be visiting *him*. James smiles and I see his mouth say the word hello and ask how she is before he steps back to let her in. The door closes.

My heart pulsates in my chest, James is with *her*. No wonder he didn't kiss me, why have a burger when you can have a sirloin steak like the ginger *Megan Fox*. Wait… why am I thinking about James and not George?

There's still a few weeks to go so Nay could give my plus one to someone else, someone much more deserving, do I really need to bring one? This has been way more hassle than it's worth with way too many red flags.

'I can't actually fucking believe this? That's it, I'm texting her right now, the skank, and to think that we bloody stuck up for her in the group chat for rooting that married man,' Brie squawks. She always sounds way more Aussie when she's angry, it makes me smile despite my predicament. It's the day after my visit to George and we're sitting in my living room making the most of Nancy-Ella's nap time. It's so nice to have Brie over again, even if it's not under the best circumstances.

'No, don't, she's not actually done anything wrong has she? If she's with James… he's a free man.' She must be with him, she probably met him through the married man, Sammy. Urgh, does that make James just as bad? Has he stolen her from him? What a mess.

'Hmm ya reckon?' Brie narrows her eyes and squints at me, her mind ticking and seemingly not convinced.

'Yeah, I think so, I don't know? Anyway we can't just text her and say we saw her. I'll look like a psycho stalker.'

'True, I'll have to think about that one.' Brie attempts to frown but I notice her head is as smooth as a baby's bum so the frown never happens. Oh the perks of working in aesthetics.

'There's nothing to think about, I think maybe I'll just go on my own.'

'Really? Yeah, I'd just ghost that George if I were you. If you say he once took nearly a week to reply to you then he isn't worth the time it takes to shit, mate.'

'Oh, I don't know, I'd feel awful ghosting someone, it's a bit mean and so final. I've never done it before.'

'It's easy, just delete their number and never speak to them again. Bish, bash, bosh,' Brie says, brushing off her hands with each word.

'Have you done it before? Ghosted someone?' I ask.

'Yeah, sure I have, maybe before it was called ghosting, for sure. Just cut the drama out. Life's too short to waste on flaky men who don't deserve to be in the vicinity of the air we breathe. Plus he sounds like a fuck-boy, James had no reason to lie to you about that, he didn't even know you were dating him,' Brie says, and I know that she's right.

I seem to attract these flaky men, they feed me little bread crumbs and I can't seem to get enough of them. Billy was a flaky man, he's probably less flaky now that we're separated but I know that's for the sake of our child. My keenness for flaky men is probably to do with dad and the birthday breadcrumbs he used to feed us as kids. We'd get so excited over his yearly card with a tenner in, Mum must have been so upset, raging even, but she never showed it.

'Anyway enough about my shit show of a mission to get the perfect plus one, what's going on with you?' I ask, grateful for the distraction from my own shockingly poor love life.

'Okay, I'll tell ya but it's gonna cost ya another cuppa and a whole packet of those special biscuits.'

Minutes later I pad back into the room carrying a tray with a pot of tea, milk, two ready-made cups of tea and a packet of those special biscuits. Brie moves her eyes to my elegant, white China teapot.

'Just in case we want more tea, cute isn't it?' I say, admiring and stroking the teapot whilst I set the tray down on the coffee table.

'Yeah, if you're the queen or my grandmother,' she jokes. 'No, it's actually quite cute,' she says, as she picks it up and tops up her tea. 'Is the word, bijou?' Brie pauses, takes a quick sip of her tea then wolfs down an entire biscuit, then another. She takes another slurp of her tea then inhales deeply, composing herself.

'So, I'm moving back to Oz soon, like a week after Nay's wedding and I'll be gone,' she says, then stuffs in another biscuit.

'Are you joking?'

'No,' she says, through a mouth full of biscuit.

'Why?' I croak. My best mate, my partner in crime is leaving me.

'I've just not been happy for a while, babe. I want to go to the beach. I miss my parents. I want my family to be brought up where I was, not in sunny Swindon. No offence.'

'None taken, but we aren't that far from the beach,' I say meekly, knowing full well we are at least an hour away from even a crappy beach, nothing that compares to those dreamy Australian sands.

'I know babe, but it's not the same. I want the beach on my doorstep and I really miss my mum, visiting once a year for two weeks just isn't enough anymore.'

'What does Nick think about moving to Oz?'

'He's excited, it's something we've been discussing for a while.' Discussing it for a while and she didn't feel comfortable telling me because I was too busy being consumed with all my shit. 'I can take the business there; it may take a little while to build up clients again but it'll be right. And Nick's a carpenter so he'll have no worries getting business.'

'Yeah,' I agree and smile with what I hope looks like encouragement but inside I'm devastated that she's going.

'Plus, I'm pregnant.'

I almost spit out my tea.

'You're pregnant? When? How?' I say, aware that my eyes are almost popping out of my head.

'Yeah, I know. Us that didn't want kids, we weren't being very careful.' She makes a face. 'We found out about a week after the hen do when my hangover was still hanging around. Felt so guilty for downing all those shots.' Brie winces again then rubs her hands on her stomach.

'Oh. My. God.' I lean forward to hug her with a biscuit still in my hand.

'We want to keep it, we're actually really excited. I know I've changed my mind about wanting kids but that's allowed, right?' she asks, as we finish hugging.

'Of course, there are no rules. You're allowed to change your mind,' I say, holding back the tears. 'Hey, it will be a good excuse for me and Nancy-Ella to come and visit you in Oz.'

'Thanks, babe. That would be amazing. Lads on tour with kids! Special edition,' she says, punching the air. 'I knew you'd understand, I should have told you earlier I know, but I wanted to get things finalised first. It was stressful getting everything ready and I think my hormones weren't helping which probably explains my overreacting rage on the phone to you that time, sorry babe,' she says, looking at me, biting her lip, her eyes welling up with emotion. 'Also, I know I was a bitch about Krissy. I'll admit I was a tad jealous of your flourishing friendship, she's taking you away from me before I've even left the bloody country.' Brie taps me on the leg playfully and I shake my head in disagreement.

'No one could ever replace you,' I say, wiping away a tear. 'But Mum's going to be the most upset,' I tease. 'Who's going to do her face?'

'Don't worry, I'll recommended some people to her, make sure she doesn't go to someone dodgy and end up looking like Jackie Stallone or Pete Burns.' Brie winks and we both giggle despite our watery eyes.

Chapter 20

The next few weeks go by quickly but also painfully slow at the same time. Billy being surprisingly helpful, offering to Nancy-Ella an extra night so Brie and I could go out for a meal. Work often felt like I was moving in slow motion, despite having lots to do. I couldn't stop watching James, his furrowed brow, and longs legs sticking out from underneath the table were a comforting sight to behold. I was dying to ask him if he was with the ginger *Megan Fox* but shyness and pride got the better of me.

Andrea decided to go on a last-minute familiarisation trip to The Isles of Scilly which left James and I swamped preparing proposals and site inspections. Our Baywatch proposal was accepted by the client which was fantastic news, they really loved the little souvenir touch that James thought up. Andrea was very pleased with us and surprised us with a wine and pizza lunch delivered to the office. I only had a couple of sips of the wine as I didn't want to end up saying or asking anything I'd regret.

James spent the whole of lunch being extra nice to me whilst I pretended everything was fine. He did confide in me that he'd let his housemate go and he was feeling happier about that. Ha! Now the creepy George can do his creeping elsewhere. Other than that James has been visibly a little stressed looking and on the phone a lot talking to clients regarding the restaurants and pubs idea. He said something about a gay couple giving him grief but when I asked what about, he wouldn't go into detail.

He's also been receiving a lot of phone calls on his mobile. He'd accept a call then swiftly take his clandestine conversations out of the office, pacing up and down the car park outside talking animatedly and waving his hands around. I've never seen him so passionate looking; I'd often watch him ruffle his hair and have to stop myself from running over to ask what it's all about. The phone calls seemed to have slowed down now and at the end of one of the phone calls, he came into the office with a big smile pasted onto his face. It then dawned on me that he's probably been talking to the Ginger *Megan Fox*. Every time he went outside after that I had to stop myself from scowling at him. I was annoyed, not just because he was more than likely sorting out his love life during work time but mainly because I was jealous.

After a challenging day mumming it with a tempestuous toddler, I crawl into bed with a fresh Winnie the Poo nighty on (it's still too hot for PJ's, okay) and turn on my beloved *Love Island*. One of the new girls has waltzed into the villa and instantly stolen another girl's man, his head turned so fast he almost gave himself whiplash. The other girl has been with him since the start and now she's in bits, lost without him. I stifle a sob and take a large double bite of my *Double Gold Caramel Billionaire Magnum*.

They were my favourite couple.

'Ouch.' I hold my hand up to my head as it pulsates

with painful brain freeze from the ice-cream. I know just how she bloody feels. Well actually not quite because James was never mine in the first place but it's close enough. 'Ouch.' I hold my throbbing head as my phone pings with a message from George. A month ago my heart may have skipped a beat seeing his name flash up, the curly mysterious stranger, but not anymore.

George: *Hey, so sorry but I'm going to have to decline your invitation to come to the wedding as your guest. It all just feels a bit too much too soon and I'm not ready. Hope we can still be friends, though? It's been fun x*

Oh for fuck's sake. I've been dumped by the one person I've been trying to ghost. I knew I should have got in there first. I go to reply with *no worries, I was thinking the same myself* or words to that effect but decide that silence is probably best. Even typing something like that sounds bitter and I'm not, not about him anyway.

I stuff the rest of the Magnum into my mouth and it melts like a dream, no brain freeze this time. At least he was honest, I expect it's the most honest he's been since we've been dating. I pick up my phone to message Nay to tell her that despite my best efforts I won't be bringing a plus one but then almost shit myself at what comes next.

BANG. BANG. BANG.

The sound comes again before I realise that it must be the door but who would be banging on my door at this time of night? Oh God! It's probably Dan, he's got his tag off and has come to chop my body up into tiny little pieces before stuffing me into my own freezer.

Not if I can help it.

I crawl out of bed and feel underneath for the cricket bat I keep tucked away for emergencies. Gripping it with both hands, I run with my head down low over to the window. Slowly, I move my head up, using my fingers to slightly open the slats in the blind. Without opening the window, I can just about make out a head, he appears to be jumping up and down. The head doesn't look like it belongs to Dan, unless he's in disguise that is. This guy has long hair. Who have I dated with long hair that might be seeking revenge? I mentally go through all my recent dates as I grip the bat tightly. No one springs to mind. My conscience is clear. My danger signals diminishing, but who could it be?

BANG. BANG. BANG.

I lean forward and open the window. I must stop him before he wakes up Nancy-Ella, he probably has the wrong house or something. I'm being ridiculous thinking it's a stalker but I keep the bat in my hands just in case.

'Can I help you, mate?' I say with my best deep voice, in the hope that I sound like a big burly man, not to be messed with. I hold the bat up just enough so it can be seen next to my wide, scary looking eyes.

'Shit, when did your voice break?' The long-haired stranger says through laughter. 'It's *me* you wanker, let me in, I'm dying for a piss and put the fucking rolling pin away, you mad bitch.'

'CHARLIE!' I scream out of the window before carefully re-hiding the cricket bat that I must admit doesn't look that menacing now that he's just called it a rolling pin. My feet pelt down the stairs and it's the fastest I've moved for days. As I reach the bottom I slow down for fear of slipping and pulling something; that would not be a good idea with a wedding coming up. Opening the door with a huge grin on my face, I pull my brother into a biggest of bear hugs.

'I've missed you so much! You're back,' I squeal into his ear. He's home. My brother is home.

'I am and I love you, but first… piss,' he says, as he dumps his bags down and runs past me to the toilet. Whilst he's in the loo, I quickly run upstairs to check on Nancy-Ella. I'm shocked to see her sleeping peacefully in her cot, not even all this commotion, my screaming and my man voice has woken her. I'm glad because this is an occasion to celebrate, for adult time and copious amounts of wine. Hooray!

'Like what you've done to the place, sis. Looking good,' Charlie says, as he stands appraising my home. He's got a suntan and his sun-bleached hair tucked behind his ears, has grown long and wavy, even since the photos he sent me of him and Gethin.

'Oh, thanks, I just wanted to make it our own after Billy left, you know, which seems like a lifetime ago now,' I say, marvelling at my brother.

'Yeah, you look fab too! Look at you!' Charlie holds my hand and twizzles me around.

'Really? I'm wearing a nighty?' I say, with a scrunched-up face as I pull at my nighty with both hands to show Winnie the Pooh and all his friends.

'You're glowing darling, it's in your eyes.'

I throw my head back and laugh. 'Such a charmer. Anyway, what are you doing back? I mean I love the surprise, okay I kind of hated it as it was a bit scary but love that you're back.' I prod him in the arm to check that he's real and he prods me back on the forehead.

'Yeah, sorry about that, my phone died hours ago and I didn't want to go to Mum's in case she has Jeff over.'

'She's told you about Jeff?'

'Oh yeah, she felt she had to after you met him by accident in the shops that time.'

I don't tell him that it wasn't in the shops but at her house after a quickie. I'll let Mum save some face on that one. 'Yeah, probably best.' I smirk. 'Anyway! I'm so excited you're back, I'm going to open a bottle of wine and then you can tell me everything you've been up to in the past year. No filters.'

The last time he was back it was only for a week so I have to make the most of his visits, savouring every word he says and every story he tells like it's my last bar of chocolate.

'Okay, you little mentalist.' Charlie laughs as he slumps down on my sofa and takes his shoes off. Moments later, I arrive back in the living room with a bottle of wine, two glasses, two bottles of water, a sandwich and some nibbles as I assume he's dehydrated and hungry from the flight.

'Here you go, broski.'

'You're amazing, sis.' Charlie wolfs down the crisps and sandwich before downing a whole bottle of water. I pour us a glass of wine each, in readiness for our gossip dump.

'One wine coming up…' I finish pouring his glass then push it over to him on the coffee table.

'Oh no, sorry, not for me thank you, you go ahead though.'

'What? No wine?'

'Yeah, I'm AF now, didn't I tell you?'

'What's AF?' I ask, worrying that it's some rare debilitating illness.

'Alcohol free.' Charlie shrugs. 'Gethin inspired me, I was wary at first but I was getting too old for my hedonistic partying ways and alcohol was really taking its toll on me, mentally and physically. I won't go into detail but I think it was giving me these massive painful piles,' he says, pointing to his arse and going into way too much detail anyway. 'And I over shared way too much, you know me, I don't need alcohol to do that.'

'Well, good for you,' I say, handing him another bottle of water.

'Yeah, it's been liberating and much cheaper on the purse.'

'I bet, and where is the lovely Gethin?' I ask, looking around as if I expect him to jump out at any moment and shout *surprise* in a very Welsh accent.

'We actually flew back together,' Charlie says. 'He came out to see me again, stayed for a week but when the time came for him to leave I just couldn't part with him. We couldn't part with each other. You've got to take a leap of faith when you know you've found the one,' he says, with a big grin.

'Yeah, so where is he?' I ask impatiently.

'Oh he's back in Swansea, thought it might be a bit much to turn up in the middle of the night on your doorstep with a man in tow.' He hugs himself. 'Plus I wanted to spend some quality time with my family before I introduce you to my beloved. This Guncle needs to see his gorgeous niece.'

I smile at my brother as his eyes twinkle with love. The last time he saw her in person, she was just a few months old.

'I'm so pleased you're home. You couldn't have come at a better or worst time.' I pause then take a sip of my wine as I watch my brother raise both his eyebrows at my ominous statement.

What comes next is a load of word vomit from me explaining that in my quest to find the plus one after many disastrous dates, George is no longer my plus one because he dumped me before I could ghost him. I continue to gabble on that I've met a man who I think is the one but most definitely will not be my plus one or maybe even be my one as I've left it too late and now the ginger *Megan Fox* has got in there first, plus I've also snogged his soon to be ex-housemate who is also George. I admit, after a few too many glasses of wine, that I've caught feelings for James and it's only taken a dance off, strip show, sharing a bed twice, dating his housemate and bloody working together for me to realise it but now it's too late. I've missed the boat and the ginger *Megan Fox* has hopped on it; she's set sail on Tilly's dream. Literally.

'Wow, so you're going to sit back and let ginger *Megan Fox* take your man?' Charlie asks, after my large info dump.

'Well. He isn't exactly *my* man, is he?'

'Of course he is, you two have been thrown together, it's serendipity. Meant to be. For fuck's sake, can't you see?'

'You're a poet and you didn't know it,' I joke.

'Seriously, you can't just sit back and let her take your life. You need to do something.'

'I think I have to take a back seat on this one, don't you?'

'Hmmmmm, not necessarily,' he says, as he reaches forwards, opens another water bottle and takes a sip. 'Try thinking that something wonderful is always on the verge of happening and eventually, it will. Worked for me.'

'Yeah, as if it's that easy,' I say.

Chapter 21

'Morning,' I say as I drop my handbag down by my desk, whilst trying to remain as casual looking as possible. Inside my heart is beating so loudly, I fear he might hear it.

Control yourself, Tilly; he is off limits.

'Morning,' James says, then looks up at me with his twinkling brown eyes. My mind turns to us on the yacht watching the sunset, Mr half-moon eyes. They're so rich, like chocolate and I could just drink them up and stare at them for days. I realise I've been staring at his eyes for much longer than is normal, so I break eye contact, sit down and busy myself with shuffling papers around on my desk.

'Hey, I've been meaning to tell you,' he continues, with a hint of a smirk. 'While I've been setting up the Baywatch event, I told one of the surf guys that you found a Coolsbay stone in your hair and he said that it was supposed to be good luck if a stone finds you.'

'Really? Must be special then.' I raise my eyebrows in a horrible attempt to flirt with him. No, don't do that, he has a girlfriend remember, the ginger *Megan Fox*. I imagine myself hissing like a cat when I see her at the wedding next week. Must practise my happy, nice face in the mirror before seeing her again. Must remain neutral.

Gracious.

'Maybe,' he smiles. 'Good weekend?'

'Yeah, it was actually. My brother surprised me by turning up on my doorstep in the middle of the night.'

'No way.' He leans forward, seemingly interested in knowing more.

'Yeah, I've not seen him in person for over a year so it was really cool.'

'Nice,' James says, suddenly distracted by his laptop. 'Fuck.'

'You alright?'

'I knew he was up to something, I should have insisted and gone back to meet with them when the client showed up to view it.'

'Who?'

'Arrgh shit, this is not good.' James stares at me with a distressed look in his eyes then holds his head in his hands. 'Andrea's going to blow her lid.' He leans back in his chair and closes his eyes. 'Arrrrgh,' he moans.

'Anything I can help with?' I grimace. Here I am, your knight in shining armour or rather your single mum in a slightly see-through blouse and pencil skirt.

'The owners have been difficult and now they've poached our clients, it wouldn't matter so much if it was a small business but it's *Sovereign Wide*,' he says, with a wince before the penny drops that he's talking about his small bespoke conferences in pubs/restaurants venture.

'They're one of our biggest accounts,' I whisper, as I feel the colour drain from my face, not meaning to make him feel bad but knowing how big a deal it is. If we lose them then we're pretty much out of business. We can't afford to lose them, or one or both of us will loose our jobs.

'I know. I actually feel sick. FUCK! I knew this job

wasn't for me.' He throws his hands up in the air before they land on his head and he begins to literally pull his hair out.

'Stop. Look, I'm sure we can salvage this but you need to tell me everything, start at the beginning.'

'Okay, the company is Latte Baby, you know that swanky coffee shop just outside Marlborough?' I feel the bile rise in my throat as he continues to speak. 'When I phoned them I thought they were a restaurant and after I'd done my pitch he sounded really keen. I tried to backtrack when I found out they were only a coffee shop but he insisted that he'd be able to source whatever the client needed in the way of refreshments and equipment and he could seat a minimum of thirty in his conference room. I went to check it out and was sold, the coffee was pretty delicious too.'

Now it's my turn to put my head in my hands. 'Oh My God.'

'I know, I'll sort it out, I have to,' James says.

'No it's not that, that's my ex, Billy's coffee shop. I knew he was up to something.'

'Billy and Timmy? But they're a couple? They seemed really sound guys at first but they're just a couple of dishonest, money grabbing twats,' James says, as I shake my head, not wanting to compute what he's just said about Billy and Timmy being a couple. Keeping our jobs is top priority for now so I'll deal with that bombshell later.

'Okay, so what's *Sovereign Wide* said?'

'They went to visit the coffee shop to explain their requirements and Timmy exposed our rates. I told him not to discuss rates with them and only requirements, knew I should have been there to keep an eye on things. Anyway, *Sovereign Wide* have just sent an email to say they're going to go direct with the venue as they're on a budget with their monthly meetings and the coffee shop have offered them a fucking deal.' He bangs his fist down on his desk and the whole thing shakes.

'What? No, they wouldn't do that. They can't do that. *Sovereign Wide* aren't stupid they know we charge a fee for our venue finding and organising. They're loyal.'

'Not, any more. Looks like I've well and truly fucked it.'

'Forward me the email,' I say in an even tone.

I spend the next hour and half being put through to various different people before I finally speak to Mandy who I've been dealing with for years. She's stepped away from organising the monthly meetings and a new girl, Marie is now doing it. She's obviously out to impress and save the company money, unaware of the relationships that have already been built with suppliers, including us. Mandy apologises profusely and says that she will have a serious chat with Marie regarding the monthly meetings and will let her know that all dealings must go through us. She doesn't understand why Marie was booking direct and I insinuate that the venue has been a little naughty, because I don't want to get Marie into trouble. Mandy knows that it's cheaper to go directly and probably not too much more work but with the bigger events that they book through us, we save them a hell of a lot of time and frustration. Mandy is thankfully all about the bigger picture and I have never felt more grateful to her.

'Right, it's all sorted I think, we just have to be patient and wait for Marie to contact us, Mandy's having a word with her as we speak.'

'What, just like that?' James asks, a worried look still in eyes.

'Yes, just like that. I've known Mandy for years; she wouldn't want to jeopardise our relationship as we've got her out of a few sticky situations in the past where their event organisers have fucked up and we've stepped in to save the day. I'm fairly confident it will all be sorted now.'

'You're amazing, thank you,' he says, as I try not to blush.

'I'm going to ring up those guys at Latte Baby and give them an ear bashing. It's bad business,' James says, already picking up the phone.

'It really is but if you don't mind, I'd like to do the ear bashing on this occasion.'

James puts the phone down and nods. He doesn't question why because I think the look on my face says it all. Gay? A gay couple. He has to have it confused, surely.

'James,' I say slowly.

'Yes.' He meets my gaze and gives me a lovely warm smile.

'What makes you think Billy and Timmy are a couple?' I'm trying my best not to look emotional about it.

He visibly winces then speaks. 'Umm, without going into detail they were very tactile and Timmy kept referring to Billy as his partner.'

'Yeah, business partner,' I say, with a glimmer of relief that James may have got it *very* wrong.

'No, Tilly, I'd say they're definitely a couple,' he says quietly, as he watches my face. 'I saw them holding hands,' he whispers.

'The bastard,' I squeak, as tears betrayingly sting the back of my eyes. I don't want to cry over him, I've spent way too many months doing that already. It's just such a shock.

James gets up from his desk and rests a hand on my

shoulder, I shrug it off so he pulls up a chair and sits next to me.

'I'm sorry,' he says and I shake my head at him.

'It's just a shock, right under my nose the whole time, what a couple of wankers,' I say, still not believing it.

'Yep.' James presses his lips together then motions the wanker sign with both hands. It's so wrong it makes me giggle through my tears. He laughs too then gets up and marches over to the fridge, pulling out the half drunk bottle of wine that Andrea sent us.

'Here, have this, take the edge off a bit,' he says, handing me a small glass.

'Thanks.' I take a sip as James gently rubs my back. It's just a brief couple of seconds but his large hand leaves a burning, yearning imprint on my body that sends tingles all up my spine. Not now, Tilly. He's spoken for and he's just a work colleague. Boundaries.

'Better?' he asks, sitting down opposite me, studying my face. I wonder what he's thinking.

'This wine is rank.' I make a face followed by a smile. 'But thanks for the thought.'

'It is pretty rank but I thought it was just me not being a wine connoisseur.' He grins as I hand it back over to him, takes a sip and makes a face too. 'Yeah, I thought it was bad the first time but now it's even worse. Sorry.' He grimaces.

'It's okay,' I say, thinking what a cheapo Andrea is with the wine.

'Hey,' James says, leaping up from his chair. 'I know what will cheer you up.' He marches over to the Radio and turns it up, just as he does so *Ebeneezer Goode* by The Shamen comes on and he looks at me in mock shock as if to say this was meant to happen. He begins to troop in time to the music, his big feet slapping on the floor like a couple of kippers. I snort and giggle away the tears as he begins to perform big fish little fish, carboard box before throwing himself on the floor to perform a full break-dancing arrangement. I mean, I knew he could move but this is quite impressive. He finishes the performance in a head stand, his feet not far off reaching the ceiling. Tears are still falling down my cheeks but this time, I'm in hysterics.

'Thanks, I appreciate the effort,' I say through laughter, as James turns down the radio then sits back down.

'All worth it to see you smile again,' he says. 'Listen why don't I take you out for a drink tonight? I want to say thank you as well for what you did with *Sovereign Wide* and treat you to some better tasting wine,' he says.

I notice his cheeks look flushed but it's probably from all the dancing or does he feel a little self-conscious, maybe? As I open my mouth to reply, Andrea marches through the door with a face like thunder.

I'm about twenty minutes into the journey when I realise that I've driven past my house. In fact I don't even get to my street because my mind is racing with thoughts of Billy and Timmy. Yes that's right, I'm on the way to the bloody coffee shop. It appears that I'm going to confront them, my body has taken over and made that decision for me and has autopiloted me here.

After Andrea arrived she told me to go home early as she needed to have a private urgent meeting with James. She's probably got wind of the *Sovereign Wide* problem somehow, that's the thing with Andrea she just seems to know everything no matter how much you try to hide it from her. She's like a mother, but I guess the company is her baby and when anything goes wrong she does take it very personally. At least James can give her the good news now, hopefully Marie has emailed him to reinstate the meetings and it can all be forgotten about.

I pull up to the coffee shop and catch sight of the new sign, it's bolder, brighter and much more out there than the last sign. Just like those two, I think bitterly as I remember all the times Timmy has been in my house having a *meeting* with Billy. Christ he was even there when I went away on the hen do, he was probably in my house the whole-time playing house with the father of my child. The thought makes me sick to my stomach. I sit in my car for a few moments not sure of what I'm actually going to do. Why am I here? What will it achieve? I decide on the only logical thing that I can do; I strut into the coffee shop and order the most obnoxious coffee I can think of.

'Hello, can I have a triple, hobbit-sized, half-sweet, non-fat caramel latte with soy milk please, and extra cream?' I say to the smiley girl behind the counter. They've employed more staff, a sign of them doing well. Too well.

'Yes of course, to have in or take out?' she asks, not fazed by my ridiculous order, poor girl probably gets them all the time. I suddenly feel guilty.

'In fact, it's fine, just make it a normal latte, no frills. And I'll have it to take out please.' I smile, thinking I can make a quick escape if I need to. 'Are Billy and Timmy around? I ask casually, as she faffs around making my coffee.

'Just out on lunch, having a meeting but they should be back any minute.' She nods towards the door behind me then continues to finish making the coffee. Moments later my drink is presented in front of me. 'Oh, here they are now.' She waves at Billy and Timmy as I stay facing her, sipping my latte.

'Oh hello,' I say with a big, bright smile as Billy and Timmy clip-clop over to the counter in matching shoes and crisp white shirts. How on earth did I miss this?! 'Just wanted to check out the conference room, you know, for our client.' I narrow my eyes at Billy who frowns then smiles.

'Which client?' he asks coolly as my eyes move to Timmy who has gone a deep shade of crimson and is now looking at the floor. His jaw tenses a few times before Billy speaks. 'Let's go out the back,' he says, as he clocks Timmy's expression.

Whether it's shame or embarrassment, Timmy should feel both. I grab my latte and we follow Billy to the little office and we shuffle around until each of us are seated in a chair. Timmy is balanced on a little stool that looks like it might give way at any moment and I secretly hope it does.

'Well, what can I do for you, Tilly?' Billy asks, with a smug flick of his hair.

'How about tell me the truth.' I'm calm as I look between both men feeling like a school teacher with two naughty kids.

'You've lost me,' says Billy.

'*Sovereign Wide*, they were booked in via us to have a monthly meeting here and I've just been informed that you have encouraged the client to go direct to you and cut us out.' I fold my arms and wait.

'Yes, and what's wrong with that?' Timmy says, seemingly having composed himself from earlier.

Billy moves his body to face Timmy as his mouth drops open, this seems to be news to him too.

'Lots of things actually,' I say. 'For a start, it's bad business to poach our client. We also have a long, established relationship with them and exposing our rates, tempting them to come direct to you has jeopardised that,' I say, as both of them blink at me and fold their arms to mirror mine.

'Why didn't you come to me first? Talk to me about it?' I turn to Billy.

'Umm James approached us. I was excited for the business. I wanted to surprise you with the fact that we were working with you,' Billy says, with a croak in his voice and I almost feel sorry for him. 'We were just waiting on signing the contracts with James.' He looks at Timmy with a hurt expression, Timmy juts out his jaw and continues to look forward.

'Well, I found out today, through my colleague that you'd backstabbed us.' I cross my legs, pointing them away from him. 'But you'll be pleased to know that *Sovereign Wide* are still going to meet here but they'll continue to go through us, that includes their requirements.' I turn my gaze to Timmy. 'James will be in touch with the contracts soon and if there's any other funny business then I'm afraid we'll have to find them another venue and I might make that general knowledge to all my other clients too.' I wave my finger between the two of them, now feeling like a stern headmistress making threats of expulsion.

'Of course, we wouldn't jeopardise that would we, Tim?' Billy says. as he glares at Timmy then quickly kicks him in the shin.

'No,' Timmy says flatly, looking at the floor. 'Sorry Tilly, it won't happen again.'

'Great, glad that's all sorted, oh and by the way congratulations.' I let the words hang in the air to see if either cotton on. They don't.

'For what?' Timmy asks, looking up.

'For finding love, for finding each other.' I smile as Billy flicks his hair over and over as if he's a robot glitching. 'I'm happy for you both but equally as happy for me that I didn't agree to work here. I mean, how awkward would that have been and also how stressful for you two, trying to keep it a secret and sneak about behind my back.' I throw my hands up in the air in mock shock and they both stare back at me in silence. 'I'll see myself out, bye.'

And with that, I jump up, turn on my heel and walk out of the room, leaving them both staring open mouthed at me.

Chapter 22

Today it's Music Bums again. I've messaged Krissy and she still hasn't replied, although I hope to see her there. Now Brie's going I could use a friend now more than ever and I like Krissy, she's funny and her heart's in the right place. I just hope she's okay. I get Nancy-Ella ready and savour dressing her in the cute little romper suit that Brie bought her from one of her trips back to Oz. Soon she'll be too big for this, soon she'll be too big for romper suits. But for now, I'll just enjoy it. I stuff her little wriggly toes into her socks then stand her up.

'You look beautiful, baby,' I say, before dropping a kiss on her squishy cheeks.

'Boofull Nanyella,' she says, jumping up and down and I giggle. She's so cute even if Billy is her father.

'Come on then, are you ready for Music Bums?'

'Yeaaahh.' Nancy-Ella squeals and claps her hands together. She really does love this class, even if the thought of her touching a musical instrument does bring on severe anxiety in me, my little bruiser comes first.

'Come on then, little miss heavy hands, no throwing any instruments today, okay? Gentle hands, not heavy hands.'

'Heavy hands, heavy hands,' she sings almost goadingly. This child of mine understands more than she lets on, I'm sure.

♥ ♥ ♥

We arrive at Music Bums and Krissy is already sitting in a different spot, chatting with the other mums. We tend to stick to the same mats each time; it does become a bit territorial like that as sad as it sounds, but she's purposefully moved, not to sit by me. And she looks away when I look over. I'm baffled as to what I've done to upset her.

Nancy-Ella and I sit in our usual spot and focus on the teacher and the class. The next forty-five minutes go by very slowly without Krissy to laugh with, I try to enjoy my time with Nancy-Ella but it's bugging me. *The wheels on the bus go round and round, round and round, round and round.* I try catching her eye a couple of times but nothing. *The wheels on the bus go round and round, all day long.* She doesn't even bat an eyelid when Nancy-Ella bonks a little boy on the nose with the bells and she doesn't join in with the rampant roar of laughter when Nancy-Ella says, '*Oh bugger,*' right afterwards which she then says on repeat for the rest of the class. It's really bugging me and what's bugging me much more is why it's bugging me so much. The class finishes and I make a shameless beeline for her as she exits the door.

'Hey Krissy, how's things?' I give her a big wide grin.

'Hey,' she says, without looking at me and continuing to walk away with Arthur on her hip.

'Are you alright?' I ask, getting a little closer.

'Yes, why wouldn't I be?' Krissy stops, shakes her head then tries to turn off again.

'Krissy.' I'm just going to come out with it. 'Have I done something to upset you?' I frown and Krissy sighs heavily as if she's been holding her breath for the entirety of the class. She hoists Arthur further up onto her hip whilst she studies my face and I think I see her soften slightly.

'You really don't know?' she asks, and I shake my head vigorously. She grabs my arm and leads me over to the corner of the leisure centre hallway. She studies my face again then sighs. 'You dropped me in it.'

'Huh?'

'The hen do, you talked about the hen do on the double date and dropped me in it. Steve doesn't know that I went, remember?'

'Oh, was I not supposed to say anything?' I frown, baffled.

'No. I knew I should have reminded you before you came over, telling you when you were drunk probably wasn't the best idea.'

'Krissy why are you hiding it from him?' I almost laugh, is she joking?

'Ugh, he gives me so much grief, Tilly, it's just easier this way. I said I was staying at my mum's for the night to have a nice relaxing break. Mum covered for me but you didn't.' She points accusingly. I hoist Nancy-Ella up onto my hip and lower my voice.

'Hang on a minute, firstly I don't remember you telling me that the hen do was supposed to be this huge secret - and by the way it's very weird that you have to keep that from him. And secondly you gate crashed our room and didn't pay your share. Brie and I deserve an apology for that as well as Gemma and Nay.' I hoist Nancy-Ella up again probably a little too aggressively and she reaches over and pulls Krissy's hair.

'Ouch. Nay said it would be alright, said someone was pulling out, I asked her,' Krissy says.

'Alright, but can you see how it might have upset us. We paid for the room?'

'Yes,' she whimpers, her eyes filling up. 'I just wanted to have a good time, a night without worries. Sorry, sorry it was wrong, selfish even.'

'It's alright,' I say, feeling sorry for her as I notice the reception team staring at us.

'I'll buy you girls a drink at the wedding yeah, call it evens.'

'Sounds perfect.' I smile. 'But wouldn't Steve have found out about the hen do at the wedding? That you went to it?'

'Oh, he's not coming. Nathan's coming in his place, Steve doesn't mind.' She gives me a big, toothy grin.

'Oh right, okay.'

'Coffee?' Krissy says and I nod, deciding not to question the arrangement any further but all I can say is I'm so glad I didn't get caught up in it. An image of Nathan seductively squeezing teabag juices onto Steve's face flashes into my mind. I think there's more to that little threesome than meets the eye.

Today is the big day, Nay is getting married. I'm so excited for it and it's all made a little better by the fact that I do now have a plus one. Okay he's not my dream man, far from it but he's reliable, funny, good company and has also offered to drive because he's alcohol free. Yes, it's my brother, Charlie. Nay was delighted when I asked if I could bring him, *way better than any of the weirdo's you've been dating*, she'd said as I filled her in on my disastrous quest to find the plus one.

Everyone loves Charlie and is keen to catch up, so it's

a win. It's definitely not what I imagined when I set off to find my plus one a few months ago but I'm happy and I'd much rather bring him than any other man. After I told Charlie about Timmy and Billy he said he wasn't surprised then proceeded to phone several of his friends in Swindon to see if they knew Timmy, '…*because every gay knows a guy that knows a gay that knows a guy,*' were Charlies words. He howled with laughter when one of his friends described Timmy as the community penis, apparently he was a bit of a naughty boy when he was younger. Yuck. I never would have said that about Timmy but then again I don't really know him because all he's done is scowl at me since they started working together and now it's clear why, he was jealous.

Since I admonished them for exposing our rates, Timmy has actually been a lot more agreeable. He even pulled me aside when they came to pick up Nancy-Ella one day and said thank you for stopping the family days out as it was making him feel awkward. I told him it was no problem and thanked him for dating Billy and taking him off my hands. It was tongue in cheek and I only meant it a little bit.

'Alrightyroo lads, looking hot,' Brie booms, as I answer the door to her and Nick. They look like the perfect power couple with Brie in her tangerine dress and Nick with his matching tie. Charlie and I are also matching in sage green, Charlie said he wanted to wear sage to compliment the fact that we're bad ass witches. I think he meant bitches but I agreed anyway, green looks good on us.

'Oh my God, hi guys. Oh Brie, you look gorgeous. Look at your bump.' I lean forward to give her a hug and afterwards she pats her belly through her figure-hugging dress. 'Yep, he's growing in there alright. Still looks like

I've just eaten way too many pies but I'm sure I'll be a blossoming whale in no time.' She laughs then looks at Nick.

'She will with the amount she's eating, sent me to the shop for a tin of *Roses* the other night, I didn't even get a look in,' Nick says, laughing.

'What can I say, this baby's hungry.' Brie shrugs before giving Nick a little dig in the ribs.

'Just buy two tins next time Nick, and hide the other one for yourself,' Charlie stage whispers.

'Good plan, my man,' says Nick, patting Charlie on the back.

'Right, let's go and see our friend get married,' I squeak, as I close the door behind us.

We arrive at the venue forty minutes later; a gorgeous old barn with loads of pastel bunting hung up outside. I admire the rolling fields that look like various shades of green carpet surrounding the whole barn, there isn't a house anywhere to be seen. It's stunning. From the car park we're ushered by one of the groomsmen to the side of the building and taken round a corner then through a red and pink rose decorated archway where the outdoor ceremony takes place. There's at least one hundred white wrought iron chairs evenly spaced out with pink ribbons tied to the last chair on the inside row. Red carpet runs down the whole of the aisle and at the end of it another archway sits. It's white and covered in more roses but this time they're white and pink. With the beautiful Wiltshire countryside as the backdrop and the pretty ceremony space, it takes my breath away and I can't help but let out a little gasp.

'Don't tell me, this is what you would have,' Charlie says, as he clocks me drooling at the aesthetics of everything as we're shown to our seats.

'Yes, maybe something similar, but with way less people,' I whisper. What am I saying? Since when did I have an opinion on weddings, well it appears I do now I've seen this.

A trio of violinists begin to walk down the aisle playing a catchy tune. My eyes squint trying to remember what it is, as I scan the room for the other hens. I find a familiar backs of heads then Gemma, Vanessa and Lisa with their partners, Samantha is sitting next to Gemma with no plus one. Probably too spoilt for choice so decided on none, I think bitterly, before telling myself off for thinking about me. Today is about Nay and Mark.

I almost don't recognise Nathan and Krissy when I spot them. Krissy's wearing an enormous hat that keeps hitting Nathan on the head as she leans in to talk to him. She must feel my eyes watching her as she turns around and gives me a little wave.

'Spice Girls, *If You Want to be My Lover*,' Charlie whispers in my ear. I mouth *oh yeah* at him because we really shouldn't be talking now.

Naomi enters the room and this time it's the whole room that gasps; she has one of those mermaid tail dresses that hugs her figure in all the right places. She glides down the aisle and we all wait with baited breath as Mark waits then melts for her.

Soon the vows are said. I hold my breath as the registrar asks if anyone knows of any lawful reason why they shouldn't wed. My eyes are drawn to Samantha, aka the ginger *Megan Fox*, she steals all the men so why not this one. I hold my breath as I wait for her to stand up and ruin the day. *Oh shut up, Tilly. Stop getting jealous about*

James and move on. You're far too busy for a man anyway.
Samantha doesn't stand up, no one does and there are
no dramas apart from Nay's nan hysterically crying as she
gets wheeled out in her wheelchair. Bless her.

The wedding breakfast flies by with plenty of rich
food, champagne, giggles, amusing speeches and even an
apology from Krissy to Brie about gate crashing on the
hen. It was lovely to see and I even get a bit emotional
and end up hugging them both.

'To old friends and new,' I slur into their faces, as
Charlie replaces my champagne with water.

Next, we're all ushered outside for awkward achy feet
photos as the barn gets turned around for the evening
party. The day quickly fades into night and the evening
guests begin to arrive. The band begins to set up and
much to Charlie's delight, it's a K-pop band; Nay loved
the one on the hen do so much that she cancelled her old
band for this one.

'Apparently they were the first K-pop band formed in
the UK, she must have paid a fortune for them,' Charlie
says, fangirling hard as he drags me up onto the dance
floor along with Brie and Nick.

It makes me smile to myself then a little giggle bursts
out of me as an image of James feeding the fish with his
vomit pops into my mind. The K-pop band were so
fascinated by it, photographing the event like it was a
special Coolsbay ritual.

'What are you laughing at?' Brie asks.

'Nothing, just reminded me of something on the hen
do,' I say, and with that Brie slut drops to the floor and
I throw my head back with a huge guffaw. She may be
pregnant but that certainly isn't stopping her.

We throw out our best dance moves as the band
performs some nineties classics including *Push It* by Salt

n Pepa. Afterwards, I go and find a place to sit down, suddenly my legs feel very heavy and I feel sad. Everything's reminding me of James.

I miss him.

'What's wrong, sis?' Charlie asks, as he comes to find me.

'Ahh just this song, I'm missing the person I last danced with this to.'

'Oh how did they dance?' he asks.

'They trooped,' I say, with a little shrug.

'Like this?' Charlie gets up and begins trooping as a crowd begins to form around him.

I clap and giggle as he gives the performance of a lifetime. James and Charlie would really get on. Before I know it, I'm pulled into the middle. Ahh fuck it, I think, as I pull out my best troop to showcase to the crowd.

As I move around in a circle trooping to my best ability something catches my eye. I see him first, then Samantha. His curly hair and boyish smile do nothing for me now but they are certainly doing something for Samantha as I see them sneak off towards the toilets, holding hands as he kisses her on the neck. It's George and he's come as the ginger *Megan Fox's* evening plus one. The cheek! I wonder if she even asked Nay if he could come. Either way, they are welcome to each other and actually suit each other more than they realise.

I slow down trooping as I process the information then instantly speed up again as *Ice Ice Baby* begins to play and my body catches up with my mind. She was at their house to see George, not James. She got my bloody sloppy seconds, I smile.

But more importantly, she isn't seeing James.

Chapter 23

Monday rolls around all too soon and I'm back in the office again at an ungodly early hour. It's the Baywatch event today so it's back to Coolsbay to oversee it after I've checked my emails and made a plan with James. It's nice that we can oversee this together, I would have felt nervous doing it on my own after two years off. Nervous bubbles of excitement begin to dance around in my stomach before I mentally pop each and every one of them. Boundaries, Tilly! But the giddiness won't go away. I'm happy, happy that James is seemingly unattached. An image of his amused half-moon eyes flashes across my mind as I open the door to the office, grinning like a Cheshire cat.

'Ah, Tilly, good morning,' Andrea says. She gives me a tight lipped smile and a funny look as if to say *what are you so happy about?*

It feels strange seeing her in here. It's been a while since she's been in the office as recently she's either been out on the road or on holiday. What's also odd is that she's sitting at James's desk and there's no sign of James. She looks tiny behind his huge desk. The sound of her typing frantically with her long nails hitting the keys hurts my head and reminds me that I have a two day hangover from the wedding, not to mention my legs still aching from all that trooping. An image of me trooping around in a circle with a big crowd watching flashes into my mind's eye and makes me cringe. Why do I think I'm the world's greatest dancer when drunk?

'Morning Andrea, good weekend?' I drop my bag down and switch my laptop on before treating her to a beaming smile that hopefully conveys that I'm switched on, fresh-faced and ready for the day.

'Good, thanks, you?' she asks, but doesn't wait for my answer. 'Umm before you get set up can I have a word? Her head peeks over her laptop. Uh oh, she has the two-line frown. Not a good sign.

'Of course.' I drag a chair over to her desk and plonk myself down. Why does this not feel good. I give her another winning smile.

'James is leaving,' she announces, without smiling, before blinking furiously at me. I wait for her to elaborate, she doesn't.

'He's leaving?' Oh God I hope he wasn't sacked for the *Sovereign Wide* thing. I was sure that would be sorted. Inside I wince about my conversation with Billy and Timmy – what if they ignored everything we said and went direct anyway. I'll literally kill them.

'Yes.' She shrugs, making a straight line with her mouth, seemingly not impressed.

'Oh, that's a shame,' I say, hoping she can't hear my heart beating fast in my chest and hoping she'll just bloody elaborate. Why is he leaving!?

'Yes, it is, I had a good feeling about him too,' she says, with a dismissive wave of her hand. 'So now I'm having to try and find a replacement but at least you'll be back to three days a week soon, so I guess there's that,' she says, more to herself than to me.

'I will be, so why is he leav…'

'Right,' Andrea cuts me off. 'So, I just wanted to fill you in. I'm now incredibly busy as I'm sure you can understand, even busier than before so I'll need you to run the Coolsbay event on your own. Is that alright? It didn't need two of you anyway, I should have thought of that in the first place,' she says, with a wave of the hand.

'Yes of course, no problem.' Andrea gives me a small smile, nods and begins to speed type again. When Andrea doesn't want to divulge information there's no point pressing her for it and I have to respect that, she's my boss. Boundaries. But that doesn't mean I can't text James.

After getting all my stuff ready for Coolsbay and silently shitting my pants, I get in the car and send James a text.

Me: *Hey, just had a meeting with Andrea. You're not working here anymore? What happened? P.S. I'm doing Baywatch on my own, no Hasslehoff to help.*

I drop my phone back into my bag and fish out my sunglasses. Shit, I've only got my heart shaped sunglasses again, not very professional looking, I'll have to squint at Baywatch. My stomach does an ominous flip.

Please can it not be *Sovereign Wide*, we can't lose that account. I switch on the radio to try and find some relaxing music to calm me down as I begin my journey to Coolsbay. What will I do without James at work to laugh with? To troop with? I was looking forward to coming back three days a week but now it will just be me and Andrea until she employees some new idiot. James was the only good decision she's made in terms of employment. A groan escapes me as I think of Fabien and his predecessors, I'm not looking forward to that. What will I do without James?

Oh, stop stressing, Tilly, and concentrate on the road.

You are not Silly Tilly any more. It will be fine, it will all be fine. Charlie's words begin to resonate in my head. *You just have to think like something wonderful is always on the verge of happening and it more than likely will.* Yes, something wonderful, something wonderful. Not doom and gloom, something wonderful, Tilly. Baywatch will be wonderful.

I finally arrive at Coolsbay and drop my stuff off at the hotel. I'm staying at the B & B again but this time on my own.

'No James this time?' Fern, the manager asks. 'I was disappointed when he cancelled his room, was looking forward to swapping some scone recipes,' she says, smiling. 'He said his nan was from Fowey in Cornwall and she taught him to bake.' Baking? Of course he does. Could he be any more lovely?

'Yeah, it's a shame he can't be here today, but duty calls,' I say, with a salute then wonder what the hell I'm doing as a huge eel swims around in my stomach, prodding all of my organs. I pray that she doesn't ask any more questions and she thankfully doesn't.

'Drop your bags here and I'll get them sent up to your room at check-in time,' she says kindly, probably sensing my nerves.

'Thanks so much,' I reply.

'Doing anything nice?' she asks, with a raise of the eyebrow as if she knows something I don't.

'Just overseeing an event, team building and dinner,' I reply.

'Ohh lovely, have fun.'

'I'll try.' Something wonderful. Something wonderful.

With a clipboard in hand, I march up to the beach hut to find the surf school and manager. Everything seems to be set up just right. Fifteen surfboards, check. Surf school instructor, check. Sea, just the right amount of choppiness, check. Next, I pull the treasure maps out of my bag and count them again just in case my bag has accidently eaten one. They're all there plus a few spares. Check.

The delegates begin to arrive and I hover around handing out bottles of water and making a fuss of them before the event begins. I explain about the treasure hunt and the search for the elusive Coolsbay stone which is met with an air of competition and comradery. I continue to explain that in teams of two, people should mark off all of the landmarks. First team wins a bottle of champagne and a certificate each. If they find the stone then that's great but of course it's not mandatory. The manager, not one for joining in, explains that he is going to visit a relative who lives nearby and will be back when they've finished. I breathe a sigh of relief because I won't have to make small talk with him for two hours. Sometimes unsociable people are the best.

I wander along to a beachside café and grab myself a cold drink before sitting on a bench along the promenade. It's a beautiful day and I can make out little ships dotted about on the horizon which makes me smile. I wonder how Gerald is and where Tilly's dream is setting sail to now. My phone buzzes in my bag. Two missed calls from James and a text.

James: *I'm so sorry you're having to do this on your own. Andrea was really upset when I handed in my notice and told me that I should leave with immediate effect, I tried to reason with her but she was having none of it. I hope it's going well? P.S Sovereign Wide is fine, all sorted and no need to worry.*
Me: *It's going fine thanks, but why are you leaving?*

James: *It's for the best, the job wasn't for me and I've been offered something else I can't turn down but I'd still like to thank you for saving my arse, if you'll let me.*

I stab at my phone to switch it off, irrationally angry at James for abandoning me. What does it matter if I've saved his arse or not now?

The delegates start to come back in dribs and drabs, two young women being the winners. They squeal at their prize and contemplate opening the champagne now, I manage to talk them out of it by saying that the booze and surfing might make them sick before telling them the story of my ex-colleague and how the fish ate his vomit. Ha! Take that, James.

Once everyone is back, one of the delegates pulls me aside to tell me that she has a fear of the sea and the creatures that inhabit it and that she doesn't want to do the surfing. I tell her that's fine and we sit together, we chat about the treasure hunt and I fill her in on all of the sights of Coolsbay. She tells me a bit of office gossip and I'm friendly but careful not to say too much. We have a good laugh and I'm pretty certain she's still had a good time despite not being able to join in with this part. I tell her about my dealings with the Coolsbay stone and finding it stuck in my hair and she laughs. I feel a little sorry that she couldn't go surfing but it appears you can never please everyone with things like this, even in a really small team. The surfers come back drenched and exhausted and thankfully with no injuries. Phew. I can finally relax a little, once I've checked their hotel and everything is set out correctly for them, dinner will take care of itself and I will be pouring myself a very large glass of well-deserved wine.

I pad back to the B & B, and surprise myself by being

a little disappointed to find that I'm not staying in the same room. It's smaller, with a single bed, but it still has a wonderful view of the sea. I message Andrea to tell her that everything has gone without a hitch so far and she sends back a thumbs up and a smiley face. I decide to have a shower and wash off today's travel and hard work. I'll only have to be at the delegates' hotel for half an hour or so and then I can leave. If I wanted to, I could even drive back home tonight, maybe I won't have that wine, be alcohol free like Charlie.

I change into a nautical, navy circle dress and after drying and styling my hair, I tie a yellow head band around my head in a bow then put on some yellow wedges to cheer myself up. I probably wouldn't wear this in Swindon, afraid of being judged in my own town, but I feel like I can wear what I like here, be who I want to be and besides I'm by the sea so I want to match with it.

My phone reminds me that it's time to check the hotel guests and dinner so I make my way over to the venue to meet with the restaurant manager and check the tables. I place their name cards down and give out the little Coolsbay stones in their twee little rope bags. No one found the elusive stone so it was just as well James thought of this idea and it's a nice touch too, a little keepsake to take with them from their team building event.

He was thoughtful and kind and funny but also a bit of a dick for leaving without telling me, he obviously didn't think very much of me as a colleague or a friend. Oh well, onwards and upwards. I bump into the manager on my way out who thanks me for a brilliant day and compliments the hotel rooms. I paste on my biggest gracious smile and wish him a pleasant evening, asking him to call me if they need anything. The sun is slowly beginning to set as I leave the venue and I check my watch; everything has gone to plan and on time. That wasn't too bad at all, James did a great job of planning that event and I did a great job at overseeing it. We made a good team, I think sadly. Now I can finally relax and maybe cry a little into my wine, perhaps I won't drive home tonight.

My yellow wedges slap the pavement as my feet grow heavy and tired. I've only had them on a little while but all the running around today has made my feet ache. I bend down and take them off, managing to stuff them into my bag before I pad along the promenade back to the B & B, barefooted.

'Nice feet. Lost your shoes? You can always borrow mine if you want to, anytime you like,' a cheerful male voice calls out. I'm definitely not in the mood for shit chat up lines and I sigh and wearily turn my head, ready to give whoever it is a mouthful.

'No thanks!' I shout. 'And why don't you just piss o… oh.'

James beams as he leans back against the railings and bites his lip, he's smart in a white shirt and navy trousers; his expressive Mr half-moon brown eyes twinkling in the evening sun. He looks annoyingly, incredibly sexy. He's watching me in amusement as the sea dances behind him, laughing with him.

'What are you doing here?' I ask, in shock.

'I'm taking you out for a drink to say thank you,' he says, as I look at him with my mouth hanging open. I quickly close it, aware that I might be resembling a gormless fish. 'Come on.' James walks over to me and stands in front of me for a moment before suddenly leaning towards me and wrapping his arms around the tops of my legs and slinging me over his shoulder in a fireman's carry. I scream.

'What are you doing? Get off, I've got a dress on, my knickers,' I squawk, as I try not to laugh and scream at the same time.

In the end I just give in, clinging onto my dress for dear life as he marches with me on his shoulder. His delicious scent infiltrates my nostrils as I hang upside down. We pass people on the promenade who cheer and clap which only adds to my giddiness and hysteria. Just as I get the fear he's going to dump me in the sea, we stop and he carefully puts me down.

'Tilly's dream.' I gasp as I take in the beautiful view of the yacht once again.

'Yep,' James says, watching me and chewing the inside of his lip.

'Gerald, helloooo?' I call out towards the boat.

'No, Gerald's not here. He's let me borrow it for the evening.' James holds out his hand as he helps me onto the boat.

'Oh, right,' I say, as he motions for me to sit down.

I watch as he opens the drawer and pulls out a bottle of champagne and some glasses. It all feels very familiar but also not.

'How did the event go?' he asks casually, as though we do this all the time, hang out on yachts.

'Good, went perfectly well.' My feet tap on the floor with all the nervous energy. He looks so hot. I don't know what to do with myself, I might end up throwing myself overboard from the shock of it all.

'Great, nobody had to share a hotel room or a surfboard then?' He laughs nervously as he hands me a glass of champagne, his expression changing when he sees my face. 'Look, you're probably wondering what the hell is going on,' he says, as he watches me narrow my eyes at him. 'I wanted to say thank you for helping with the *Sovereign Wide* thing but also I handed in my notice because I couldn't work with *you* anymore.'

'Charming, it was only for one day a week anyway.' I fold my arms as he sits next to me and touches my shoulder briefly. It leaves a tingling mark and I cover it with my hand to stop the feeling. Bloody body betraying me, who does it think it is?

'Yes, but soon to be more and you're way too distracting,' he says, as I turn the other way and look out onto the ocean. 'Tilly,' he whispers.

I study the sea as the word 'Yeah,' gets stuck in my throat.

Then it all happens so fast as I feel his finger and thumb gently pull my chin towards him. My stomach lurches and tumbles then I'm lost in his kisses and the feel of his stubble in my hands. The waves crash around us then he pulls away from me, keeping one hand resting tenderly on my knee.

'Can't you see, I want to be around you, all the time, just not at work. If you'll let me, that is.' He bites his lip as his eyes search my face. I take his hand in mine and study it, enjoying the feeling. I feel so safe with him. Content. There's no way he'd throw me over the edge of this yacht.

'Just not at work?' I smile as I grip his hand firmly and he pulls me in closer.

'Just, not at work. I can't have you bailing me out all the time for silly mistakes, it's my job to save you.' He nods towards me.

'Deal, but I quite enjoyed saving you, I was your powerful queen and besides the event today went perfectly and you planned all of that so give yourself some credit,' I say, stroking his wrist, enjoying the feeling of his hand in mine. 'Is that what all the phone calls were about?' I say, pulling away from him. 'Sorting out a new job?' So he wasn't planning his life with someone else.

'Yes, were you watching me?' He smiles, stroking my hand with his thumb.

'Couldn't keep my eyes off you,' I admit, biting my lip as James positions himself towards me.

'The first night I saw you in Coolsbay, I was smitten with you, even when you refused to kiss me because I'd beaten you in the dance off. Then you insisted on staying in my bed because you had no bed on the hen do. I wanted so badly to see you again but you didn't seem interested at all. I felt like you hated me but I knew you were from Swindon so I figured if I saw you again, maybe it was meant to be.'

'You old romantic. Wait… I told you I was from Swindon?'

'Yeah, how drunk were you?'

'Very, too drunk. I might go AF.'

'What's that?'

'Never mind. I didn't hate you, but you did piss me off, laughing at my lizard face in the morning. I admit it was a massive overreaction on my part, probably not helped by my huge, grumpy hangover and I wasn't sure whether we had, you know… which made me cross. But I realise I was more cross with myself for not remembering.'

'No, we didn't, not even a kiss. You just hogged the bed all night, just like our work trip,' he laughs. 'I couldn't believe my luck when I ended up working with you, as cheesy at that sounds.'

'I have something to confess though.' I take a deep breath, feeling the need to get everything out in the open now.

'What is it?'

'I dated your housemate for a bit, we did kiss but then I found out what a snake he was, you were right. Sorry about that.' I wince but James just shakes his head, his eyes sparkling with amusement.

'I don't care about all that, he's been on a date with pretty much every woman in Swindon, even your mate, I think.' He gives me a silly grin then kisses my forehead. I lean in closer to him, relishing his warmth and smell.

'Yeah, the ginger *Megan Fox*. It's a bloody small world, isn't it?' I say, thinking about all the serendipity that's been thrust upon us as the evening turns cooler and he wraps me up in his arms.

It really is,' he murmurs. Then we watch in silence for a few moments, just holding each other as the sun begins to disappear into the sea. 'And I have a feeling, Tilly Loveberry, that you're going to be a massive part of *my* world.'

Chapter 24

Five months and ten days later

We squeeze ourselves onto my three-seater sofa whilst Charlie arranges the laptop on the coffee table so that everyone can be seen. It's my work laptop but Andrea has allowed me to take it home for the first time ever. She said I can use it for personal use too as long as it's not for anything too untoward. It made me question what she thinks James and I do in our spare time and paranoid that the yacht incident has somehow got back to her. I wouldn't be surprised; she does seem to know everything. Andrea has finally forgiven James, she's a sucker for a love story and I managed to convince her to let me help with the recruiting process for fear of recruiting another flaky man (no offence James). We've now hired a lovely woman with years of event experience and she fits into the team nicely.

'Anyone for another glass of wine?' Mum asks, holding the bottle up and wobbling it in the air before pouring another for herself and Jeff.

Mum looks so much more like herself these days, much better. She's binned the filler and now just has facial peels, and I have Jeff to thank for that. He told her he preferred a much more natural woman and that filler in her lips was sometimes like kissing two slugs. Needless to say that put her off getting any more done for a while. Thanks Jeff.

'Not for me thanks, Mum, I've had enough,' I say, as James runs his hand down my back making my whole body tingle. I don't want to be too drunk later, we're kid free, if you catch my drift. Nancy-Ella is at Billy and Timmy's and James's boys are at their Mum's, who by the way seems lovely. She was understandably a little icy at first but is now beginning to thaw.

'You should get some of the AF wine, Lil,' Gethin pipes up in his strong Welsh accent, as Charlie attempts to sit next to him on the sofa. He can't squeeze in so he settles for the floor, seconds later Gethin joins him, resting a hand on his knee. 'Some of it is soooo good, you can't even tell the difference apart from the hangover and the drunk feeling.'

'Hmm maybe, darling.' Mum nods along in agreement as she takes another swig of her wine and winks at Jeff.

'Isn't that the point though?' James tilts his head. 'To get that drunk feeling?'

'You don't need it, life is enough to get drunk on.' Charlie stares into Gethin's eyes and Gethin smiles a gooey smile at him. If you were to tell me that by the age of thirty-seven my brother would be tee-total and settled down in Swindon, I would have laughed until I peed my knickers but he is and it appears he and Gethin couldn't be happier. They're even in the process of buying a house together in Wichelstowe. I may have lost Brie to Australia but I got my brother back. Krissy and I still keep in touch but only really for play dates with the kids, something tells me she's far too busy with two men to entertain.

'Okay, it's ten o' clock, everyone quiet.' I lean forward

and click on the link directing me to *Zoom*. We all watch in anticipation as the screen fizzes and pops until an image of Brie, Nick and their eight-day old baby, Rocky, appears in front of us.'

'Alrighty-roo people,' Brie croaks in a sleepy morning voice, as she and Nick wave at the screen. They are both in their dressing gowns. Rocky is dressed up as a sailor and he looks like the perfect little bundle of joy.

'Oh wow, he's beautiful, so much hair!' Mum coos.

Brie smiles and strokes the top of her baby's head before inhaling his smell. I wish I could smell that baby smell. I sense James watching me out of the corner of his eye as my ovaries begin to scream.

No!

One and done. One and done.

'Yeah, he's just gorgeous, isn't he? Our perfect little pudding,' Brie agrees.

'So gorgeous, congratulations again guys,' I say, because I've seen a dozen photos of him already. Brie even rang me during labour high on pethidine to tell me that one of the male nurses looked exactly like the foot fetish guy that I once went on a date with. Needless to say, the male nurse was horrified when she asked him to prove it by showing her his feet. I'm not sure what showing her *his* feet was going to prove but Nick gently reminded her that she can't ask strangers to strip.

'Brie, can I just say, you look amazing for someone that's just given birth. Congratulations guys,' Charlie says, as Gethin nods along. 'He's so adorable.'

'Thanks Charlie, babe, had a little pre-birth face freshener, peel, plump and prune.'

Mum looks at Jeff and makes an oooh noise, but he shakes his head and mouths, 'you're beautiful,' to her, and she melts back into his arms.

'Sorry we're not dressed but I thought it more important that this little guy be looking his best rather than us,' Brie continues.

'Everything's an effort at the moment,' she winces, probably still feeling sore.

'Oh no, don't worry about that, it's seven o'clock in the morning there and you've not long had a baby for God's sake,' I say. 'He's so lovely, little Rocky. How are you guys getting on?'

'Ahh mate, I love him so much but it's a lot harder than I thought.' She looks directly at me and sniffs. 'My hormones have been all over the joint, I think on day four when my milk came in, I went crazy and cried for two days straight. This poor guy has been a saint,' she says, throwing a thumb at Nick. 'Why does no one tell you this shit?'

Sensing her stress the baby starts to cry. Nick takes little Rocky and gently rests him on his shoulder, rubbing his back in a soothing manner until he stops crying.

'Ah the baby blues darling, it will pass in a few weeks, just make sure you take plenty of baths and try and rest when the baby rests.' Mum says.

But sleeping when the baby sleeps is easier said than done and I know that all too well. 'Just take each day as it comes, there's no right or wrong. I couldn't sleep when Nancy-Ella was born, I was a massive mess but the days soon pass and you'll soon recover, be patient with yourself.'

'Thanks babe. So now I know what the big deal is all about, I owe you an apology.'

'Oh, no need,' I say, waving her away as she begins to well up again.

'So birth story,' Mum says. 'I want all the gory details, blood, guts the lot.' She leans forward, puts her elbows on her knees, then rests her chin in her hand, ready for the show.

'MUM!' Charlie screeches. 'You can't ask her that!'

Gethin looks horrified as all the colour drains from his face.

'Why not?' Mum asks.

'Of course she can, but maybe we'll save that for us girls hey, Lil?' Brie smiles and Mum does an exaggerated nod, tapping the side of her nose. She's drunk, she never would have asked that if she were sober.

We stay on *Zoom* for a while longer until little Rocky begins to cry again but this time he won't be soothed. Brie tells us all she's going to attempt to feed him but will do it off camera as sometimes it makes her cry too. We take that as our cue to say goodbye to Brie, Nick and little baby Rocky and shortly after to each other.

'Urgh, I'm so tired,' I groan, as we finally manage to get Mum out of the door at gone midnight. She decided to tell us all her own birth stories which was both horrifying and amusing at the same time.

'Me too, wish we were getting the kids later tomorrow so we can have a nice lay in,' James says, as he begins to kiss my neck and I close my eyes, enjoying it. We're picking the kids up early and taking them to *Peppa Pig World* for the day, much to the boys' dismay but James tells me that they will secretly love it. We'll see.

'You think I'm going to let you share my fancy new bed?' I tease, as he picks me up and I wrap my legs around him.

We had to get a new bed when he moved in, his feet hung out of the bottom of mine and his bed broke when he dismantled it for the move. We've been living together for two whole weeks now and it's been chaotic but also happy, fun and fulfilling.

We reach the top of the stairs and I smile at the painting of the Coolsbay coast I finished just before he moved in. I surprised myself with how well it turned out. I wanted to paint our portraits but James said he couldn't look at a huge painting of himself every day like he was some sort of lord and why don't I paint something more aesthetically pleasing. I told him that he was very aesthetically pleasing and he just laughed. Painting Coolsbay was definitely out of my comfort zone but I'm so glad I did it as it's where it all began. Us.

James continues to kiss my neck again as we enter the bedroom, then looks at me intensely with his dark, half-moon eyes. I kiss him back, enjoying the sensation.

Hmmm, perhaps I'm not that tired after all.

Sleep can wait a little longer.

The End

From the author

Thank you so much for reading my book I really do appreciate it. I'm an Indie Author, part of a small family run imprint (Tamarillas Press) and not backed by a big publishing company. Every time a reader downloads one of my books I am genuinely thrilled.

If you've enjoyed my book then please feel free to post your review on goodreads, Amazon or both. I cherish every rating and review, they really do make my day and encourage other potential readers to try my books.

We've worked hard to eliminate typos and errors but if you spot any please let us know.
TamarillasPress@outlook.com
Belle Henderson

Belle Henderson

Belle Henderson loves to read and write. She lives with her family and her rambunctious beagle in Wiltshire. She absolutely loves hearing from readers so please feel free to connect with her via email or on social media.

Email: bellehendersonauthor@gmail.com
Instagram: Instagram.com/bellehendersonauthor/
Facebook: facebook.com/bellehendersonauthor/
Goodreads:
https://www.goodreads.com/author/show/18999602.Belle_Hend erson
Tiktok: https://vm.tiktok/ZMesW9RQA

Other books by Belle Henderson

What happens when you find yourself
homeless and relationshipless?

YOU GROW GIRL

BELLE HENDERSON

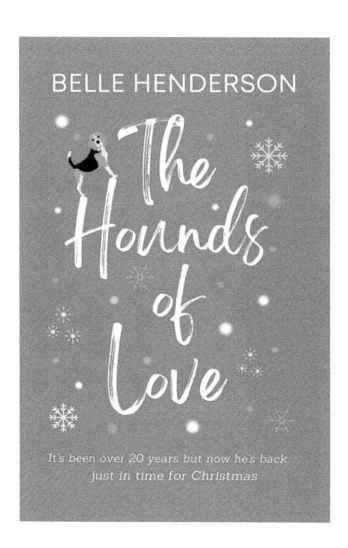

BELLE HENDERSON

The Hounds of Love

It's been over 20 years but now he's back...
just in time for Christmas

BELLE HENDERSON

What's eating FELICITY FROST?

A quirky tale of love, forgiveness
and finding your people

BELLE HENDERSON

Livin' La Vida Lockdown

Life got hard but
then love got interesting

BELLE HENDERSON
& CJ MORROW

We
can
Work
it out

Two people,
one
opportunity

Printed in Great Britain
by Amazon